THE CHESS PLAYERS

by

J. D. MALLINSON

Inspector Mason novels:-

Danube Stations
The File on John Ormond
The Italy Conspiracy
The Swiss Connection
Quote for a Killer
Death by Dinosaur
The Chinese Zodiac Mystery
A Timeshare in France
Beyond Budapest
City Conspiracy

WAXWING BOOKS, NEW HAMPSHIRE

CHAPTER ONE

It was a blustery day in the early spring when Fabien Leroux made his way along Bayswater Road towards Marble Arch. Masses of cumulus cloud scudded across the sky above the verdant acres of Hyde Park, immediately to his right. He paused to observe the progress of play in a soccer match between what appeared to be rival school teams, with small groups of adults he took to be a mixture of parents and teaching staff shouting encouragement. He checked his watch. He was fifteen minutes early for his appointment at noon, time enough to hang around for a while in the hope of seeing a goal scored. Soccer was not a sport he was very familiar with. At his private school in Quebec, in common with many other fee-paying schools in North America, they had played rugby. Until this moment, in fact, he had only occasionally watched soccer games on television; so he was much intrigued to see a live match. There being no score after ten minutes, he continued on his way, arriving at The Wheatsheaf Inn at just turned midday. It was a large Victorian building facing Hyde Park, just south of the area known as Speakers' Corner, where practiced and amateur orators were accustomed, chiefly on a Sunday morning, to air their views on all manner of subjects, whether political, religious or philosophical. There was also a fair number of outright cranks.

On entering the popular pub, he noticed in the far corner of the lounge bar a gentleman somewhat older than himself sitting with a pint of beer, while gazing out through French windows onto a walled-in patio garden sporting crocuses and early daffodils. The man wore a fake carnation in his buttonhole, which provided the Canadian a means of identification. Ordering a pint of Banks's bitter at the bar, he crossed the room to join him. At his approach, the older man rose in greeting.

"Monsieur Leroux?" he genially enquired.

The younger man nodded.

"Please take a seat."

The two men sat facing each other, weighing each other up across the narrow table as they sipped their ale.

"Sorry I cannot offer you lunch, Monsieur," the older man said. "I have a prior arrangement to meet my niece at Paddington Station. She is coming down from Bristol today to interview for a place at Queen Mary College."

"In what field?" Leroux politely enquired, thinking he would order a pub meal later.

"I don't think she is quite sure herself," came the rather ironic reply. "She is torn between modern languages and psychology, as far as I can gather."

"It is quite difficult, these days," his visitor said, "to choose a college course with good job prospects. Computer science and I.T. seem to be all the rage nowadays."

"You can say that again, Monsieur Leroux, but try

telling that to my niece. Now, to get down to the business in hand. You claim to be ex-military?"

The younger man nodded.

"I served with the Royal Canadian Navy, mainly on Arctic patrol vessels," he explained.

"So you are fully conversant with the use of firearms?" the older man enquired.

"Marksman, first-class," Leroux confidently replied.

His interviewer nodded in evident satisfaction at that information, before taking a generous quaff of Grolsch lager. He was a heavily-built man clad in a dark suit with a light-blue shirt and club tie. His rather swarthy complexion was crowned with thinning gray hair, neatly styled. Fabien Leroux took him to be a professional man in his late fifties. Why, he wondered, would he be hiring a hitman?

"The fee," the older man then announced, without ceremony, "is ten thousand pounds."

"For just the one hit?"

"There may be more than one," came the considered reply. "It depends on circumstances partly beyond my control at this juncture."

The Canadian was much intrigued at that remark, implying as it did the prospect of an extended stay in Britain. As this was his first visit to a country his French-Canadian parents had never shown much enthusiasm for, it augured well for the future and for his new line of work following dishonorable discharge from the navy. He raised his glass and thoughtfully sipped his beer.

"And for additional services?" he prompted.

"Five thousand for each case, Monsieur Leroux,"

came the reply. "Are we in business?"

"Absolutely," came the immediate reply.

"Your initial target is the owner of a store named Max's Hardware at Stepney Green. On exiting the Underground Station, turn left and you will find his premises in the first row of high-street shops."

"Stepney Green?" the Canadian quizzed, with a puzzled look.

"You are familiar with the Underground system, I take it?"

"To some extent," he bluffed, since he had hardly used it in the short time he had been in London.

"Where are you staying, Monsieur, as a point of interest?"

"At a small hotel in Bayswater."

"Take the Central Line from Queensway to Mile End. Once there, switch to the northbound District Line to Stepney Green, which is the next stop after Whitechapel. The proprietor leaves his store promptly at 8.00 p.m. He locks the front door and secures the metal window shutters before accessing his car, a white Volvo sedan parked at the curb."

"I am to approach him during that short interval of time?"

The older man shook his head.

"That will not be possible, Monsieur Leroux," he explained. "Stepney High Street at that hour is still quite busy, with evening shoppers, restaurant clientele, cinema-goers and the like. Not to mention the local police patrol, which can take place at any hour."

"What is the alternative?" the Canadian enquired.

His hirer took another swig of ale, replacing his

4

glass firmly on the table, as if to emphasize his point.

"Directly opposite the row of shops stands a block of municipal buildings, which have an extensive roof garden. It was installed some years ago, I understand, as part of a trend to reintroduce nature into urban areas. It was also aimed at offsetting traffic pollution."

The ex-navy man gave a knowing smile.

"Part of the modern green agenda," he remarked. "It is catching on in North America, too, by converting, for example, wasteland and disused railway tracks into urban parks."

"The roof garden is open to the public," the other said, seemingly little interested in urban renewal. "You can reach it by lift from the ground floor. No one will challenge you."

"But wouldn't I be visible to the public below, when I reached the rooftop?" Leroux objected.

His hirer smilingly shook his head, saying:

"The shrubbery is by now quite mature, Monsieur. And at that hour, it will already be growing dark. You will have sufficient cover. After the hit, take the elevator back to the ground floor, exit and enter the public library next door. Occupy yourself reading one of the daily newspapers or a magazine until the street hubbub has died down. You should then be able to return safely to the Underground station.

"Sounds straightforward enough," Fabien Leroux remarked, impressed by the older man's attention to detail.

"You have suitable weaponry?" his hirer then

pointedly asked.

"I can obtain a rifle with a telescopic lens and silencer within a few days, from a contact I have at Brixton."

"Today is Thursday, Monsieur. Visit Stepney on Monday evening. I shall be tied up early next week. I suggest we meet again around noon on the following Wednesday. I shall bring your fee in cash."

"We are to meet here?" Leroux optimistically enquired.

The older man shook his head.

"It would be better to vary the venue," he said. "This place is convenient for you, I am aware, since you are staying at Bayswater. But next week, we shall try The Black Prince near Victoria Station. It is always very busy at lunch-time, with rail commuters and local office staff, so we shall be inconspicuous. And by the way, in all future dealings you know me simply as Q."

With that, he raised his glass again, drained it and rose to leave.

"I must hurry," he said, "to catch up with my niece. They do a good steak-and-kidney pie here, if you care to stay for a bite to eat. It is home-made. I can recommend it."

Fabien Leroux rose to his feet and firmly shook the man's hand.

"You can have complete confidence in me, Q," he assured him, thinking he would act on the culinary tip.

"I sincerely hope so," came the quick reply.

*

From his modest accommodation at Leinster Hotel on Queensway, Bayswater, Fabien Leroux spent the next few days familiarizing himself with his new environment, visiting Hyde Park and Kensington Palace Gardens, which were close-by. On the Saturday, he made a trial run on the Underground to Stepney Green, before taking the train down to Brixton, a borough on the south side of the Thames. His contact there, Jeb Sinclair, was an ex-navy colleague who had moved to England two years ago to work as a security specialist at London's financial center, known as the City. They had dinner at a Thai restaurant and a round of drinks at one of Sinclair's favorite pubs, The Ram's Head, reminiscing on time spent together in the Royal Canadian Navy. Sinclair was much intrigued by his friend's request to borrow a weapon, but did not press him for details. Fabien Leroux left Brixton on the last train back to Victoria Station with a modern folding rifle concealed in his rucksack.

On the following Monday, after an early dinner at a Greek restaurant on Queensway, he took the Tube to Stepney Green, arriving there at just turned 7.30 p.m. On leaving the Underground station, he took a left turn, as directed by Q, soon locating Max's Hardware along the row of Victorian-era commercial buildings, many of them still open at this hour. The hardware store was placed between a Chinese take-away and a bookshop, both of which were brightly lit and seemingly well-patronized. Pedestrians moved briskly along the sidewalks, to and from the Tube station and in and out of the various amenities. His hirer was correct in surmising that a direct approach to the target would be unfeasible in such a lively neighborhood. Leroux crossed High Street and entered the municipal buildings on the opposite side. He took the lift to the roof garden and made his way through rather dense shrubbery to the low parapet overlooking the street. From there, he had an unrestricted view of Max's Hardware.

A glance at his Accutron wristwatch told him that it was now 7.50 p.m. It was already dark. He drew his rifle from his rucksack, methodically assembled it, adding a silencer, and took up his position by the parapet. From there, he could clearly observe the proprietor through the gap above the varied window display. The man was of fairly short stature, middle-aged, with a good head of graying hair. Leroux followed his movements closely, as he locked cabinets, emptied the cash till, switched off the lights and finally stepped out into the street. As he secured the shop door and began lowering the metal window shutters, Fabien Leroux raised his weapon to his shoulder and took careful aim. As his index finger squeezed the trigger, he was startled by a sudden noise to his right, farther along the extended rooftop, which caused his arm to jolt slightly. His target immediately collapsed. The Canadian hurriedly crouched down behind the parapet and listened intently. The initial noise was followed by a series of low giggles, persuading him that whoever was there was not aware of his presence, nor had they heard his shot. He remained motionless for several minutes, concluding with a rueful smile that the sounds likely came from a young courting couple. So much for Q's insistence that the rooftop would be deserted.

He gingerly retraced his steps to the elevator, crouching below the shrubbery to remain unobserved. On regaining the ground floor, he entered the public library and crossed to the newspaper rack. He chose a copy of *The Guardian,* which he had occasionally read on-line during his navy service, and took it to a table by the window, in order to observe the scene in the street outside. A small crowd had gathered by the hardware store, but the angle of his view did not afford sight of the victim. He assumed that, even with the sudden distraction on the rooftop, his aim had been true.

Some ten minutes later, at the sound of an ambulance siren, patrons of the reading room rushed to the window, to see what was afoot. Fabien Leroux joined them, observing the scene with grim satisfaction as paramedics placed the victim on a stretcher and lifted him into the ambulance. He waited several minutes after the vehicle had departed, before quitting the building and striding back towards the Underground station. Once aboard the southbound District Line train, he congratulated himself on a job well done. On reaching Queensway, he would celebrate with a pint of Guinness at The Dublin Arms. The mysterious Q had not got it quite right, he reflected, with a wry smile. The roof garden was probably quite often used by young couples romancing under the stars; the facility was ideal for the purpose. It was a stroke of luck his presence there had gone undetected.

*

Inspector George Mason was nearing the end of his evening shift when a call came through to Scotland Yard from the duty sergeant at Stepney Green police station. There had apparently been a firearms incident. Mason cursed his luck, as he phoned his wife Adele to tell her he would be late for dinner, before heading out to his car. Twenty minutes later, in light evening traffic, he reached his destination, cruising along the high street until he noticed police tape cordoning off the area in front of Max's Hardware. He pulled up at the curb, stepped out of his car and approached the uniformed officer stationed there.

"What do we have here, Constable?" the Scotland Yard agent enquired.

"There was a firearms incident, Inspector, around eight o'clock this evening," the officer informed him.

"Involving whom?"

"The proprietor of the hardware store, an individual named Maxim Brodsky, was shot while leaving his premises."

"What was the outcome?" Mason enquired.

"The victim was unconscious, but apparently still alive, when they took him by ambulance to East London General Hospital."

"That would be at Wapping, just south of here, I believe?" the detective surmised.

"Correct, Sir," the officer replied.

Mason looked askance at the pool of blood on the sidewalk and glanced towards the darkened building.

"Were there any witnesses, Constable?" he asked.

"Several pedestrians rushed to the scene immediately on seeing Brodsky collapse," came the reply, "including the owner of the local bookstore."

George Mason thanked him and entered the adjoining premises, finding the proprietor on the point of closing for the night. He showed ID and introduced himself.

"Melvin Farrer," the owner returned.

"Tell me what you know of the incident, Mr. Farrer," the detective urged.

"On hearing the commotion outside," the other explained, "I rushed out to see what it was all about. I found my neighbor, Max Brodsky, lying face-down on the sidewalk, blood coming from a wound to his back."

The detective stepped back into the street, accompanied by the bookstore owner.

"If Mr. Brodsky was securing his premises at the time," Mason said, noting the half-drawn shutters, "the shot must have come from across the street, to strike him in the back."

Farrer nodded agreement.

"In which event," Mason continued, "the shooter would need adequate cover. How could that be on a busy street like this?"

Melvin Farrer indicated the block of buildings opposite.

"Those are municipal offices, Inspector Mason," he said. "Some years ago, the borough council had a roof garden installed. It holds mature shrubs which are difficult to make out from street-level in the dark. But you can access the facility by lift."

George Mason glanced upwards, noting the dim outlines of vegetation on the roof.

"That would provide good cover," he agreed. "Have you noticed anything suspicious in the neighborhood recently?"

Melvin Farrer shook his head.

"Strangers, for example?" Mason prodded.

The bookseller thought carefully for a few moments.

"There was someone who made a distinct impression on me," he eventually replied. "That is not to suggest he was in any way involved in this crime."

"Go on," the detective urged.

"Last Saturday afternoon, as I was rearranging my window display with the new spring stock, a tall, athletic figure with tanned features, aged around forty, strode by. He paused momentarily to glance at book covers. Our eyes briefly met."

"What you are implying, Mr. Farrer, is that this individual was not typical of the people one would normally come across on Stepney Green High Street. He stood out, in fact?"

"I would go along with that assessment, Inspector," Farrer judiciously remarked. "We have a fair number of Asians living in this community, as well as immigrants from East Europe. I would not place the man in either category."

"Would you recognize him again?"

"Assuredly so," came the emphatic reply.

"Now, about the victim, Mr. Farrer," Mason continued. Were you aware of any threats he might have received? Did he confide in you any concerns or misgivings?"

"Max just seemed his normal self to me, Inspector," Melvin Farrer replied. "He generally kept much to himself, to tell the truth. But he was invariably courteous and friendly. We usually met first thing in the morning, while opening up our stores. We would chat for a few moments about this and that, usually the weather outlook. He mentioned nothing untoward to me when we spoke this morning, Inspector, so I cannot help you there."

"You have been most cooperative, Mr. Farrer. I thank you for it."

With that, he took leave of the bookstore owner and the duty constable and drove to the general hospital at Wapping. On entering the reception area, he introduced himself and was quickly greeted by the almoner.

"Mr. Brodsky is now in the operating theatre," the official said.

"Is his condition critical?" the detective enquired.

The almoner shook her head.

"The bullet fortunately missed his vital organs," she said. "He is expected to make a full recovery. He should be out of here in a matter of days, unless something else turns up in the course of our examination. That is always a possibility."

"Let us hope it is a straightforward procedure," a concerned George Mason said.

"His wife Linda is in the waiting room, Inspector," the almoner added. "Second door on the left, if you wish to have a word with her."

The visitor thanked her and made his way down a short corridor hung with prints of Impressionist paintings. He found Linda Brodsky sitting on a straight-backed chair while glancing at a travel program on the television.

"Mrs. Brodsky," Mason began, "let me introduce myself. Inspector George Mason, from Scotland Yard."

The woman rose from her seat. She was several inches shorter than the detective, clad in a print dress and loose-fitting beige jacket. She glanced at him appealingly, with an anxious expression.

"How could such a terrible thing happen?" she complained.

"Your husband is most likely out of danger, I believe," the detective reassured her.

"Thank goodness for that," Linda Brodsky exclaimed.

He motioned for her to sit, occupying the chair next to her while turning down the television volume.

"The sooner we get to the bottom of this the better," he continued. "I am hoping you can assist me in my enquiries."

"I shall assist you in any way I can, Inspector," she replied.

"It strikes me as a targeted assault," Mason said, on reflection, "rather than a random incident."

"But who on earth would want to harm Max?" the woman protested. "He was one of the friendliest people you could meet."

"Did he have any enemies, in so far as you are

aware? Or did he receive any threats?"

"Not to my knowledge, I can assure you, Inspector Mason."

"How long have you known your husband?" he then asked.

"We have been married – very happily, I can add – for twenty years."

"How did you happen to meet him, Madame, may I ask?"

"Is such a question really relevant, Inspector?" a slightly piqued Linda Brodsky asked.

"It helps to get as much background as we can," he explained. "I am aware this is a difficult time for you and I ask for your understanding."

The woman glanced downwards and shifted her position, before saying:

"Of course you are quite right to ask questions, Inspector," she said, more calmly. "We met through an introductions bureau at Whitechapel. I have always been a little self-conscious of the fact."

"What do you know of his background?" Mason then asked.

"Max never spoke about his past," she replied. "It was decidedly off-limits."

"But you must have formed some impressions, from his surname for instance," the detective persisted.

Linda Brodsky returned an ironic smile.

"It had occurred to me, Inspector, that he might be Jewish. Perhaps a Russian Jew. But he never practiced any religious observances, to my knowledge. He never went to a synagogue, or kept any of the major Jewish festivals."

"Did he eat kosher foods?"

Linda Brodsky shook her head, with the beginnings of a smile.

"Your husband could therefore have been what is called a secular Jew."

The woman slowly nodded.

"Assuming your husband was, in fact, of Jewish origin," Mason continued, "he may have wished to conceal his ethnicity."

"You mean in view of the rise in anti-Semitism in the West in recent years?" she pointedly put it to him.

George Mason nodded.

"On the European Continent more so than in this country, I should imagine," he ventured. "We have a very good record of welcoming Jewish immigrants into Britain, particularly in the nineteen-thirties."

"Those fleeing Nazi Germany?"

"Precisely, Mrs. Brodsky. Sigmund Freud was among them. He arrived here in 1938 and established a replica of his Vienna clinic at Hampstead Heath, which is now the Freud Museum."

"How interesting, Inspector," she remarked, while glancing at a view of St. Tropez on the television.

"His grandson, Clement Freud, used to have a regular spot on television," Mason added.

"You are referring to the celebrity chef?" came the intrigued reply. "I would never have connected the two, Inspector Mason, but I do recall seeing him quite frequently on the box. I enjoy cookery programs. Clement Freud was quite a character, in many ways."

"You can say that again," the detective said, rising to his feet. "Now, if you should need a lift home, I could offer one. I have my car outside."

Linda Brodsky shook her head emphatically, before saying:

"I shall wait here until Max comes safely through the operation. Then I shall return home by taxi, as it will probably be too late for the Underground. Tomorrow morning, hopefully, I shall be able to speak with him."

"My best wishes to you both, Mrs. Brodsky," her visitor said, rising to take his leave.

"Thank you, Inspector Mason," she replied, turning the television volume back up.

The Scotland Yard agent made his way back to the reception area and placed a request for the bullet from the victim's body to be kept back for him. He then drove to his West Ruislip home, reaching it just before half-nine for a supper with his forbearing wife Adele.

CHAPTER 2

Three days later, Fabien Leroux made his way by
Tube to Victoria Station. He was in a buoyant frame
of mind, anticipating a substantial fee from the
person he knew only as Q. On arrival at the busy
terminal, he crossed the concourse and exited on
Victoria Street, to locate The Black Prince, the pub
where the mystery man was expecting him for
lunch. A short walk brought him to his destination,
which he quickly recognized by the large sign-
board swinging in the breeze. It depicted an
imposing figure in medieval armor. On entering the
bar-lounge, found his contact already seated at an
alcove table, tackling *The Times* crossword.

"Bang on time," the older man said, laying his
newspaper aside. "Grab a seat and let us order lunch
at once. I have limited time at my disposal."

The Canadian did as he was bid and studied the
menu. As the waitress hovered near their table, he
requested a pint of Watney's Bitter and a quiche
Lorraine with endive salad. His companion, already
nursing a gin-and-tonic, ordered steak with French
fries.

"This is a very nice pub," Leroux remarked. "But
what an unusual name it has."

"The Black Prince was a Prince of Wales active in
the thirteenth century," Q explained, "famous
mainly for his exploits against the French at Crecy.

I hope you will not mind the anti-French associations, as this is one of my favorite haunts."

"Not at all," came the reply. "My parents strongly supported an independent Quebec, but I have no particular beef against the British. They have done more than most countries in advancing civilized values."

"Quite true, Monsieur," the other agreed. "Britain is rated the most prominent soft power in the world, for the spread of its language, literature and traditional values."

His guest nodded in agreement. The meal soon arrived, occupying their attention as the pub began to fill with patrons from the nearby offices and stores. Conversation between the two men centered on neutral topics, including the freshman niece, of whom Q was evidently fond. He said that she had opted for a dual-honors course in French and Psychology. Fabien Leroux was pleased to hear that, but if he was expecting a wad of banknotes to cross the polished table, as he nudged his empty plate aside, he was in for a disappointment.

The older man took more time finishing his lunch, promptly ordering coffee for two.

"I expect you read the newspapers yesterday?" he then said, almost off-handedly.

The Canadian, somewhat bemused at the question, shook his head.

"I was out of the country for a few days," he replied. "I decided to pay my uncle a visit. He lives near Paris."

"There were reports in the press about an incident at Stepney Green on Monday evening. Maxim

Brodsky was taken to East London General Hospital with a gunshot wound. Apparently, his condition is not critical."

The last remark was issued as a challenge. Leroux's jaw dropped.

"How do you account for that, Monsieur?" Q continued, with a frown.

The ex-navy man shifted in his chair and glanced warily at his table companion.

"I was sure I had made a clean hit," he remarked, uneasily. "I saw him drop to the ground and waited, as you suggested, in the local library until the local paramedics arrived."

The older man returned an ironic smile.

"So much for your vaunted marksmanship," he said. "I had expected better."

"There was a sudden noise on the far side of the roof garden," Leroux explained, "just as I was squeezing the trigger. It took me by surprise and must have affected my aim."

"Why would there be other people on the roof after dark?" Q pointedly enquired.

Fabien Leroux returned a wry smile.

"The noise was followed by giggles," he said, "most likely from courting teenagers."

"Romance under the stars?" the other mused aloud, with a more indulgent smile.

"It would be the perfect place for a tryst," Leroux added. "It is probably used quite often by local youth, a factor we had evidently not allowed for."

Q carefully weighed the other's words, conceding to himself that he was partly responsible for the cock-up. He sipped his coffee in silence for a few moments, deep in thought.

"There can, of course, be no question of a fee in the circumstances," he said, eventually. "But all is not lost."

A deflated Fabien Leroux looked expectantly towards him.

"What is your experience with explosives?" Q then enquired.

"I have used them in the navy," the other replied. "But only in training sessions. Never for real."

"Well and good," came the satisfied reply. "Now is your opportunity to put your training to good account."

Saying that, he reached into his wallet and drew out a slip of paper, which he slipped across the table. Leroux glanced quickly at it. It contained a name and a telephone number.

"Contact this person as soon as possible," Q instructed. "He will supply you with a suitable device. Further instructions will follow in due course, by text message. And no misfires this time!"

"I shall do my level best to meet your requirements," the Canadian assured him, as the older man quickly settled the lunch bill and rose to leave.

Fabien Leroux immediately ordered a second beer, keen to enjoy the atmosphere of a popular London pub. The young waitress had also caught his eye. With her trim figure and dark hair tied back, she struck him as possibly an immigrant from East Europe, one of the large number who had migrated to Britain in recent years in search of better job prospects. It rankled that Q had not coughed up the agreed fee, as he could use the money following his trip to France. He resolved to do better next time.

*

"Any leads on the Stepney Green incident?" Chief Inspector Bill Harrington asked George Mason immediately after lunch that same day.

"Not very much, so far," his colleague replied. "I called at the hospital on Monday evening while the victim was in surgery. I spoke with his wife Linda, who was naturally much distressed."

"It has all the markings of a professional job," the senior man said. "Was she aware of any threats recently made against her husband?"

George Mason shook his head.

"Or was there anything in the victim's background that might reveal a motive?"

"Linda Brodsky knows very little about Max's personal history," Mason informed him. "He told her not to probe too deeply."

"That could imply," Harrington thoughtfully remarked, "that there were aspects of his past that he preferred to keep quiet about."

"Or that he wished to forget, Chief Inspector."

The senior man raised his eyebrows at that canny remark, while slowly nodding his head in agreement.

"Linda's impression, however," George Mason continued, "was that her husband may have been of Russian Jewish origin."

"In which event," Harrington said, "there may have been any number of things he wished to keep under wraps."

"Very true, Chief Inspector," Mason agreed. "I shall go over to Wapping first thing tomorrow morning. I expect Max Brodsky will be sitting up in bed by then. He may be more inclined to talk to me than to his wife about his background."

"Now that his life has been threatened," the other added, "he may well be more forthcoming."

"We shall see what transpires," George Mason said, rising from his chair with the feeling that this could develop into a very interesting case.

*

Later that same afternoon, Fabien Leroux was enjoying the view from the window of the express train to Brighton, as it sped through the dormitory towns and rural villages south of London to cross the Sussex Downs. He had rung the telephone number Q had given him and he was now on his way to meet Dirk deGroot at Pavilion Hotel. He rechecked the text message his enigmatic employer had sent to him. He was to give certain specifications to the Dutch explosives expert, take delivery of the bomb soon as it had been assembled and await further instructions. The Canadian felt a keen sense of relief, as he purchased a cup of tea and arrowroot biscuits from the refreshment trolley, that he was being given a second chance. It would be an opportunity to redeem himself after the botched attempt on Monday evening. He was also in desperate need of funds, having spent liberally in Paris in anticipation of a substantial fee. He preferred to use cash, rather than credit, to leave no trail.

On reaching his destination, he found he had time for a brisk walk along the sea-front, at a resort with strong associations with British royalty. The bracing sea air was welcome after some days in the metropolis; the cawing of the gulls was music to his ears, as they swooped out of the sky for morsels of food children threw to them. There was a sprinkling of early-season tourists on the pebble beach, but no bathers in the still rather chilly waters of the English Channel. On locating Pavilion Hotel, he exchanged pleasantries with the smartly-uniformed commissionaire and entered the lounge bar, which was already quite full of guests sampling drinks before dinner. He ordered a glass of lager and turned to notice someone waving to him from the far side of the room. Taking him to be his Dutch contact, Fabien Leroux crossed the patterned carpet and joined him at table. They shook hands warmly.

"Pleased to make your acquaintance, Monsieur ....?" deGroot began.

"Leroux," his visitor said. "Fabien Leroux."

"Dirk deGroot," the other rejoined. "I am terrible with names, but I rarely forget a face."

"I tend to be the other way round," Leroux confessed. "Better with names than with faces."

"In fact, I am so good at remembering faces," the Dutchman went on, "that I could probably land a good job at Scotland Yard."

"You can't be serious!" an amused Fabien Leroux

exclaimed.

"In view of my current activities, I expect not," came the reply. "But I was very interested to learn that the police have recently established a facial recognition squad. It seems that some people – and they are comparatively few in number – have a special talent for recognizing faces. From a grainy image, caught on camera or on closed-circuit television, they can instantly identify the person in question if they pass him in the street."

"Wouldn't the authorities need large numbers of cameras to achieve results?" his visitor queried, with a strong hint of skepticism.

"British cities are chock full of cameras," the other replied, with a broad smile. "Don't you doubt it, Monsieur. Surveillance of the general public going about their daily business has really taken off in recent years. It has paid off, too - quite handsomely by all accounts - in terms of successful arrests."

"I am surprised to hear that," Leroux remarked, "in a country with a long tradition of civil liberties."

The Dutchman sipped his beer with a knowing look.

"It is all down to terrorism, Monsieur," he said. "It is becoming a major concern in many European capitals. Libertarians, of course, strenuously object to ubiquitous surveillance, but to no avail."

"I have often read about Europe in *Journal de Quebec*," his visitor said. "Especially regarding recent terrorist incidents in England and France."

Dirk deGroot nodded in agreement.

"Very regrettable," he remarked. "But come, my

25

friend, let us not dwell on the downside. Drink up and I shall go to the bar for refills. We can then get down to serious business."

Fabien Leroux made no objection to that. He raised his glass, which was almost half-full, drained it and handed it to his companion. deGroot returned with fresh pints of lager some minutes later, complaining of slow service at the crowded bar.

"Tell me something of your background, Monsieur" he said, on regaining his seat.

"I served several years in the Royal Canadian Navy," Leroux informed him. "Mainly on patrols in the Arctic, including on a minesweeper searching for World War 11 mines drifting in the North Atlantic."

The Dutchman appeared impressed.

"So you have some experience with explosive devices," he observed, with satisfaction. "What type of thing do you have in mind today?"

"Q has mentioned a car bomb," the Canadian replied.

"A very interesting character, Q," deGroot remarked. "I have had few direct dealings with him. To be quite frank, I have never known how to place him. We have some mutual acquaintances, so I imagine it was one of them who referred him to me."

"He struck me as a typical city gentlemen," Leroux remarked, "with his dark business suit and club tie."

"I should say there is a lot more to him, behind that conventional persona he presents to the public."

"But you can meet his requirements?" his visitor

then asked, wondering what the Dutchman might be hinting at.

"Assuredly," came the confident reply. "In fact, you and I shall assemble the device together. It will be a useful learning experience for you. Most of the materials are to hand, except for the timer. I shall need to place a special order for it across the Channel."

"How long will that take?" a concerned Fabien Leroux enquired.

"About a week to ten days," deGroot informed him. "This is my cellphone number." He jotted it down on a beer mat and passed it across the table. "Ring me early next week, with a view to arranging a second meeting. I live in a brick-fronted apartment building called Ullswater House, facing the Brighton Station. You cannot miss it."

"Sounds good," Leroux remarked.

That settled, they sampled their ale in silence for a while, observing the build-up of patrons around the bar. As the hour of seven approached, most of the hotel guests began drifting towards the dining-room. Fabien Leroux's thoughts turned to food, as he had only eaten a ham sandwich at midday.

Dirk deGroot seemed to read his mind.

"I know an excellent Lebanese restaurant downtown," he said. "If you care to join me, Monsieur, we could have dinner there and afterwards visit one of my favorite clubs. It is noted for both traditional and modern jazz, featuring a visiting a quartet from Memphis all this week."

That proposal was music to the Canadian's ears in more ways than one. He readily acquiesced, saying:

"The last train for London leaves at 10.48 p.m. I checked the schedule at Victoria Station when buying my ticket."

"So we have a good opportunity to spend the evening together and get to know each other," the Dutchman said, "ahead of our joint effort in the near future."

*

George Mason's first task on Thursday morning was to visit the hospital at Wapping, just north of the Thames. On arrival at Scotland Yard, he took time to clear a backlog of paperwork and perform a few other routine tasks, to allow the heavy rush-hour traffic to subside. He then headed east along the Thames embankment, arriving at East London General Hospital at just turned ten o'clock. If he was expecting to interview Maxim Brodsky, however, to learn something of his background and business affairs, he was disappointed.

"Mr. Brodsky has suffered a relapse," the almoner informed him.

"How could that be?" the surprised detective asked. "He was supposed to be out of here within days, according to his wife Linda."

The hospital official regretfully shook her head.

"The bullet pierced his right lung," she explained, "causing partial collapse. This was not apparent during the initial diagnosis."

"Can you enlarge on that?" a concerned George Mason asked.

"It means that air is escaping from his lung and

building up outside it, exerting pressure."

"Which would affect his breathing?"

"Precisely, Inspector," she confirmed.

"So what is the prognosis now?" he enquired.

"The condition is treatable," the woman said, matter-of-factly. "We have had similar cases before, at infrequent intervals, admittedly. They usually result from vehicle accidents."

"When the driver was not wearing a seat belt, for example?" Mason said, quickly cottoning on.

The almoner returned a wry smile.

"That is generally the case," she replied, "I regret to say."

"So Mr. Brodsky will be laid up here for the near future?"

"For at least two weeks, I should estimate," came the reply. "We do not keep patients longer than the minimum necessary, owing to the demand for National Health Service beds."

"It is a sign of the times, unfortunately," her visitor remarked, "cutting back on welfare services generally, in the government's austerity program."

"The surgeon, Dr. Arrrowsmith, asked me to give you this," the almoner then said, handing him a small plastic zip-lock bag containing what the detective immediately realized was the bullet extracted from storekeeper's body.

"Thank him for it," he said, as he turned to leave. "I shall be in touch with you again, in due course."

"Good day, Inspector," the woman said. "And thank you for your concern."

CHAPTER 3

Yuri Orlov liked to spend time tending his garden before setting off to work his afternoon shift, starting at two o'clock. Especially at this time of year, there was lots to do ahead of spring plantings. Having cleared the borders by the stone path leading to his front door, to make room for the variety of bulbs he wished to plant, he took a break mid-morning. His attractive wife Daphne brought him fresh coffee and chatted for a while about her plans for the day. Left to himself again, he sipped his warm drink and peered out over the box hedge towards Dulwich Academy, a private school endowed centuries ago. He was a man of stocky build, just short of six feet tall, with a buzz-cut and rather angular features. As he observed with casual interest a game of soccer in progress on the school playing fields, he felt a keen sense of satisfaction about his current circumstances. He and Daphne had moved into their house on leafy Oak Lane about three years ago. The country setting of Dulwich Village, just eight miles south of the Thames, suited them both admirably following years in an apartment house in East London, close to Tilbury Docks. It afforded opportunities for outdoor pursuits in a pleasant middle class neighborhood.

Daphne was nine years his junior. A straw-blond

woman of much slighter build than he, she had a part-time job at the local library, allowing her time to shoulder voluntary work servicing the less-affluent areas of South London. She was also a keen member of the local art club, exhibiting watercolor paintings there, often of the flowers her husband cultivated in their spacious garden. Nearby Dulwich Art Gallery was to her mind the village's most appealing amenity, which she visited quite frequently throughout the year. She especially liked to take family visitors and old friends from London there, ending up in a tea-room clung with magnolia vines for light refreshments. Their only child, Ivan, had moved up to Manchester two years ago, to help manage catering services for one of that city's premier league soccer clubs.

On finishing his coffee, Yuri Orlov handed the empty cup back through the kitchen window, just as his wife was about to leave for the library, where she worked flexible hours. In good weather, she preferred to cover the relatively short distance by bicycle. He watched as she wheeled the vintage machine out of the garage, waved to him and set off at a fairly brisk pace along the country road. He spent the next hour or so trimming the shrubbery, before calling it a day. He cleaned his tools carefully and stacked them in the shed. He then took a quick shower and went down to the diner-kitchen for the light lunch Daphne had prepared for him. On weekdays, it was usually cold cuts with salad, unless there were left-overs from the previous evening's dinner. Daphne always cooked generous portions, especially of meat loaf or tuna-fish pie, which were among his favorite dishes.

While so engaged, he switched on the television to watch the midday news on the BBC, which was soon interrupted by a bulletin from the Metropolitan Police. The spokeswoman, a young sergeant named Alison Aubrey, was appealing for information about a shooting incident at Stepney Green, over two weeks ago. A rifle bullet, presumably fired from the municipal roof garden, had struck a storekeeper on the opposite side of High Street. The victim's name was not revealed and the police claimed to have no leads in the case so far. They were treating it as an isolated incident, similar in character to a recent case of random shooting at vehicles on the M4 motorway. Yuri Orlov smiled to himself on hearing that, while remarking how attractive the young officer was. He was skeptical of her theory, however. That sort of incident was surely more likely to occur in America, he considered, where firearms were readily accessible. England, by contrast, had strict gun-control policies. But Scotland Yard more often than not had the right angle on things, pointing to what could become a disturbing new phenomenon, that of the lone gunman at loose among the general population.

After his lunch, he read the newspaper for an hour before heading off to work. Backing his car out of the driveway, he turned into Oak Lane and proceeded in a westerly direction towards the South London borough of Tooting Bec. As he drove, he congratulated himself on the recent favorable turn of events in his life. Some years ago, he had enrolled as a mature student at University College,

London, to obtain a bachelor's degree in physics. That background had led to a series of junior research positions before he managed to land the post of department head at the Cybernetics Institute, a government-funded research center coordinating several academic disciplines. His job was to ensure smooth cooperation among scientists with sensitive egos, who were highly-trained in their respective fields and jealous of their own specialisms. Diplomacy and tact, as much as scientific credentials, were the main requirements of his job.

*

A little after one o'clock that same day, Fabien Leroux met Q at Roebuck Inn, Chelsea. They served themselves from the cold buffet and occupied an alcove table in the lounge, well out of earshot from the pub regulars crowding the bar area.

"Are you well-prepared for your next mission?" the older man asked, forking a slice of smoked trout.

"I do believe so," the Canadian assured him. "But I have one small problem."

"And what might that be?" came the truculent response.

"I am almost completely out of funds. I had counted on receiving the agreed fee for the Stepney job."

Q chewed his mouthful thoughtfully and helped it down with a swig of Perrier water, while eyeing his companion skeptically. Fabien Leroux glanced down and fidgeted with his fork, separating some large prawns from their brittle shells. The older man's attitude then appeared to soften a little.

"I can make you an advance on your next assignment," he declared. "Two thousand pounds, in fact. The balance will be paid on successful completion."

On hearing that, Leroux felt a keen sense of relief and smiled in gratitude, as his table companion reached for his wallet and peeled off some large-denomination banknotes.

"I had a notion you might ask for money," he remarked. "So I came prepared. Now tell me how you fared at Brighton."

"It went very well," the other replied. "I met with Dirk deGroot and discussed our precise requirements. He said he needed to order a special timer from the Continent. He did not say where."

"I can hazard a guess," Q opined. "That is a very specialized field, with very few operatives."

"On receipt of the timing device," the Canadian went on, "he invited me down to Brighton to help assemble the device. I stayed there for two days."

"What did he use for a timer?" the older man enquired.

"A digital alarm clock," Leroux informed him. "It was connected to the explosives and placed inside a metal container."

"Wouldn't it move about precariously, when handled?" Q wanted to know.

"Dirk deGroot thought of that," came the reply. "The whole package was wrapped in fabric, to prevent movement and any possibility of the wires disconnecting. A magnet was then attached to the container, so it will be a simple matter to fix it to the underside of a vehicle."

His hirer, seemingly satisfied with that account, finished his lunch in silence. He then ordered coffee for two. Fabien Leroux ate more slowly, absorbing the convivial atmosphere of the pub. He then paid a quick visit to the men's room. Meanwhile, Q had spread a map of South London on the table.

"Your next target works at Cybernetics Institute, Tooting Bec," he explained. "The address is 17 Regent Street. Where are you keeping the device, in the meantime?"

"In my hotel room at Bayswater."

"Isn't there a risk that room service might chance upon it?" the other testily enquired.

The Canadian shook his head.

"I placed it inside a shoe box in the wardrobe," he said. "It has a secure lock and I removed the key."

"Well and good, Monsieur," Q said, with evident satisfaction. "In that case, when you retrieve the device, take the Central Line Tube from Queensway to Tottenham Court Road, where you switch to Northern Line South. On leaving the Underground at Tooting Bec, immediately turn left and continue for two blocks along Waverley Road. Regent Street will be the second turning on the right."

"How will I recognize the victim's car?" Leroux asked.

"It is a light-blue Ford Sierra, registration number YBU 425Y."

"What about on-site security?" Leroux wanted to know.

"It is fairly lax," the other replied. "The Cybernetics Institute exists purely for academic research. Practical applications, which would be the more obvious targets of espionage, are conducted at a different facility. It is somewhere in the southwest. In the county of Wiltshire, I believe, not all that far from Stonehenge."

"Where will the vehicle be parked?"

"Right behind the main building, in the main parking lot. The Institute shuts promptly at 9.00 p.m. Nobody is permitted to stay beyond that, for security purposes. Your target will proceed immediately to his vehicle for the drive home."

"Where does he live, as a point of interest?"

"At Dulwich Village."

"I know of it!" the other enthused. "It is the home of Dulwich Academy. When I was at high school in Quebec, they sent their rugby team over for a series of friendly games."

The older man seemed unimpressed.

"There are many famous schools in England," he curtly remarked. "They call them public schools, for some odd reason. They are, in fact, private establishments for the children of the elite. The hoi-poloi attend state schools, where tuition is free."

There was a rather awkward silence for a few moments, before the Canadian said:

"So I should set the alarm clock for, say, 9.10 p.m.?"

Q carefully considered the matter, before nodding in agreement.

"The target should be well on his way home by then," he said. "If the bomb were to explode in the

36

Institute parking lot, it would cause absolute mayhem."

Fabien Leroux returned an understanding smile.

"You evidently wish to limit collateral damage," he said.

"Exactly, my dear sir," the other agreed. "We are not in the business of mass murder, after all."

*

Later that same day, George Mason caught up with Detective Sergeant Aubrey, who had been called out to a domestic abuse case at Clapham Common, just south of the Thames.

"There has been a response to your appeal on television for information about the Stepney Green incident," he told her, as she was writing up her report.

"So soon?" she said, agreeably surprised.

"A teenager rang through about an hour ago," Mason explained. "He claimed to have noticed a tall figure moving towards the elevator through the shrubbery on a rooftop garden facing the hardware store. Shortly afterwards, he heard an ambulance siren. He peered over the parapet to watch the ambulance stop on the opposite side of the street. There was a man lying on the sidewalk, with a small crowd gathering round him."

"Most interesting, George," Alison Aubrey remarked. "Yet why hadn't he come forward with this information sooner?"

George Mason returned an amused smile.

"It seems he was doing a spot of courting with his

girlfriend. Her parents are apparently quite strict and he did not want them to find out that they had been up on the roof garden. It could be that the pair had been having regular trysts up there under the stars."

Alison smiled indulgently.

"Just typical young kids," she said, "and good luck to them. It was big of him to come forward at all. Could he provide a useful description?"

"I am afraid not," her senior replied. "It was already dark and the shrubbery would have obscured his view."

"Can his girlfriend add anything?"

"He wants to keep her out of it," Mason replied. "In fact, he would not even disclose his own name."

Sergeant Aubrey rose from her desk and crossed to the Keurig coffee machine, to fix herself an Italian Roast.

"So what have we learned from that?" she asked, as the coffee percolated.

George Mason perched himself on the edge of her desk and considered the matter.

"This new information, Alison, makes it look less like a random incident, as the media recently implied, and more like a targeted hit, for whatever reason. Max Brodsky was lucky to survive."

"How is he doing?" Alison asked, stirring measured amounts of cream and sugar into her mug.

"The bullet pierced his lung, causing partial collapse, a condition the almoner described as pneumothorax. He will be in hospital for quite some time, apparently."

"In that case, I shall pay his wife a sympathy

call," Alison said.

"That is a very good idea, Sergeant," her colleague agreed. "I feel sure she will appreciate it."

*

On parting company with the enigmatic Q, Fabien Leroux took the Underground back to Bayswater, glad to have some funds in his wallet. On reaching Queensway Station, he turned right along Bayswater Road and entered Nordic Spa. A fitness fanatic, he made good use of the exercise facilities there, did push-ups and weightlifting before heading to the sauna. A glance at the thermometer told him that the temperature inside the chamber was a hundred-and-five degrees Celsius. It was a bit lower than he would have preferred, to get a good sweat, but he shrugged and made do. As he lay prone on the wooden bench, staring up at the charred beams on the low ceiling, he mentally went over the instructions Q had given him. All seemed perfectly straightforward, with no possibility of hitches. Unless, of course, something unforeseen occurred, as had been the case at Stepney Green.

A second bather entered and immediately began ladling water onto the stove. This caused clouds of steam to rise to the ceiling and descend on the bare shoulders of the bathers. Leroux tensed himself, absorbing the impact of the hot droplets and the sudden spike in temperature. After twenty minutes of stoic endurance, he quit the chamber, took a cold shower and relaxed for a while on a comfortable bed in the recovery room, where he ordered a pot of

Ceylon tea with toast. On leaving Nordic Spa feeling fully refreshed, he crossed the busy road and entered Hyde Park, walking as far as the Serpentine for some useful exercise, before heading back to Leinster Hotel. On reaching his room, he switched on the television news on the off-chance there might be a report of the incident at Max's Hardware, Stepney Green. Since nothing was said, he felt confident that he had not been observed on the roof. Those giggling teenagers had no doubt been too wrapped up in themselves to take much notice of anything else.

He unlocked the wardrobe and retrieved the contents of the shoe box, taking a few moments to adjust the timer, before placing the device in his backpack. Pouring himself a stiff drink from the mini-bar, which he was pleased to note carried Jack Daniels, he consulted his Underground map to confirm Q's directions to Tooting Bec and left the hotel. A short walk brought him to La Pergola, a two-star restaurant in the Michelin guide, where he enjoyed a leisurely dinner and read the newspaper. There was a brief account of the Stepney incident, stating that the Metropolitan Police were continuing their enquiries. So far, so good, was his reaction. Allowing himself ample time to reach his destination, he quit the restaurant and proceeded along Queensway to the Underground station. The subway trains were much less crowded now, he was pleased to note, than during the rush-hour, when commuters were often crammed together like sardines in a can.

On resurfacing at Tooting Bec, he took a left, as

directed, walked two blocks along Waverley Road to reach Regent Street. He soon located the premises of Cybernetics Institute, quickly noting the large parking lot behind the building. As it was not yet dark, he continued along the thoroughfare, thinking to pass half an hour or so in a local pub. He duly came across an Irish joint named O'Grady's, where he ordered a half-pint of Guinness, enjoying the piped Irish music in the main bar, while observing with much interest the pub regulars. Some were throwing darts; others were playing dominos, clattering their chips noisily on the bare wooden table. The rest engaged in lively chatter round the bar, with a strong hint of Irish brogue. What a pleasant way to spend an evening, he mused, as he contentedly sipped his chilled stout. English pub life, he considered, had a lot to recommend it, for its sheer conviviality.

Noting through the windows that night was drawing in, he drained his glass, quit the pub and made his way back towards the research institute. It was difficult in the darkness to discern the colors of vehicles in the parking lot. It was several minutes before he identified the Ford Sierra with the registration number YBU 425Y. Crouching low, since lighted windows overlooked the area, he withdrew the explosive device from his backpack and attached it by magnet to the underside of the vehicle. He then quickly regained the shadow of the building, checked that there was nobody about who might have observed his movements and regained Regent Street. Mixing with the light pedestrian traffic, he calmly made his way back to Tooting Bec

Underground station, taking the northbound Northern Line to Tottenham Court Road. He would spend the remainder of the evening in the West End, he decided, to savor some of its storied nightlife.

*

Daphne Orlov had a problem. Since it was a fine evening, she had cycled over to Herne Hill, a community two miles north of Dulwich, to have dinner with her library colleague, Gillian Smart. They discussed, among other matters, summer vacation plans. Gillian and her husband Bill sometimes made joint trips to Europe with the Orlovs. This year, they were planning to take a Viking cruise on the Danube, from Vienna to Budapest, spend some time in the Hungarian capital and then proceed by rail to Prague. Both couples were eagerly looking forward to the experience, their first joint trip in three years. The Smarts, both keen hikers, also liked to make frequent use of the timeshare they had acquired in Snowdonia, North Wales. Shortly before nine o'clock, as she was about to set off home, Daphne discovered that she had a flat tire. Hoping that it had merely deflated for some reason, as cycle tires are wont to do, she tried to revive it with her hand-pump, as Gillian Smart looked on.

"Must be a puncture," her friend sympathetically observed.

Daphne Orlov looked crestfallen.

"How on earth shall I get back home?" she complained.

"Bill would gladly have driven you," Gillian said. "But he is working late this evening and won't be home before eleven."

"I suppose I could walk it," Daphne said. "It's not all that far, thirty minutes at the most."

Her colleague shook her head, decisively. Glancing at her watch, she said:

"It would not be safe enough, Daphne, in the dark. It is almost nine o'clock. Why don't you give your husband a call, to pick you up. He should be leaving work any minute now."

"A good idea, Gillian," the other said, as she wheeled her bicycle back into the front garden, closed the gate and joined her host indoors. "What is the exact time?"

"It is now 8.56."

"I shall have to wait until he actually leaves the Institute. No personal calls are permitted during working hours, unless for an emergency."

"A flat tire is hardly that," Gillian joked. "Let us have a tot of brandy while we wait."

She crossed to the wall cabinet, took down a bottle of Armagnac and poured two good measures.

"I got this on my last visit to Provence," she said. "Bill, who knows his cognac, rates it highly."

"Nice tipple," her friend agreed, on taking a sip, feeling that it soothed her nerves.

*

Promptly at 9.00 p.m., Yuri Orlov emerged from the main entrance to Cybernetics Institute, in company with the other employees, the research scientists and administrative staff, who were mainly female. The janitor secured the door behind them and switched off the porch lights, in line with the government drive for economy in official buildings. As Yuri walked towards the parking lot, thinking what a fine starlit evening it was, his cellphone rang. He stopped in his tracks and lit a cigarette, while listening to his wife explain her predicament.

"No problem, Daphne," he assured her. "I am just leaving work and shall call by Herne Hill on my way home."

"What should I do about my bicycle, Yuri?" his wife asked.

"We can put it in the trunk and see if I can fix the problem at the weekend. You probably ran over a nail. It is easily done."

"I cannot remember when I last had a puncture," she remarked. "I do not even know if we have a repair kit."

"I imagine there is one in the garage somewhere," her husband told her. "It's a nuisance, but it can't be helped. Did your evening go well?"

"Absolutely!" came the reply. "Gillian and Bill are very keen on the idea of a Danube cruise. They think it will be great fun."

"Glad to hear it," Yuri said. "We should make a deposit on it without delay, to avoid disappointment. These river cruises tend to book up early."

"I shall mention that to Gillian before you arrive, dear. See you soon."

"Give me about twenty minutes, Daphne."

With that, he rang off and remained on the

forecourt to finish his cigarette, glancing now and then up at the stars, wishing he could identify more of them. His knowledge of the heavens was very limited and he had long been promising himself an evening course in astronomy at Clapham Polytechnic, if only his work schedule would allow it. With a final glance at what he took to be Orion, he stubbed out his cigarette and rounded the corner of the building to reach the parking lot. That was the last thing he recalled about that particular evening.

*

George Mason arrived at the Regent Street premises at just turned 9.25 p.m., accompanied by a team from Forensics. They were met with a scene of devastation in the parking lot of Cybernetics Institute. Twisted pieces of metal and tire shards strewed the ground. Wreaths of acrid smoke still hung in the air. Curious onlookers were kept well back.

"What have we here?" the detective asked, turning to the chief forensic officer, Walter Stopford.

"It looks very much like a car bomb," Stopford replied, as firemen were extinguishing a blaze in a vehicle at the center of the parking lot.

The police team warily approached the vehicle, which continued smoldering when the flames were doused.

"It is – or was – a Ford Sierra," Stopford announced, examining the rear of the car, while his assistant combed the area for clues.

"Any injured parties?" Mason asked the head fireman, a burly individual whose rough-hewn features wore a grim expression.

"The paramedics left just minutes before you arrived," he informed him. "The only victim, a middle-aged male, is on his way by ambulance to South Wimbledon Hospital."

"Any news of his condition?"

The fireman gravely shook his head.

"He was struck, apparently, by a piece of metal," he said. "Probably the door of the target vehicle. The explosion occurred about ten minutes after the Institute closed for the day. Other personnel had fortunately cleared the area by then."

"A stroke of luck," the detective remarked. "Otherwise this would have been a scene of carnage."

"You can say that again, Inspector," the fireman said, turning to supervise his crew's activities.

The janitor, who had lingered in the background to watch the unfolding of events, approached the two officials and introduced himself.

"What light can you shed on all this?" George Mason enquired.

"As I explained to the fire officer," the man replied, "I heard a loud explosion as I was on my rounds inside the building, shutting down computers and locking doors, prior to leaving. That usually takes me about twenty minutes. I was about half-way through my routine when the incident occurred."

"That would be at approximately 9.10 p.m.?"

The janitor nodded.

"Do you know the identity of the injured party?" the detective then asked.

"It was Yuri Orlov," came the confident reply.

"How can you be sure of that?"

"I spotted him on the forecourt as I was closing the front entrance. He was speaking on his cellphone while smoking a cigarette."

"Is that his car that was targeted?"

"I do believe so, Inspector, if it was a Ford Sierra. The other staff would have left promptly," the janitor said.

"Your own vehicle was not parked here?"

"I live nearby, Inspector Mason, so I generally come by bicycle. I leave it by a side entrance used mainly by cleaners and tradespeople."

"Do you happen to know Mr. Orlov's next-of-kin or his home address?" Mason asked him.

The janitor, a wiry man in his late fifties, shook his head.

"Details like that are stored on the office computer," he explained. "I could admit you inside the building, but I do not have the website password. Only the Institute director and his deputy have it."

"Thank you for the help you were able to give," Mason said, turning to Walter Stopford as the janitor walked to the far side of the building to retrieve his bicycle.

"After my assistant has gathered useful fragments," the expert informed him, "we shall take them to the laboratory for a thorough examination."

"Let me know if something significant turns up,

Walt," the detective said, casting a final glance over the scene before heading back to his car. "The fire service are the best to deal with all this. There is very little I can do before we get some hard evidence."

"Grab an early night, while you can, Inspector Mason," Walter Stopford said. "My assistant and I shall be here for quite some time."

"On the way," the detective replied, "I shall pay a quick visit to South Wimbledon Hospital."

Twenty minutes later, following a drive in light evening traffic, he pulled up outside the hospital. While driving, it had struck him as curious that both targets in these recent incidents had Russian surnames. Could there be a connection, he wondered, or did the difference in the method employed discount that? It would be interesting to see what Forensics came up with, before drawing any conclusions on that score. On entering and showing ID, he was directed to a waiting area. Ten minutes later, a senior nurse approached him.

"You are enquiring about Yuri Orlov?" she asked.

The detective nodded and rose to his feet, to greet a tall, fair-haired woman with a brisk manner.

"Mr. Orlov is in intensive care," she informed him.

"The nature of his injuries?" a concerned George Mason enquired.

"Severe concussion, plus trauma to the right shoulder and neck, Inspector."

"Is his condition life-threatening?"

The senior nurse shook her head, with a half-smile.

"The patient will, however, be with us for quite some time," she explained. "We would expect him to make a full recovery in due course, absent further complications."

"I am very pleased to hear that," George Mason said. "Now, about his next-of-kin?"

The nurse passed him a well-worn driving license, with fraying edges.

"This is the only personal document we found among his effects," she informed him.

The detective made a note of the address, handed the document back to her and made to leave the premises.

"I shall be in touch," he said, "probably tomorrow morning, after making enquiries."

"Thank you very much, Inspector Mason," the nurse said, on parting. "That will be most helpful."

Half an hour later, George Mason arrived at 5 Oak Lane, Dulwich. On alighting from his car, he approached the house and rang the doorbell. The occupant opened the door, reacting in some surprise at the presence of a complete stranger.

"Inspector George Mason, of Scotland Yard," he said.

A look of alarm spread across the petite woman's features.

"Step inside, Inspector," she said. "I was on the point of contacting the police. I tried to reach my husband by telephone from Herne Hill, where I was visiting a friend, but without success. I arrived home by taxi a few minutes ago and expected Yuri to have arrived home from Tooting Bec. He clocks off promptly at nine o'clock."

The detective accepted the offer of a seat facing her in the parlor of their comfortable home, noting a painting of what he took to be Cornish Riviera on the opposite wall.

"I am afraid your husband has met with an accident," he said, as gently as he could. "He has been admitted to South Wimbledon Hospital."

Daphne Orlov reacted in alarm.

"I had the feeling something had happened to him," she tearfully said. "I must get to him straight away."

"That would not be practicable, Mrs. Orlov," Mason rejoined "He is currently in intensive care. Better wait until tomorrow morning, when the picture will be clearer. I shall get my assistant, Detective Sergeant Aubrey, to pick you up and drive you down to South Wimbledon."

"What exactly has happened, Inspector Mason?" Daphne demanded. "I need to know the truth."

"A bomb was attached to the undercarriage of your husband's car," he explained. "Luckily for him, he had not yet reached it. It seems he was struck by flying metal as he entered the parking lot."

Daphne Orlov gasped aloud, rose from her chair and paced the room agitatedly.

"How could such a thing happen?" she protested. "How could anyone wish to harm my husband? We live a quiet life here in Dulwich and do not interfere with other people. I am at a complete loss to understand this."

"Please calm yourself, Mrs. Orlov," Mason urged. "We shall get to the bottom of it, all in good time. It is getting rather late now. I advise a good night's rest. We shall catch up with each other in the morning, after you have visited the hospital. I may have a few questions to put to you, if you are agreeable."

Daphne showed her visitor to the door.

"I shall do anything in my power to assist you," she emphatically replied, having regained some of her composure.

"Good night, Mrs. Orlov," her visitor said. "Sleep well!"

"Good night, Inspector Mason. And thank you for coming."

CHAPTER 4

The next day, George Mason arrived at Oak Lane, Dulwich at just turned eleven o'clock. Detective Sergeant Aubrey and Daphne Orlov had just got back from South Wimbledon. Daphne immediately made fresh coffee, which she served with digestive biscuits to her visitors in the parlor.

"What news from the hospital?" George Mason solicitously enquired.

"Yuri is in a stable condition," Daphne replied. "I thank God for that. But he is still in intensive care, so unfortunately I was not able to see him. I left a bunch of daffodils from our garden, to be placed at his bedside."

"We discussed the situation with the medical staff," Alison Aubrey added. "Mr. Orlov's condition is not considered to be life-threatening."

"That is a lucky break," Mason said. "It could easily have gone the other way."

"It was a good thing my phone-call caused him some delay as he was leaving the Institute," Daphne remarked. "A flat bicycle tire saved the day, after all."

George Mason smiled at her nice sense of irony. He sipped his coffee thoughtfully, grateful for the warm drink on a cool mid-April day, while glancing through the window at the spring flowers in the front garden.

"Do you know of anyone who would wish to harm your husband, Mrs. Orlov?" he enquired.

His hostess shook her head.

"As I indicated last evening, Inspector," she replied, "this is a complete mystery to me."

"Yuri has not received any threats," Alison asked, "in so far as you are aware?"

"If he did," came the reply, "he has certainly not mentioned anything of that disturbing nature to me."

"Were you aware, Mrs. Orlov, of the incident about a week ago at Stepney Green?"

"I may have seen something about it on the news," she replied. "So many untoward things happen these days, no particular incident readily springs to mind."

George Mason cleared his throat and said:

"The target in that incident also had a Russian surname. He was called Maxim Brodsky. He is recovering from a gunshot wound at East London General Hospital."

Daphne Orlov's eyes opened wide in surprise.

"You are suggesting there may be a connection?" she queried.

"It is at least a remarkable coincidence," Sergeant Aubrey remarked.

"Many Russians live in London nowadays," Daphne said. "They even have Orthodox churches and their own schools."

"That is very true," Mason agreed, thinking of millionaire immigrants. "Did your husband, whom by his name I take to be of Russian extraction, have much contact with fellow nationals?"

"Not in a day-to-day context," she replied, refilling their cups. "But he certainly did at Christmastide."

"Can you expand on that, Mrs. Orlov?" Alison asked.

At that, Daphne rose from her chair and stepped into a room towards the rear of the house, returning minutes later with a large desk diary, which she placed open on the coffee table.

"Russian Christmas follows the old Julian calendar," she explained. "It is celebrated about three weeks after the European festivities. Yuri was accustomed to sending greetings cards to some of the people listed in this diary."

The two detectives peered with much interest at the short list of names.

"Are these people somehow related to your husband?" George Mason asked. "Or are they just friends and acquaintances?"

"Yuri never spoke much about them, to tell you the truth, Inspector," came the rather bemused reply. "And I did not ask, for fear of prying."

"You yourself are not of Russian extraction?" the detective sergeant prompted.

Daphne Orlov essayed a thin smile at the question and shook her head.

"I am British, born and bred," she said, "hailing from Bournemouth. I met my husband on a guided tour of the Dutch bulb fields, organized by Globus Travel."

"How romantic is that!" Alison said.

Their hostess smiled again, more broadly, reassuring them that she was slowly coming to terms with the recent tragic occurrence.

"We are both keen gardeners," she said. "I suppose it was flowers that brought us together and helped us bond."

"As I can appreciate from your lovely garden," Alison remarked.

"Thank you," Daphne replied. "Yuri devotes a lot of his spare time to it."

"You definitely have no idea of Yuri's link with the individuals in this diary?" George Mason asked, nudging his coffee cup aside.

"I got the impression," she said, "from the odd remark Yuri made, that they all knew each other back in Russia. During the Soviet era, as a matter of fact. They all left the country around the same time. 1989, I think it was."

"That is assuredly most interesting," Mason observed. "Were they perhaps all members of, say, a theatre troupe, a trade delegation, or something along those lines?"

"I have no idea what their connection was," their hostess replied, "to be perfectly honest with you."

"Yet they seem to have left as a group," Alison Aubrey said, "in the way that Soviet nationals on foreign tours or assignments sometimes defected to the West."

"You mean groups attending conferences, for example, Alison?" her senior put in. "Or musicians, such as members of string quartets? Or athletes even?"

"Something along those lines, Inspector," his young colleague replied.

"I should like to pursue this idea further," Mason

then said. "May I make a note of these names and addresses?"

"By all means, Inspector," came the reply. "Most of them live in London. They may be willing to open up on their shared history."

The detective read off the names.

"We have a Mikhail Konev and a Dmitri Smirnov, both of whom have a London address. Maxim Brodsky also appears here, by a most interesting coincidence."

"He being the person targeted at Stepney Green?" Daphne Orlov nervously enquired.

"Correct," Mason tersely replied. "And it may be that these other individuals are also in danger if, as seems to be the case, they are linked by a common thread."

"How dreadful would that be!" their hostess exclaimed.

"The last-named here, a Pavel Belinsky, does not appear to have a current mailing address," Alison Aubrey remarked. "The entry has been partially erased."

"Yuri may have lost touch with him," Daphne suggested.

"Which could very easily happen," Mason considered, "in the circumstances. People often move on, to new jobs, new cities. He could have gone to the Continent, or even farther afield, say to America, in the intervening years."

"Or they could have had a disagreement," his young colleague suggested.

Daphne Orlov thought about that for a few moments, before saying:

"Either is possible, I suppose. Only Yuri could fill you in on that."

Her two visitors then thanked her for the refreshments and rose to take their leave.

"We shall be in touch, Mrs. Orlov," George Mason said, pausing on the threshold with an admiring glance at the blooms in the front garden, "as soon as we have some definite leads. Your husband will be in good hands at South Wimbledon. After teaching hospitals like St. Bartholomew's, it is one of the best hospitals in the London area."

"I am gratified to hear that, Inspector Mason," she replied. "And I look forward to hearing from you again, in due course, so that Yuri and I can continue to lead our lives without this kind of threat hanging over us."

"Amen to that," Alison added.

*

Mikhail Konev was accustomed to taking his lunch-break in the staff canteen, where a warm buffet was usually served. On filling his tray with a helping of shepherd's pie, a chocolate mousse for dessert and a bottle of Perrier water, he chose a table by the window overlooking several acres of lawn, fringed with birch trees just coming into leaf. He preferred to eat alone on this particular day, leaving his colleagues to chat among themselves. It would help him gather his thoughts for the afternoon, when an important client of Philpot's Advertizing Agency was due to arrive, by prior appointment.

While eating, he reflected with satisfaction that he was approaching his twentieth anniversary with Philpot, one of the leading firms in its field. Over the years, he had risen to the rank of senior account manager, specializing in the catering and brewing industries. This afternoon, he would meet with the managing director of Tadcastle Ales, who was arriving by train from Leeds. The Yorkshire brewer was about to begin promoting its products - mainly premium beers – for the first time in Russia, which was thought to present a promising new market.

Mikhail had been named by Philpot management as the key executive to handle the initial advertising campaign. He spoke fluent Russian and was familiar with the terrain as well as the habits of his former countrymen. It would be a matter of somehow weaning them off strong liquor and promoting the attractions of English beer, aware that high-profile German and Dutch brewers had made significant inroads into the Russian market in recent years. He had already had some limited success in introducing British products into East Europe, notably in Poland and Bulgaria. The Czech market, amply served by its celebrated pilsners, had proved more resistant. And good luck to them! Mikhail Konev was not a man to cry over spilled milk...or was it spilled beer? He finished the main course, reflecting that it had likely been made with New Zealand lamb, so tender had the meat been. He quickly ate his dessert, gulped down his mineral water and went back up to his office on the third floor, where he fixed himself a Sumatran dark roast and gathered his thoughts for the meeting ahead.

One hour later, his client arrived. Edward Marsh was a well-built man in his mid-fifties, with a ruddy complexion in testimony to decades of sampling his own products. A typical no-nonsense Yorkshireman, his manner was brusque and to-the-point. The account executive bade him take a seat facing him across a desk sporting amateur golf trophies and a set of chessmen.

"Had a good trip down, Ted?" he genially enquired.

"The Inter-city service took just over two hours," his visitor replied. "The buffet car did a passable lunch, to help pass the time."

"I have been considering your advertising needs carefully," Konev continued. "Selling English beer to the Russians will take a lot of careful groundwork."

"I am aware," the brewer drily remarked, "that they have generally gone for stronger liquor, particularly vodka."

"But did you know, Ted," the executive replied, with a twinkle in his eye, "that Russian women are increasingly seeking Muslim husbands, on the grounds that they do not use alcohol? I read that recently in an article in *The Times*."

Edward Marsh returned a look of amused surprise.

"Is alcohol as serious a problem as that?" he asked.

"I am afraid so," came the reply.

"Then we could be doing a lot of people a lot of good by converting them to Tadcastle Ales."

"The question, Ted," Konev pointedly replied, "is

how best to achieve that objective."

"What are your preliminary thoughts on the matter, Mikhail?"

"I think we should emphasize the Britishness of the product. Most foreigners have a positive view of Britain. Our advertising campaign should be quintessentially English."

"You are not suggesting using the royal family, for heaven's sake, are you, Mikhail?" the brewer half-seriously enquired.

The account executive smilingly shook his head.

"That would be a great idea, Ted, if we could get the royals to cooperate. Instead, we can feature soccer, for instance. The English Premier League is known all over the world. Teams like Manchester United, Tottenham Hotspur and Chelsea have dedicated fans in Moscow, St. Petersburg and other Russian cities."

"I am beginning to get your angle," his client said, approvingly. "How about cricket, too? There is nothing more English than that."

Mikhail Konev was not so sure about that.

"It might work, to a limited extent," he dubiously remarked. "But, unfortunately, foreigners rarely understand the game. I was in America recently, for instance. Americans are totally baffled by it."

"That would certainly be a drawback, Mikhail.," the other agreed.

"Aside from soccer," the advertising executive continued, warming to his theme, "we could feature prominent London landmarks."

"Such as the Tower of London, Big Ben, Buckingham Palace and the Houses of Parliament?"

Mikhail Konev nodded, saying:

"They are easily recognizable and would add a touch of class to your product, Ted. You might consider featuring them on bottle labels, for example."

Edward Marsh leaned back in his chair and thought about that, just as a junior member of staff entered to serve tea. The account executive did the honors, pouring the milk first, followed by premium Darjeeling.

"Sugar, Ted?" he asked.

His visitor shook his head.

"You can't beat a nice cuppa," he said, grateful for the pick-me-up after the long rail trip and commute across London.

"Except perhaps with a Tadcastle Export Premium," Konev ingratiatingly remarked.

"Now you are talking, Mikhail! But I rarely touch liquor before seven in the evening."

Konev thoughtfully sipped his tea, allowing his preliminary ideas to sink in.

"Will your promotion budget extend to a trip to Moscow?" he eventually asked.

His client rose from his chair and crossed to the window, still clasping his cup of tea. A large flock of starlings caught his eye. He followed their antic movements as they spiraled over the lawn and headed north.

"Migrating birds," he remarked. "A sure sign of spring."

"Wonderful to see," the other said. "Last year, we put out feeders for them, attracting a variety of species, including hummingbirds."

The Yorkshireman regained his seat.

"Your suggestion about fresh labeling sounds promising, Mikhail," he said, little interested in ornithology. "But what would be the objective of a trip to Russia?'

"Mainly to sound out the media – the newspapers and television stations – and to get a general feel of the place. The British Embassy should be able to give us some useful pointers, too."

Edward Marsh judiciously nodded.

"We might go together," he said, taking to the idea. "I have often wanted to visit Russia. With your background, Mikhail, you would be the ideal guide."

"It is a while since I was last there," the executive replied. "It will have changed quite a bit over the past twenty years."

"But you still speak the language?"

"True enough, Ted," Konev agreed. "I could hardly forget my native tongue, even though I have scarcely used it since coming to Britain."

"Your wife is not Russian, I take it?"

"Hillary is from Yorkshire, like your good self," came the reply.

His visitor beamed approval.

"By all means bring her along," he urged. "I shall ask Marjorie to join us, too. We shall make it a foursome and combine business with pleasure. My wife would be very keen to attend a performance of the Bolshoi Ballet, for example."

The account manager could not have expected a better outcome to his meeting with an important client. He had often wished to revisit his homeland, curious about the changes that had taken place there since the collapse of the Soviet Union. Including Hillary in the venture was also had its attractions. She would be thrilled at the prospect.

"I shall make enquiries regarding travel arrangements," he said, rising to lead his visitor on a tour of the graphics department, where they were preparing promotional materials for current advertising campaigns.

"Make it for the beginning of May," the Yorkshire brewer suggested. "But not for the May Day Parade, to avoid the crowds."

"And the military hardware!" the other quipped.

As he rose from his chair, the visitor pointed to the chess pieces laid out on the board.

"That is a nice set, Mikhail," he remarked. "Is it for show, or do you actually play the game?"

"Not as much as I did back home in Moscow," Konev replied. "But I do visit my local chess club, from time to time, when I have a free evening."

"I sometimes dabbled in it at college," Edward Marsh acknowledged. "I have not played much since, except occasionally with my son. Do you have any particular model for your game?"

The executive thought about the question briefly, before saying:

"I used to study the theory of the game in earlier days, when I was a more serious player. Nowadays, the local competition is rather limited, compared to the scene back in the USSR."

"I can appreciate that," the other said. "Which chess player did you most admire in those days?"

"The Latvian grandmaster Mikhail Tal," came the

unhesitant reply. 'He was world champion in 1960. A leading exponent of Queen's Gambit Declined."

"A bit above my level," his client confessed, as they left the room.

*

Earlier that same day, Fabien Leroux left Leinster Hotel and took the Northern Line Tube to Tooting Bec, retracing his steps towards Cybernetics Institute. A sort of morbid curiosity impelled him to revisit the scene, even while acknowledging that it would have been more prudent to keep his distance. Checking that the parking lot was deserted, he ventured into it, noting the darkened patch of asphalt at the center. Bits of car debris still strewed the ground, confirming the success of his criminal enterprise. Q would be very satisfied with the result, he mused, as he made a casual inspection of the area, before heading back to the Underground station. From there, he took the northbound line a few stops to Elephant & Castle, where he had arranged to meet Q for lunch at the Horse & Jockey pub.

"Greetings, Monsieur," the older man coolly began, as the Canadian crossed the lounge bar to join him at a corner table. "What will you have to drink?"

"A pint of bitter," Leroux said, noting with unease Q's cool demeanor.

On Q's return from the bar, they studied the menu, opting for steak pie with French fries. Leroux crossed to the service counter to place the order. He was handed a ticket with a number on it that would be called out when the meal was ready.

"You followed my instructions to the letter," Q said. "I will grant you that, and I take full responsibility for the outcome."

From the older man's tone of voice, Fabien Leroux sensed that something was very amiss.

"Is there a problem?" he anxiously asked.

Q took a swig of beer before answering and glanced around to make sure other pub patrons were not within easy earshot.

"The target had not reached his car by the time your device exploded," he remarked, with a deep frown.

"You mean that he escaped harm?" the Canadian asked, with a look of incredulity.

Q returned a half-smile.

"Apparently, he was seriously injured by the blast," he replied. "Struck by flying metal as he entered the parking lot."

Fabien Leroux shifted uneasily in his seat, while coming to terms with this unforeseen setback.

"So where is he now?" he enquired.

"According to the newspapers," the other replied, "he is in intensive care at South Wimbledon Hospital. My sources tell me that the outlook is uncertain. He may or may not survive."

"Something must have delayed him leaving the

Institute," Leroux opined.

"Evidently so, Monsieur," came the terse reply. "But do not blame yourself. As the great Scottish poet, Robert Burns, once wrote: *The best-laid schemes of mice and men oft gang a-glay.*"

The Canadian returned an amused smile on hearing that. He would never have suspected a poetical touch from this mysterious and sinister individual. Then again, he mused, how much did he really know about the man, who revealed nothing of himself and not even the names of the targets? He relaxed inwardly. All, apparently, was not lost. Their meal number was announced. He went to the busy serving area to collect it, noting as they tackled the tasty dish how much Q enjoyed his food, which he ate in silence.

On eventually nudging his empty plate to one side, the older man said:

"On future occasions, you will need to employ a different method. Explosives are messy. I hate disorder of any kind."

Fabien Leroux was relieved to hear that there would be future occasions, since he badly needed the money.

"A pistol is perhaps the most reliable method," he replied.

"See if you can get hold of one, from your contacts here in London. I do not keep a private arsenal."

"My ex-navy friend at Brixton has a useful stock of firearms. He is bound to have a pistol or revolver."

"Well and good," Q replied, taking a satisfying

swig of ale. "Now pay close attention, Monsieur. It helps that the two previous targets are out of circulation for the time being. It is not quite the desired result, but it is provisionally useful."

"When is the next assignment due?" Leroux asked.

"Not for at least two weeks," came the reply. "I shall be out of the country on official business for the rest of the month. In the meantime, you could be doing some research on the next two possible candidates."

"Who might they be?" an intensely curious Fabien Leroux enquired.

"Their names do not matter," came the curt reply. "It is better, in fact, and much simpler, if you just regard them as targets. While I am away, I shall text you the relevant addresses. Locate them and observe as much as you can of their daily routines and those of other members of their households – wives, children, in-laws etc."

Saying that, the older man drained his glass before reaching into an inside pocket. He drew out a wad of high-denomination banknotes and passed them across the table.

"This should keep the wolf from the door for the time being," he said, as he rose to leave.

Left to himself, Fabien Leroux quickly counted the money. It was about half the agreed figure, he ruefully noted. But it would have to do, in the circumstances. He crossed to the bar for a refill, content to pass the next hour or so in the convivial atmosphere of the pub, while wondering what Q meant by 'official business'. That seemed to suggest government affairs, but how could a public official, if he was indeed such, be instigating hits against citizens of London? This was the United Kingdom, after all, not some banana republic. The plot grows thicker, he mused, as he called Jeb Sinclair on his iPhone to learn what time he would be home from work. He could then go down to Brixton to could discuss handguns.

CHAPTER 5

In the early evening of the following day, George Mason dispatched Detective Sergeant Aubrey to Shoreditch, to inform the Smirnovs of the attempts on the lives of Brodsky and Orlov. She was also to try to find out what she could about the connections linking the group of Russian emigres. He himself, after informing his wife Adele that he would be late home for dinner, took the Tube to Cockfosters, arriving at 110 Sevenoaks Road at just turned six o'clock. Mikhail Konev, who had just got home from work, reacted in some surprise at the arrival of a member of the Metropolitan Police, inviting the detective into the sitting-room of a semi-detached house in a mixed commercial and residential neighborhood.

"To what do I owe the honor of a visit from Scotland Yard?" he asked, with a puzzled look.

"Are you aware, Mr. Konev, of attempts made recently on the lives of Maxim Brodsky and Yuri Orlov?"

A look of dismay spread across the man's intelligent features.

"No, Inspector," he emphatically replied. "I was certainly not aware of that."

"There were reports in the newspapers and on television," the detective said.

"I have been far too busy to pay much attention to

the media," the account executive replied.

"I believe they were acquaintances of yours," his visitor prompted.

Konev reacted with unease at that remark, wondering how his visitor could be aware of something like that. George Mason, noting the man's hesitation in replying, added:

"My understanding, Mr. Konev, is that you left the Soviet Union as a group in 1990 and that you have kept in fairly regular contact since arriving in this country."

A hesitant smile spread across the Russian's face.

"Your sources of information are correct, Inspector," he said. "But the contacts between us are very limited. We are accustomed to exchanging greetings cards for Russian Christmas. And that's about it."

"You are quite sure of that?" Mason persisted.

"Absolutely," came the reply.

"Why would someone suddenly decide to pick off members of your group?" his visitor then asked. "Do you have a view on that?"

Mikhail Konev rose from his chair and crossed to the cocktail cabinet, pouring himself a large tot of whisky. Mason, being on duty, accepted a glass of tonic water.

"Perhaps they were just random incidents," the Russian said. "After all, Inspector, many people in London are victims of assault these days. It's the world we live in, sad to say."

"Very true, Mr. Konev," his visitor allowed. "And it may very well turn out that these were unrelated incidents. But for your safety, provisionally, and that of other members of your group, I am considering the possibility that they are connected to your common background in Russia."

Mikhail Konev added a dash of soda to his whisky, took a sip and said:

"I appreciate your concern, Inspector, and I am only too glad that my wife Hillary is not here to be party to this conversation. She is out shopping at the local mall."

"I was hoping to catch you privately," Mason said. "It had occurred to me that you all might have been members of an official tour, possibly to do with music or the theatre, and that you decided to defect as a group at some point in 1990."

A brief smile lit up the other's features.

"You are on the right lines, Inspector," an impressed Mikhail Konev remarked. "There was nothing particularly artistic in our background, however, unless you consider chess an art. We were all members of the intelligence services, and also of a chess team based at Artists' Village, in the Leningradsky suburb of Moscow."

George Mason reacted in some surprise to that disclosure.

"You got out while the going was good?" he asked, after taking a few moments to digest the information.

"Exactly, Inspector," the other replied. "We saw the end of the Soviet Union coming and decided to leave. We were taking part in an international chess tournament at Helsinki, in which we were placed second. While in the Finnish capital, we purchased tickets from Finnair, flew to Heathrow and applied for asylum in Britain."

The detective again took a few moments to digest the surprising information, before saying:

"You were all agents of the secret service, but evidently not very dedicated Communists. How could that be?"

"After the fall of the Berlin Wall," the advertising executive replied, "it became obvious to us that the Soviet Union would crumble too, sooner or later. Many of us had already lost faith in the system and the outlook for members of our profession seemed uncertain. Would a more liberal society have the same need for a secret service?"

"You were afraid of possible reprisals, too," Mason suggested, "as occurred with the East German secret police, known as the Stasi."

"That was also a factor in our decision," Konev agreed. "But it was not the main one. Our objective was to make a clean break with the system as it then was and start over in a different country with more mature values."

"And you have evidently done very well for yourself in the intervening years," his visitor remarked, "judging from your circumstances here at Cockfosters."

"Fate has been kind to me since I left Russia, I must admit," he replied. "I studied advertising and marketing at Hammersmith Polytechnic and managed to move up the ladder to my present position as senior account executive at Philpot's."

"Good for you," Mason remarked. "That is one of our leading agencies. The Metropolitan Police have sometimes used it, to help bolster their image with the general public."

"In fact, Inspector," the other went on, "I am planning to make my first visit to Russia since I left in 1990."

"In connection with your work?" the detective asked.

Mikhail Konev nodded.

"We shall be running a major promotion for Tadcastle Ales," he explained.

"The Yorkshire brewer?" an intrigued George Mason asked. "As a Yorkshireman myself, I know it well."

"We are aiming to break into the Russian market, as a niche product."

"Your will have your work cut out for you there," his visitor opined, "given the competition, especially from Holland, Italy and Germany."

"Don't we know it, Inspector!" came the reply. "We shall give it our best shot, however, using the soccer premiership and iconic London sights in our promotional campaign."

"What about the royals?" Mason prompted.

"We thought about inviting one of them to Moscow, perhaps to a function arranged by the British Embassy at which our beers would be served. But we decided in the end that royalty may be a sensitive matter with the Russians, since they lost their own royal family during the Revolution."

"You have a point there, Mr. Konev," the detective agreed. "When do you expect to embark on this interesting project, may I ask?"

"In about two weeks' time, in early May."

"We shall hopefully have made some progress in

our investigations by the time you return," Mason then said. "It is as well that you will be out of the country meanwhile. Out of harm's way, in a manner of speaking."

. "My wife and I are very much looking forward to the trip," the other said, discounting the detective's last comment. "As is my client, Edward Marsh."

"Before I leave, Mr. Konev, is there anything else you feel I should know, to help me in my enquiries?"

Mikhail Konev again rose from his chair and crossed to the window overlooking the well-kempt front lawn. He finished his drink and did not speak for several minutes.

"Is something the matter?" his visitor enquired.

The account executive turned to face him, without sitting down.

"There is one other matter you should perhaps be aware of, Inspector," he said, with a grave turn of phrase.

"Go on," the detective urged.

"One member of our group, Igor Nikolayev, died in mysterious circumstances only days after setting foot on English soil."

"Can you expand on that, Mr. Konev?" an intrigued George Mason asked.

"He collapsed while walking across Chelsea Bridge, Inspector. I do not know much about the incident, since my English at that time was too limited to read the newspapers. I subsequently heard on the grapevine that foul play was not ruled out."

"Indeed?" came the surprised response. "If Nikolyev was the victim of foul play, what might have been the motive?"

Mikhail Konev merely shrugged and regained his seat. Peering directly into his visitor's eyes, he said: "The intelligence services may have been involved."

"Because they feared he might spill the beans to the British, regarding the structure, strengths and objectives of the Russian secret service?" the detective asked.

The account executive nodded, saying:

"That is a scenario, Inspector, that cannot be ruled out."

"How interesting is that!" Mason remarked.

"That is all many years ago," Konev continued. "I would find it hard to believe that the authorities are now on our trail."

"Since any useful information you may have left Russia with would be totally out-of-date by now?"

"One would certainly think so," came the reply.

"The plot only thickens," his visitor said, downing his tonic water and rising to leave. "I shall try to contact you again shortly after your visit to Russia."

"I would appreciate that, Inspector Mason. Keep me posted on any developments. My life may depend on it."

As George Mason exited through the front door, Hillary Konev was unloading her shopping from the trunk of her Ford sedan parked in the driveway. She cast a curious glance in his direction. Her husband, however, declined to introduce them and her gaze closely followed the visitor as he entered his own car parked in the street outside and drove off. She then glanced at her husband for an explanation, but he said nothing, merely helping her bring in the groceries.

*

The next day, George Mason and Alison Aubrey were summoned first thing into the chief inspector's office for a brief conference. Fresh coffee was served. Bill Harrington was in an upbeat frame of mind. His elder daughter, Melissa, had just made the cut with the London Symphony, being offered the chair of third violin in the string section.

"You will get complimentary tickets," Alison remarked, on hearing the news.

"Aren't my wife and I looking forward to that!" Bill Harrington exclaimed, with a satisfied grin. "Now bring me up-to-date on recent casework."

George Mason cleared his throat, took a sip of hot coffee and said:

"We are acting on the assumption that the two recent murder attempts in this city are connected, Chief Inspector."

"What grounds do you have for thinking that?" Harrington challenged.

"I discovered during recent interviews that the two victims were members of a chess team who left the Soviet Union as a group in 1990. They defected, to put it bluntly."

"That is a promising start," the senior officer said, his hand hovering near his whisky drawer.

"I visited a third member of that group last evening," Mason continued. "He told me that they were all also former members of the secret service!"

"You don't say so!" Harrington exclaimed. "Did he mention ever meeting the notorious British double agent Kim Philby, who lived out his retirement in Moscow with the rank of colonel?"

George Mason smiled ironically at that remark.

"He may well have crossed his path," he replied. "But he did not mention any of the Cambridge Five and I did not think to ask."

"What other gems did this individual offer?" Harrington then asked.

"He mentioned that a fifth member of the group, someone named Igor Nikolayev, died in mysterious circumstances shortly after arriving in this country."

Bill Harrington leaned back in his chair for several moments, seemingly deep in thought. After a while, he said:

"I vaguely recall that case, Inspector. I was a rookie constable on the Sussex force at the time. It caused a big to-do in the media."

"Was foul play involved?" an intrigued Alison Aubrey asked.

"I seem to recall that there was an autopsy, Sergeant," Harrington replied. "It revealed that the victim had a small puncture in his upper left arm, sustained while crossing the Thames by Chelsea Bridge. The coroner's verdict was 'death by poison', using a little-known substance whose name eludes me for the moment."

"He was probably murdered," George Mason said. "I am wondering if the recent attacks may somehow be connected to it."

"The Nikolayev incident was twenty years ago, Inspector," Harrington remonstrated. "Surely that is all water under the bridge by now. Russian nationals come and go freely. They buy upscale property here, settle down and raise their children."

"That is very true, Chief Inspector," Alison remarked. "We have a Russian family living next-door to us in Henley-on-Thames. The two children attend Westminster School."

"All the same," Mason persisted, "the circumstances do suggest that there may be a pattern."

"Then it is up to you to discover one, Inspector," Harrington quickly retorted. Turning to the young detective sergeant, he said:

"What have you to report, Alison?"

The young officer sipped her coffee thoughtfully and said:

"Last evening, I paid a visit to the Smirnov family at Bethnal Green, to advise them to be on their guard. I spoke with Carrie Smirnov, who informed me that her husband had passed away only last year. He had been suffering from liver cancer."

"Sorry to hear that, Alison," George Mason said. "Could she shed any light on Dmitri's background?"

Alison Aubrey shook her head.

"She told me that her husband never discussed his former life in Russia. He apparently regarded it as a closed chapter."

"Understandable enough, in the circumstances," the chief inspector commented.

"I also paid a visit yesterday to Daphne Orlov at Dulwich Village. She informed me that her husband Yuri had slipped into a coma while under intensive care."

"That is a real setback," Mason said, with a frown. "I was looking forward to interviewing him."

"The prognosis is uncertain," Alison added. "Daphne is hoping against hope that he will fully recover."

"Maxim Brodsky, by contrast," Mason said, "is steadily improving. He will leave East London General Hospital in another week or so."

"Quite a kettle of fish we have here," Bill Harrington said, refilling his coffee cup while pouring himself a tot of Glen Morangie to chase it. "You two will have your work cut out."

"You can say that again, Chief Inspector," Mason remarked.

"So what is your next move?"

"There is one other person from that group we have yet to interview," George Mason said. "His name is Pyotr Alenin, apparently now living in Dublin."

"Then I suggest you go over there without delay," his superior said, "and see what he can add to the puzzle."

"May I take Alison along?" Mason asked.

The chief inspector, with an appreciative glace at the young sergeant, demurred.

"She has enough on her plate right here, for the time being," he said. "I want her to keep in touch with Linda Brodsky and Daphne Orlov. But I would not rule out her joining you in the later phases of the investigation."

George Mason thanked him for that, as he and

Alison Aubrey rose to leave. Alison went to the general office to make his travel arrangements to Dublin, while he took the elevator down to Forensics in the basement. Walter Stopford greeted him warmly.

"Good morning, George," he said. "How is the Tooting Bec business going?"

"Slowly," the detective somberly replied, as he eyed all the fascinating paraphernalia in the laboratory, the testing equipment and the accumulated evidence of various crimes.

"I have some news for you," Stopford remarked, "that may help speed things up a bit."

The detective's face lit up, as the forensics expert led him to a work table in a corner of the room, where he showed him a fragment of plastic.

"This item was recovered from the parking lot of Cybernetics Institute," he announced, with satisfaction.

His visitor peered closely at it.

"What exactly is it, Walt?" he dubiously enquired.

"It is a piece of the circuit board from the timer used in the car bomb," Stopford informed him.

George Mason peered more closely at it.

"How interesting is that!" he said.

"It became embedded in this piece of fabric during the explosion," the expert continued, indicating a shred of pale-blue cloth nearby.

"Fabric would be used to baffle the device," Mason surmised, "to prevent any movement in transit and possible detachment of the wiring."

"You've got it, George," came the reply.

The detective examined the fabric closely, saying:

"This is a good breakthrough, Walt, but where does it lead us?"

A broad smile spread across the expert's features.

"Under magnification," he jubilantly explained, "we can just make out the name of the timing device."

"Which is?"

"Apex," Stopford said. "It is not a brand I have come across before, so I contacted the C.I.A. Interestingly enough, they knew of it, having recovered fragments of a similar device used in the bombing of a U.S. military post over a decade ago."

"How extraordinary is that!" Mason exclaimed. "Do the Americans also know the manufacturer of these timers?"

Walter Stopford nodded.

"It is a Dutchman named Aad Kuipers," he explained. "His premises are on Kreuzstraat, Amsterdam."

"Is it a legitimate business?" Mason asked.

"Apparently so, George," came the reply. "Such devices are manufactured for a variety of purposes, both industrial and military. Kuipers is known to have contracts with civil engineering firms, for example. Where explosives are concerned, however, there are bound to be some gray areas."

"As in the embassy case," Mason shrewdly remarked. "As also in the current case."

"I am afraid so," Stopford rejoined.

"It looks like a trip to Holland in on the cards," his visitor then said.

"Aad Kuipers should certainly be able to tell you to whom he has supplied these devices in the recent past," Walter Stopford suggested.

"Let us hope he will be forthcoming," the detective said. "Now what about this piece of fabric?"

"We are continuing to look into it," the expert replied. "It is an unusual type of material, with special thermal qualities. We have begun enquiries with a specialist textile manufacturer in Lancashire. I am planning to go up to Blackburn tomorrow, in fact, to show them this fragment, which appears to be part of a shirt collar."

"That is most interesting, Walt," the detective said. "You could tell me the result of your enquiry when I get back from Dublin."

"Off to the Emerald Isle, George?" an intrigued Walter Stopford asked.

George Mason nodded.

"In the line of duty, Walt," he remarked. "Certainly not for pleasure."

On leaving Forensics, he went back up to the general office, feeling a bit more optimistic about the case following Stopford's discovery. Alison Aubrey poured him fresh coffee.

"The afternoon ferry from Holyhead to Dublin leaves at 2.15 p.m.," she informed him.

"Very good," Mason replied. "That means I can get there comfortably in one day, if I leave London early-morning."

"Shall I book you a ferry ticket?" Alison asked.

"By all means, Sergeant," he replied. "And I shall need to place a call to Dublin. Mikhail Konev gave me Pyotr Alenin's telephone number. Apparently, the two have more contact with each other than with other members of the former chess team."

"More than exchanging greetings cards for Russian Christmas, George?" Alison quipped.

"Apparently so, Sergeant."

CHAPTER 6

Two days later, after a light breakfast with his wife Adele, George Mason made an early start. He sped down the M4 motorway as far as Bristol, a port-city he associated with the trade in sherry, thinking of Harvey's Bristol Cream. From there, he crossed the Clifton Suspension Bridge over the River Avon to reach South Wales. A scenic drive through Brecon Beacons brought him to the coastal city of Bangor, which he reached around midday. Since he was making good time, he decided to break his journey. He parked his car and bought coffee. Afterwards, he took a stroll along the waterfront, with views of Penrhyn Castle in the background. Around one o'clock, he returned to his car and drove across the Menai Strait to reach Anglesey for the short drive to Holyhead. At the terminal for Irish Ferries and Isle of Man Steam Packet Company, he took a snack in the cafeteria before boarding a large car-ferry named *Johnathan Swift*, for the two-hour voyage across the Irish Sea, leaving his vehicle in the parking lot. The walls of the passenger lounge depicted scenes from the life of the author of *Gulliver's Travels,* who had close associations with the city of Dublin.

Pyotr Alenin, by prior arrangement, met him off the boat. He was a genial man of slim build and an intelligent, rather impish cast of features. He drove the detective to Castle Hotel, to rest awhile and freshen up, promising to call back and take him to dinner later. That allowed the visitor ample time for his purposes. He poured himself a scotch-and-soda from the mini-bar, phoned Adele to let her know of his safe arrival and switched on the television. It was a few moments before he realized he was listening to the Gaelic language, with its lilting, musical cadences. How charming, he thought, without understanding one word. He switched channels, to access the BBC for the early-evening news, mainly for the sports results. Just before six o'clock, he went down to the foyer.

Pytor Alenin promptly appeared at the appointed time. The pair strolled towards the city center, reaching O'Connell Street, the main thoroughfare, within minutes. Almost immediately on their left was a pub named Murphy's. Alenin led his guest inside, where they found one of the relatively few vacant tables over on the far side of the lounge bar, some distance from the group of young artists performing traditional Irish music for the appreciative patrons. George Mason had often wondered what an Irish pub would be like. If Murphy's was typical, he mused, it made for a very enjoyable evening. The atmosphere was most convivial, the music was delightful and he felt sure the food would be good. A waitress hovered, as they scanned the menu.

"Order anything you wish, Inspector Mason," his host hospitably urged.

It did not take the visitor long to opt for brook trout with French fries. His companion ordered Irish lamb with wild rice.

"And to drink?" the young woman asked.

"Guinness," both replied, in unison.

"Welcome to Irish pub life, Inspector Mason," the Russian said, noting his guest's evident approval of his surroundings. "Now tell me why you wished to meet me."

The detective, fixing the other with his penetrating gaze, said:

"I came to warn you of a possible threat to your life."

His host, a smile playing about his lips, returned a look of mock-disbelief.

"You cannot be serious, Inspector," he said.

"I am only too serious," came the reply. "My understanding is that you were part of a group of chess players who defected from the Soviet Union in 1990."

"Your understanding is correct, my dear sir. But that was over twenty years ago. What possible relevance could that have today?"

George Mason cleared his throat, took a quaff of his draft Guinness and said:

"Attempts have already been made on the lives of two members of your group."

"Who are?" a more focused Pyotr Alenin replied, with a questioning look.

"Maxim Brodsky and Yuri Orlov."

His host leaned back in his chair and gasped.

"What, exactly, has befallen them, Inspector?" he asked.

"Brodsky was struck by a rifle bullet outside his hardware store at Stepney Green, East London,"

Mason replied. "Yuri Orlov was caught in a blast from a car-bomb. Both men are now in hospital, hopefully recovering from serious injuries. Orlov was the more badly wounded and has since slipped into a coma."

The Russian in turn sipped his stout as he absorbed this disquieting news.

"You are implying, Inspector Mason," he said, "that the two incidents are linked?"

"That is my working hypothesis at the moment," the Scotland Yard agent replied.

"What about motive?" the other challenged.

"That is where I hoped you could assist me, Mr. Alenin," his guest replied. "Can you think of anyone, from your shared past in Russia, who would have reason to harm – in fact, to eliminate – these individuals?"

His host returned a puzzled look.

"You have me completely baffled, Inspector," he said, conclusively.

The food arrived, causing a break in conversation as the two diners tackled it while enjoying the Gaelic music. As the hands of the wall clock moved towards seven, more patrons came in from the street, filling up the few remaining tables or crowding the bar area. It struck the visitor as a regular routine of Dublin life to spend the evening in such a venue, of which there may well be scores in the Irish capital. Good luck to the Irish, he considered, that they could so enjoy life.

"I obtained your telephone number from your friend Mikhail Konev," George Mason said, after a while.

"Who has so far been unharmed, I take it?"

The detective nodded, saying:

"He is about to embark on an advertising venture in Russia, promoting English beer. He will visit Moscow early next month with a Yorkshire brewer, to vet Russian media outlets ahead of an advertising campaign."

"That could be a hard sell," the other commented, with an amused smile. "My compatriots generally favor strong liquor."

"What exactly is your current relationship with the account executive?" Mason asked.

"I run a graphic art studio here in Dublin," Pyotr Alenin replied. "He sends me commissions from time to time, to illustrate his advertising projects, even though Philpot's has a competent in-house graphics team of its own. A gesture of friendship and solidarity, mainly."

"Are you involved with the Tadcastle Ales promotion?" the detective humorously enquired.

The Russian smilingly shook his head.

"Not so far," he replied. "But it is early days yet. It may well turn out, in fact, that he seeks my angle on things, given my familiarity with the territory."

George Mason took a swig of his stout, while musing on a particular tune the band was playing, thinking he recognized it from way back.

"What can you tell me about Igor Nikolayev?" he suddenly asked.

Alenin's face suddenly clouded, as he shifted uneasily in his chair, wondering how his visitor had come by that particular name.

"Not a whole lot," he replied, rather cagily,

"except that he died in mysterious circumstances soon after arriving in England."

"Was he assassinated?"

"That would appear to be a probable explanation, Inspector Mason. In so far as I am aware, the case remained unsolved. No one was ever charged with a crime."

"That is very true, Mr. Alenin," Mason said. "It languishes in the cold cases file at Metropolitan Police headquarters."

At that point, the waitress approached them again. The Russian ordered gooseberry crumble with custard for dessert. George Mason, thinking of his waistline, settled for Irish coffee.

"Igor Nikolayev ran the French desk," Alenin then said. "Very successfully, too, I might add. He succeeded in bugging the American Embassy in Paris. There was a double agent named Lucien Monfils accredited to the French Embassy in Washington, D.C. Nikolayev was able to tip him off that the C.I.A. were closing in on him."

"Monfils evaded capture?" his guest enquired.

Pyotr Alenin nodded, saying:

"He fled to Moscow, where he was given a hero's welcome, the rank of major and a military pension."

"Interesting," George Mason commented, comparing it in his mind to the case of Kim Philby, the British double agent, one of the so-called Cambridge Five recruited by the Russians during their time at university in the nineteen-thirties. "What do you imagine may have gone wrong for Nikolayev?"

"The rumor at the time – that is, before I left the

Soviet Union – was that Igor Nikolayev had become too cozy with the French. He was known, for example, to visit Moscow bars and clubs frequented mainly by Western journalists and diplomats. He also bought a property at Antibes, on the French Riviera, where he installed his girlfriend, a young woman from Lyon."

"Do you think that the authorities came to doubt his loyalty, Mr. Alenin?"

The graphic artist concentrated on his dessert, chewing it slowly while pondering the detective's query. Nudging his finished dish aside, he said:

"Paranoia easily sets in, in intelligence circles, Inspector Mason. To some degree, everybody suspects everyone else. That is the nature of the game, I am afraid."

"I can well appreciate that," his guest remarked, sipping strong coffee laced with Irish whisky. "And some people may have long memories."

"You are suggesting, Inspector Mason," the other came back, "that there may be a connection between Igor Nikolayev's death and the recent attacks in London?"

"Purely as a working hypothesis, Mr. Alenin.," the detective replied. "One has to start somewhere."

"But the interval of time, Inspector, in itself works against such a theory."

"The time-lapse is certainly a drawback," George Mason agreed.

"I am not going to take too seriously any supposed threat against me personally," Pyotr Alenin then said. "But I appreciate your coming over from London expressly to alert me. The truth is, I have a life to live here and I intend to lead it, without constantly looking over my shoulder. This whole scenario is too vague to do otherwise."

"Have it your own way," Mason replied. "Just take some extra precautions in your daily routine. That would be my advice to you."

"That seems perfectly reasonable," the other agreed.

"One more matter, before we part," his visitor then said.

"Fire away, Inspector."

"There was another member of the group that defected in 1990, whom nobody seems to know much about."

A wry smile played across the Russian's lips.

"That would be Pavel Belinksy," he remarked.

"Correct."

"We lost touch with Pavel almost immediately," his host explained. "I have always assumed that he used London as a staging post. He could be anywhere – in Europe, North or South America, the Far East. He was a versatile linguist, who could quickly adapt to life in any number of countries."

"In that case, I shall cross him off my list of people to contact," Mason said. "He is probably well out of the picture."

That settled, Pyotr Alenin hailed the waitress, paid the bill and departed, leaving his visitor to continue enjoying the pleasures of a Dublin pub evening. George Mason ordered a refill of loaded coffee and sat back to listen to the music for a while. At nine o'clock, when the musicians laid down their instruments for a short break, he left Murphy's and strolled back to his hotel, noting that the evening had turned rather chill.

The next day, he rose early and did justice to a mixed grill at breakfast in the hotel restaurant, noting how lean and tender Irish bacon was. Since he had a free morning before catching the return ferry at 1.20 p.m., he set off to explore the celebrated city with the aid of a street-map. Heading along O'Connell Street, he took a right turn and threaded his way through the maze of narrow streets until he located St. Patrick's Cathedral, which was already quite full of early-season tourists. He joined the queue, paid the ten euros entrance fee and entered the imposing edifice. Its associations with Johnathan Swift, a former dean of the cathedral, were immediately obvious. A glass-fronted cabinet displayed first editions of his books, including *Gulliver's Travels*. Mason was amused to note that one slim volume had as its title *A Sermon on Sleeping in Church*. Probably a not uncommon feature of Sunday services at that time, he mused, when sermons could be over an hour in length.

He spent an enjoyable hour exploring Dublin history as recorded in stained-glass windows and the marble statues of local dignitaries, including a bust of Johnathan Swift, noting also that the cathedral had sheltered Huguenots fleeing religious persecution in France. Oliver Cromwell had left his mark, too, by stabling horses in the nave during his military campaign in Ireland. There were also artifacts representing local industries and the typical tourist bric-a-brac of postcards, souvenirs and mementos, the sale of which helped defray the cost of upkeep of a structure dating back to the twelfth century. Mason noted that chamber music concerts began at midday, a pleasure he would have to forego, since he would then be on his way back to the harbor. He spent the rest of the morning visiting Trinity College campus, Temple Bar and the main shopping precinct centered on Grafton Street, listening to the street buskers there playing Irish music. After a snack at a sidewalk café, he took a taxi to the port, thinking he might well bring his wife Adele for a longer visit to the fascinating city in the not-too-distant future.

*

Around the same hour that George Mason boarded the ferry back to Holyhead, Fabien Leroux took the Tube to Cockfosters, the northernmost stop on Piccadilly Line. He had spent the morning training at a gym in Bayswater, followed by a sauna bath, after which he received a text message from Q giving him the first of two addresses to vet. On the way, he reflected on his recent visit to Jeb Sinclair at Brixton. They had spent the previous evening doing the rounds of local pubs offering jazz evenings, following dinner at a Thai restaurant. His former navy comrade had registered some alarm at the request for more weaponry, wondering uneasily what sort of business his friend was getting into. He hoped it was all above board, but his attempt to elicit information had proved fruitless. Fabien Leroux kept his cards close to his chest, eventually persuading his friend, who was more than a little tipsy by the end of the evening, to lend him his old service pistol.

On reaching his destination, the Canadian perused the street-map posted at the station entrance. Following the main thoroughfare for a couple of blocks, he turned left into Sevenoaks Road and soon located number 110, a semi-detached brick-fronted house with a well-kempt front garden showing a variety of spring flowers. He was pleased to note a MacDonald's on the corner, which would afford him a good view of number 110, while remaining unobserved himself. He checked his Rolex. It was a quarter to two. Since he had not yet had lunch, he entered the fast-food joint for a Big Mac, with occasional glances towards the house, which was only about thirty yards farther along the road. His patience was eventually rewarded with a view of a smartly-dressed slim woman parking her car on the driveway before entering the premises by a side entrance. He noted that a mature beech tree overhung that side of the building; it would provide useful cover, if needed.

Having finished his meal and observing no further activity at the address, he left the restaurant and made his way back towards the Underground station, opposite which he had noticed a cinema. He checked the program in the foyer, noting that the afternoon performance began at 2.30 p.m. He would miss the start of the feature film by about fifteen minutes, but that did not bother him. It would be an easy way to pass the time until early evening. Luckily, it was an action film, his favorite genre, rather than one of those slapstick comedies the

British seemed so fond of, or a sentimental romance. When the film eventually ended, he strolled back to MacDonald's and ordered coffee. He did not wait too long before a second car, a red Subaru Outback, pulled into the driveway of 110 Sevenoaks Road. Out of it stepped a middle-aged man dressed in a light-gray business suit. The Canadian noted the precise time; it was 5.05 p.m.

He would return here around the same time for the next few evenings, he decided, to note any variations in the man's routine. The MacDonald's suited him, reminding him of home. He had always enjoyed the fare and the brisk, efficient service. As the driver of the car came round to the front entrance of the house, Leroux got a good glimpse of him. His general appearance suggested that he was not a native Briton, more likely an East European. Canada had a large, well-established immigrant population from all over Europe and the Middle East. As a result, Fabien Leroux flattered himself that he could tell a person's origin fairly reliably.

As he finished his drink, he fell to wondering what this particular individual had done to earn Q's enmity. Could he, for example, have crossed him in a business deal? Did he relate in some way to the previous targets, at Stepney Green and Tooting Bec? Ruefully recognizing that he would probably never know the reason for his own sinister entry into the man's life, nor even his name unless it appeared in the newspapers, which he rarely read anyway, he took down a magazine from the rack and browsed through it for about an hour. Shortly before six o'clock, he observed the couple leaving the house together in the Outback. Unable to follow them, he felt satisfied with this preliminary reconnoiter and decided to call it a day, opting to spend the remainder of the evening at the The Red Lion in Bayswater.

The pub was quite busy by the time he reached it at seven o'clock, after the long Tube journey from Cockfosters. Elbowing his way to the bar, he ordered a beer and chatted for a while with the bar staff, with whom he had become quite friendly in the course of several visits. Eventually, he transferred to a table with a good view of the television screen, so that he could watch the European Championship semi-final between Manchester City and Inter-Milan. Since soccer was not much played in Canada, he welcomed the opportunity to get a better idea of the game.

When the match ended in a 2-2 draw, he ordered a second pint of Watney's Bitter and fell to considering what he might do once his contract with Q was over. That could be in a matter of weeks, he considered, or it could be tomorrow. One idea which he had been mulling for a while, even before setting foot on English soil, was to use his military background to obtain work with a security company in the Middle East. The amount of money he could put by on a fixed-term contract would enable him to buy a ranch in California. His friend Jeb Sinclair was keen to share in such a venture, the idea being to open a dude ranch for European and Asian visitors and enjoy the good life in a warmer climate than their native Quebec.

*

When George Mason arrived back at Scotland Yard the next day, he went straight down to Forensics to see what else the versatile Walter Stopford had come up with in his absence.

"Did you enjoy your trip to the Emerald Isle, George?" the scientist genially enquired, interrupting his appraisal of material from a more recent crime scene.

"It was a very useful trip, Walt," the detective replied. "I can recommend the Dublin night-life. If you ever decide to go, I will give you some useful tips."

"My wife and I may well visit Ireland at some point," Stopford said. "We have overlooked it in the past. Melissa has always preferred Mediterranean resorts, for dependable sunshine."

"We could make it a foursome," George Mason suggested. "Adele, I know, would love to go to Ireland after the positive report I gave of it."

The forensics expert seemed to take to the idea.

"A tour by car might work," he said. "That way, we could take in the interesting sights."

"Like Macgillicuddy's Reeks and the Ring of Kerry?"

"Among other attractions, George, by all means," came the reply. "We shall have to give it some thought. Now, about the shirt fabric I recovered from the Cybernetics Institute parking lot."

"You managed to trace it?" the detective optimistically enquired.

Walter Stopford nodded.

"I mentioned that I was going up to Blackburn to consult one of the leading textile companies in Lancashire," he said. "They found it very interesting, saying that it seemed to be a special type of thermal material not generally available to the clothing industry."

"What would its use be then, Walt?" his intrigued visitor asked.

"The Blackburn people could not shed much light on that," the other replied. "You would need to visit the manufacturer to find out."

"And who might they be?" Mason prompted.

"Blackburn came up with a Norwegian firm, Norje-Tex, based at Oslo," Stopford replied, handing the piece of fabric to his visitor. "You should take this with you, George, as they may make specialty fabrics for any number of purposes. Niche markets come to mind. Research stations in Antarctica, for instance, oil-rigs in the North Sea or prospecting in the Arctic."

"They could certainly use thermal fabric in those places," the detective agreed, briefly sampling the texture of the fragment before placing it inside the zip-lock bag his colleague provided. "No fingerprints on it?"

The expert regretfully shook his head.

"No DNA either," he remarked. "Whoever assembled the car bomb used at Tooting Bec was probably wearing gloves."

"This is a very useful start, at least," George Mason said.

"So you will soon be off on your travels again, I expect?" the scientist remarked, with a smile.

Mason merely raised his eyebrows at that.

"Not so far as Oslo just yet, Walt," he replied. "My immediate task is a visit to Kreuzstraat, Amsterdam, to interview an individual named Aad Kuipers about the bomb timer, if you have it handy."

Walter Stopford crossed to a filing cabinet and produced the fragment of circuit board bearing the maker's name.

"Show him this, George, and see what he has to say."

CHAPTER 7

On the following Monday, George Mason made his way to Waterloo International and took the Eurostar service through the Channel Tunnel to Brussels. From there, he caught a connection to Amsterdam Centraal, arriving there at just turned midday. Consulting the street-plan on the station concourse, he proceeded along Prins Hendrik Kade as far as the Herengracht, one of a series of large canals lined with merchants' houses dating from the seventeenth century, the city's Golden Age. Walking alongside it, he noted with interest the commercial barges plying along it and the colorful houseboats moored at the canal walls. It struck him as an idyllic life-style in elegant surroundings, with all the cultural amenities of a great city close to hand. Turning at length into Kreuzstraat, he soon located Apex, on the ground floor of a former merchant's home converted to commercial use, including suites of offices on the upper floors. Aad Kuipers was surprised to receive a visitor from Scotland Yard.

"What can I do for you, Inspector Mason?" he rather warily enquired, showing the detective into a small, cluttered office adjoining the main workroom.

George Mason produced the fragment of circuit board bearing the maker's name.

"This, I believe," he began, "is one of your products, Mr. Kuipers."

The Dutchman took it and peered closely at it.

"That is correct, Inspector," he said. "It is from one of our timing devices. I would be very interested to know how you came by it."

"It was retrieved from the site of an explosion in South London," Mason informed him. "From the parking lot at Cybernetics Institute, Tooting Bec, to be precise."

The manufacturer returned a quizzical look.

"What was the exact nature of the explosion?" he enquired.

"It was a criminal act, Mr. Kuipers, targeting a car belonging to an employee of the Institute."

"That is very disturbing news, Inspector Mason," the Dutchman said.

"I am hoping you could help identify the buyer of this device," his visitor added.

Aad Kuipers returned an evasive, and rather ironic, smile.

"We supply timing devices for any number of purposes, Inspector," he replied.

"Can you enlarge on that?" his visitor asked.

"The construction industry is one of our main clients," Aad Kuiers replied. "For blasting rock on civil engineering projects, such as dams and roadworks. We also service the defense ministries of several European countries."

"Yet they could also be used for more questionable purposes," the detective remarked, "such as safe or strong-room blowing."

"Indeed they could, Inspector," the Dutchman

readily admitted, "if they fall into the wrong hands."

"Do you carefully vet all purchasers of these devices, Mr. Kuipers, before you agree to supply them? After all, terrorists could also make use of them. "

"That would not be very practicable, Inspector," came the cagy reply. "We are a legitimate business, with scores of different clients. We cannot possibly keep track of where every single item ends up after it leaves our workshop."

The man was hedging, George Mason considered. He needed to probe further.

"Surely you keep sales records," he remarked.

"Do you happen to have a search warrant, Inspector?"

"I could very easily obtain one from Europol at The Hague," Mason informed him. "But it would save me the trouble if you simply consulted your records. I should be particularly interested to learn of any sales of timers like this one to customers in the United Kingdom over the past few weeks."

The manufacturer shifted his gaze and said nothing for a few moments, as if weighing the odds of revealing clients' names. He eventually decided, with some reluctance, to cooperate, turning to a filing cabinet to draw out a quarto-sized ledger, which he placed open on his desk.

"We have made only two sales to the U.K. in the past month," he explained, after briefly consulting it..

"Which are?" his visitor immediately enquired.

"The first, on March 25th, was a consignment of ten timers to Pennine Enterprises, a construction company based at Settle in the Yorkshire Dales, who are working on the Skipton bypass. The second, on April 6th, was to Dirk deGroot, a resident of Brighton."

"A fellow-countryman then?" an intrigued George Mason put it to him.

Aad Kuipers rather sheepishly nodded.

"Would that be for a single timing device?"

"Quite so, Inspector Mason. deGroot is an occasional customer. Perhaps three or four times a year he will place a small order."

"Do you happen to know for what purpose?" his visitor pointedly enquired.

"I am afraid not, Inspector."

"Dirk deGroot does not strike me as a commercial client, Mr. Kuipers," Mason persisted. "Such people would presumably place more regular orders. Could he be using timers for bomb-making, perhaps?"

The Dutchman shifted his stance uneasily.

"Perhaps you should ask him that yourself, Inspector," he countered. "I have export clearance from the Ministry of Trade. I cannot answer for any possible misuse of my devices."

"I shall make it my business to interview this Dirk deGroot," George Mason said. "Can you give me his address?"

"I can certainly do that for you," the other replied, glad to be able to give his visitor some small satisfaction. He consulted his ledger again and wrote the client's name and address on a slip of notepaper, which he handed over.

"Thank you very much for your cooperation, Mr. Kuipers," Mason then said, pocketing the information and turning to leave.

Since it was now past noon, he called at a canal-side restaurant for the view it gave of the water traffic. For lunch, he ordered *spedikken*, a traditional dish of savory pancakes, with a pot of orange pekoe tea. Afterwards, he made his way to police headquarters, hoping to catch Brigadier Klaas Brouwer. He was in luck. The Dutch officer had himself just returned from a meeting at Europol Headquarters. He greeted his visitor cordially.

"What a pleasure to meet you again, Inspector Mason," he said, offering a seat facing him across his large mahogany desk.

"Likewise," the detective returned.

"How have things been with you since you were last in Amsterdam?" He was referring to a case of money laundering they had worked on jointly a few years back.

"Fair enough, on the whole, Brigadier," his visitor replied.

"And you are here again on professional business?"

"Absolutely," came the reply. "I am, in fact, investigating an assault made against an employee of Cybernetics Institute in South London."

"And the trail leads here?" the other asked, in some surprise

"I have just been to the premises of Apex, on Kreuzstraat," Mason explained, "in connection with a timing device used in a car bomb. Our forensic team retrieved a fragment of the circuit board from the Institute parking lot.

Klaas Brouwer raised his eyebrows at that remark.

"The timer was manufactured by Apex?" he asked, with evident concern

"Exactly," Mason replied. "I consider that the sales activities of Aad Kuipers might be worth looking into."

"Bear with me for one moment," the brigadier said, picking up the phone to place a call to the Ministry of Trade. After several minutes' discussion, he replaced the receiver and turned to his visitor.

"Mr. Kuipers has export clearance for construction and military purposes only," he said, emphatically. "Bomb-timers are categorically excluded."

"What can you do about it?" the detective put it to him.

"In view of the potential for such devices to fall into the hands of criminals or terrorists, we shall institute a special audit of Apex. If we find due cause, we can impose a heavy fine and we can also revoke his export license. He will then be restricted to the domestic market, for the Dutch military and for the construction of new dykes and other civil engineering projects."

"You are preparing, Brigadier, for rising sea-levels as a result from global warming?" an intrigued George Mason asked.

"We have no option," the other replied. "If we do not take appropriate steps in advance, we shall be overwhelmed. Our whole ethos, for centuries, has been about keeping the sea at bay."

"I can appreciate that," the detective remarked, "for such a low-lying country. Dutch expertise in that area is world-renowned."

"We may be asked to help coastal cities like New York or Miami deal with similar problems," Klaas Brouwer added, "especially if the Greenland ice-sheet melts."

"London, too, will perhaps be affected, even with the Thames Barrier now in place."

The brigadier judiciously nodded.

"The are some very interesting scenarios ahead," he remarked, "if we cannot adequately control global warming."

"That is certainly true, Brigadier. Governments are now beginning to take the matter a bit more seriously."

"Not before time, either," Brouwer said. "May I take a look at that circuit board?"

George Mason handed the fragment across the desk.

"You can use this as evidence," he said, "if needed. It was supplied to an individual named Dirk deGroot, at Brighton. I am thinking that deGroot used it as part of a bomb assembly, since there were only two customers for these devices in the U.K. last month, the other one being a reputable construction company in Yorkshire."

The Dutch officer took the item and peered closely at it for a few moments, before placing it in the top drawer of his desk.

"Thank you very much for the tip-off, Inspector Mason," he said. "As usual, you are right on the ball. Kudos to Scotland Yard."

His visitor returned an ironic look.

"I can only hope so, Brigadier," he replied. "The

Forensic Department, under Walter Stopford, has done most of the work so far."

"If you are staying in Holland overnight, Inspector," the other then said, "We could have dinner together. There is a new gourmet restaurant recently opened on the Zaandam. I have been meaning to sample it ..."

"Thanks for the offer," Mason interrupted. "But I really have too much on at the moment. I need to be back in London by tonight."

"In that case, Inspector Mason, we shall postpone that pleasure to a future occasion. Meanwhile, good luck with your investigation. We shall do our part at this end to thoroughly vet Mr. Kuipers."

With that, the Scotland Yard agent shook hands with his Dutch counterpart and took his leave.

*

The next day, George Mason was a little late reaching his office, on account of the heavy commuter traffic. After checking both his snail mail and his email, he caught up with Alison Aubrey.

"A profitable trip, George?" she asked, half glancing up from her report writing.

"Useful enough," the detective replied. "What news on the home front?"

The young sergeant turned to face him squarely.

"Yesterday, I went to visit Linda Brodsky," she told him. "Her husband Maxim has had a relapse. He will remain at East London General Hospital for the near future."

"That is bad news, Alison," her colleague

remarked.

"At least, he is fully conscious most of the time and able to sit up in bed for brief periods."

"So you were able to interview him?" her senior asked.

Alison nodded.

"Does he have any idea at all why he was targeted by a gunman?"

"Maxim refused to accept that he was a specific target," Alison told him. "He thought it was more probably a random incident, such as those that have occurred from time to time near motorways. I then mentioned what had happened to Yuri Orlov. That made him think, George. But he cannot imagine for the world why anyone would attempt to kill either himself or Orlov. He did come clean about his past in the secret service, but didn't think that could be relevant, since it was many years ago."

"It is a curious business, to be sure, Alison," Mason remarked. "Dmitri Smirnov has passed on. Yuri Orlov and Maxim Brodsky are still in hospital. Mikhail Konev will soon be on his way to Moscow, to promote English beer, interestingly enough."

"That seems to account for the whole group," the young sergeant observed.

"Except for one individual," George Mason corrected, "who has so far proved untraceable."

"Who might that be, George?" the young sergeant anxiously enquired.

"A certain Pavel Belinsky," he replied. "Pyotr Alenin over in Dublin says the group lost contact with him almost as soon as they arrived in England, so we have no means of tracing him."

"In that case, we shall have to rule him out of our enquiries," Alison said.

"That would seem to be so, Alison, regretfully. I do not like to leave any stone unturned."

"Because you are so thorough in your methods, George," she commented, with an appreciative smile.

"What about the Orlovs?" George Mason asked, pleased at the compliment.

"After visiting Linda Brodsky, I drove down to Dulwich Village to check on Daphne," she reported. "She is still very much in a state of shock and has had to take time off from her job at the local library."

"Poor woman," her senior remarked. "I take it that Yuri remains in a coma?"

"Unfortunately so," Sergeant Aubrey said. "Her friend Gillian drives her down to South Wimbledon each day to enquire about him, but there has so far been no change in his condition. I managed to catch them the minute they returned."

"It is very helpful of you to visit them," Mason said, encouragingly. "It shows that the police care."

"It is the least I can do, in the circumstances," she modestly replied.

Rising from her desk, she crossed the floor of the office to replenish her coffee cup from the large pot kept on a warmer. George Mason declined her offer to fix him one too.

"I have to leave almost straight away," he explained.

"So what is your next move?" she asked, sipping her Sumatran roast.

"A trip to Brighton would seem to be in order," he replied, "to interview a gentleman going by the name of Dirk deGroot."

"A Dutchman, George?"

"You got it, Alison," Mason returned. "And he appears to be in cahoots with a fellow-national at Amsterdam, who manufactures timing devices for the Dutch military, among other outlets."

"You are making progress, George, I am pleased to note," Alison said reassuringly, as she returned to her deskwork.

"Hopefully, Sergeant," Mason replied. "It is early days yet, with a lot more groundwork to do."

Taking his leave, he quit the building and made his way to Victoria Station, a fifteen-minute walk. Having got there, he could have kicked himself for just missing a train. The next service would not be due for another hour. He bought himself a copy of *The Guardian,* repaired to the station buffet for a coffee and caught up on the sports news, for reports on late-season soccer games and prospects for the new cricket season, especially for his home team of Yorkshire. It was almost midday by the time he reached Brighton. He took a taxi to the central police station, where he was greeted by the duty sergeant, Don Truscott, whom he had notified of his visit in advance.

"Good morning, Inspector Mason," Sergeant Truscott greeted.

"Morning, Sergeant," the detective replied, "and a fine one it is."

"A nice spell of good weather we've been having, for sure," the local officer said. "Let us hope it lasts."

"Now, about Dirk deGroot," Mason said, getting down to business straight away.

"He has been on our radar for some time," Don Truscott replied. "But we have not been able to pin anything on him. He is quite a slippery character."

"If my suspicions are correct," his visitor informed him, "I think you may be able to charge him as accessory-before-the-fact in a case of attempted murder."

"Indeed, Inspector Mason?" came the surprised reaction. "How could that be?"

"I shall fill you in on the details after I have had the opportunity to interview him," his visitor said.

"One of my staff will drive you over to his place, Inspector. He rents an apartment at Ullswater House, a high-rise just opposite the railway station."

Minutes later, a young woman constable emerged from an adjoining room and led the Metropolitan Police agent to a squad car parked outside. They chatted briefly about local topics, before she dropped him off at his destination, saying she would wait in the car for him. Dirk deGroot was surprised, but unfazed, to see him.

"Is there a problem, Inspector?" he coolly enquired, without offering his visitor a seat.

"I am enquiring into a recent bombing incident at the parking lot of Cybernetics Institute, Tooting Bec," the detective told him.

The Dutchman returned a look of surprised concern.

"Were there casualties?" he asked.

"One serious injury," Mason replied. "The victim

is now recovering, very slowly, at a hospital in South London."

"I am truly sorry to hear of that," deGroot said, with apparent sincerity. "But what has this to do with me, may I ask?"

"Our forensics team recovered a fragment of the circuit board used in the assembly of the explosive device, a type of pipe bomb. We believe that the timer was shipped to your address by a firm named Apex, based in Amsterdam."

The Dutchman's face clouded as he took an uncertain step backwards.

"How can you possibly claim such a thing?" he asked, wondering if the detective was sure of his facts, or just fishing. Mason's reply put him straight.

"I was in Amsterdam very recently," he explained. 'Aad Kuipers, the owner of Apex, informed me that he had shipped just two of his timers to the U.K. in the past month. One went to a civil engineering company in Yorkshire; the other came to this address."

Dirk deGroot crossed to the window and glanced out over the nearby railway yards, saying nothing.

"It will help your case, Mr. deGroot, if you come clean," the detective then said. "Aad Kuipers will testify in court, if need be, that you have been a fairly regular client over the past several years."

The Dutchman turned from the window and, rather belatedly, offered his visitor a seat. They faced each other across a low table featuring a carved wooden ibex and some hunting magazines.

"It is true, Inspector," he conceded, "that I have

from time to time supplied explosive devices from this address. They were used mainly for demolition purposes."

"You mean for taking down sub-par property on re-development sites and things like that?" the detective asked.

The Dutchman nervously nodded.

"I can only assume, in good faith, Inspector," he said, "that buyers of such devices are legitimate. I cannot answer for any misuse, in the manner you have mentioned."

"That remains to be seen," George Mason came back. "Assuming that you regarded the purchaser of the device used at Tooting Bec as a legitimate client, you should have no problem revealing his name."

Dirk deGroot sensed that he had been backed into a corner by his canny visitor. He shifted uneasily in his seat and said:

"He did not give his name, Inspector, or any means of contacting him."

"No doubt he also paid in cash?"

The other slowly nodded.

"Describe him to me as best you can," the detective then said.

"What struck me immediately was his accent," the other replied. "I would say it was North American."

"That could be either American or Canadian, Mr. deGroot," Mason said.

"I could not distinguish between the two, to be perfectly honest, Inspector. I rarely come across people from across the pond."

"Apart from his accent, how did he strike you?"

"He was tall and athletic-looking. Mid-forties, I should say. His features were quite tanned, as of an outdoor type. A very self-assured individual, possibly of a military background."

George Mason made a careful note of the information, thanked him and rose to leave.

"The local police will naturally want to contact you further in this matter, Mr. deGroot," he said. "I shall let Sergeant Truscott know that you have fully cooperated with me. But I must warn you that you may have placed yourself in some serious difficulty. A major concern of police authorities nowadays, as you will no doubt appreciate, is of such devices falling into the hands of terrorists, as well as criminals."

The Dutchman looked suitably chastened by those remarks.

"I shall confine my activities to the construction industry in future," he assured his visitor.

"That would be a very wise move, Mr. deGroot," Mason commented.

On arrival back at the police station, he briefed the duty sergeant, adding that if Yuri Orlov did not survive the incident at Tooting Bec, murder charges should be instigated against the Dutchman, in addition to illegal trading in explosive devices. Sergeant Truscott thanked him for the update, promising that the Brighton police would use that information to initiate proceedings against deGroot. They then chatted briefly about the local crime scene, before the woman constable drove the visitor back to the railway station. Once there, with half an hour to spare before the London train, George

Mason entered the buffet to grab a snack and finish reading his newspaper.

CHAPTER 8

When the airliner from Moscow Sheremetyevo
Airport landed at Heathrow at 10.25 a.m., a short-
statured, dapper man in his late fifties, with dark
hair smoothed back, made his way through customs
and took the Piccadilly Line Tube from Terminal 4
to South Kensington, where he switched to the
Circle Line to reach Victoria Station. On emerging
from the busy concourse, he crossed Victoria Street,
nimbly dodging the traffic, and entered The Black
Prince. It was now 11.30 a.m. and the pub was
gearing up for the lunch-hour trade serving office
and store workers in the neighborhood, together
with random visitors to London. Nearby were
several notable tourist attractions, such as
Westminster Abbey and the Houses of Parliament.
Seeing the sights, however, was the last thing on
Lev Leverkov's mind. On entering the bar lounge,
his eye quickly scanned the room before letting on
an individual of about his own age sitting by
himself at an alcove table.

"*Dobri dyen,*" he said, as the other man stood to
shake his hand.

"Good day to you too, Lev," came the response.
"Had a good trip?"

"A little turbulence over the North Sea," the
newcomer said. "Apart from that, it was a very
smooth flight in one of our new Russian aircraft."

"The Sukhoi 130?" the other said.

"It is not as roomy as the Airbus, Paul, but comfortable enough. It should help revive our aircraft industry, especially if we can corner part of the export market."

"And end the dominance of Airbus and Boeing, Lev?"

"Hopefully so," Leverkov replied, "but we are mainly looking at niche markets, like Bombadier in Canada. Now, what shall we have for lunch? I ate very little on the plane."

They studied the well-prepared menu for a few moments, before opting for game pie with mixed salad.

Paul Bell crossed the room to place the order at the service counter. On regaining his seat, he poured two glasses from a bottle of chilled Soave.

"What have you to report, Paul?" his visitor asked, sipping the Italian wine appreciatively.

"No problems to speak of at the ministry," the other replied.

Lev Leverkov returned a look conveying both admiration and approval.

"You did very well to insinuate yourself into the Ministry of Defense," he said. "It is a remarkable coup for our intelligence services."

"I prepared the ground carefully beforehand, Lev."

"I recall that, on leaving Russia for England in 1990, you went very soon afterwards to America."

"I enrolled at the University of Wisconsin, for a master's degree in Slavonic languages. On my return to England, three years later, that

117

qualification proved invaluable in obtaining a post at Whitehall. They were looking for fluent Russian and Czech speakers, in particular. By that time, too, I spoke English like a native, albeit like a native of Wisconsin."

"So you could pass yourself off very easily?" the other said, chuckling at his host's sense of humor.

Paul Bell nodded.

"I worked at it," he said, with a smug expression. "I joined Rotary and a tennis club at South Wimbledon."

"You are wearing a club tie," his visitor noted, with approval.

"I met my wife Cynthia playing tennis," Bell informed him. "Her father is a retired departmental head at the Air Ministry. Very much one of the old school, educated at Harrow, conservative in outlook and a staunch critic of modern mores. It was through his good offices that I managed to obtain the post at Whitehall."

"And in the intervening years, Paul," Leverkov said, approvingly, "you have risen up through the ranks."

"I am now chief liaison officer with NATO," the other said.

"Excellent work!" his visitor exclaimed.

At that point, their table number was called out. Paul Bell crossed to the service counter to collect the food. They ate in silence for a while, as the visitor, seemingly bemused at his first visit to an English pub, surveyed the activity around them, while tucking in to his game pie and salad. Nudging his finished plate aside, he said:

"How soon can you submit your report on NATO military maneuvers in East Europe?"

"I am in the process of finalizing it, Lev," Bell informed him. "For security's sake, I shall send it by special courier via Helsinki. Anything can happen to regular mail; it may get lost or stolen and fall into the wrong hands."

"It is as well to take precautions, Paul," his visitor said. "Your report will be of key importance to us, in view of our current political and military objectives."

"NATO is definitely aiming to increase its presence in East Europe," Paul Bell assured him.

"What we must avoid in that event," Lev Leverkov emphasized, "is a repeat of the near-fiasco that occurred in 1983."

"You are referring, Lev, to the military exercises dubbed Able Archer, which included deployment of nuclear weapons?"

Lev Leverkov gravely nodded.

"It was the closest we came to a major confrontation with the West, after the Cuban Missile Crisis in October 1962, when we installed nuclear missiles in Cuba, less than one hundred miles from the American coast."

"Nikita Khrushchev versus John Fitzgerald Kennedy?"

"Exactly, Paul," Leverkov replied, with an ironic look. "In 1983, some of our leaders thought that Able Archer was being undertaken in readiness for a nuclear strike against the Warsaw Pact. It put our relations with NATO on a hair-trigger."

"To the extent that we transported nuclear

weapons to their launchers and assigned priority targets?"

Leverkov nodded.

"It was a close-run thing," he said. "Hence the value of any information you can provide about current NATO plans. We are counting heavily on you, Paul."

"I will not disappoint you, Lev," came the confident reply.

With that, he refilled their wine glasses, while adopting a rather preoccupied air.

"Is something bothering you?" Leverkov enquired.

Paul Bell looked his guest directly in the eye.

"I am being blackmailed, Lev," he confided, with a grim expression. "Threatened with exposure, in fact."

The senior agent looked aghast, leaning back in his chair to absorb the impact of that remark, as disturbing as it was unexpected.

"You cannot be serious, Paul!" he exclaimed, after a tense pause.

"For the past few months," the other continued, "I have been receiving demands, at the rate of about one per month, for the sum of ten thousand pounds, against the threat of exposing my true background to the British government."

"You have met the blackmailer's terms?" Leverkov asked, with growing concern.

Paul Bell slowly nodded.

"I have been transferring money to a numbered account at a bank in Geneva," he explained.

"This cannot be allowed to continue, Paul," his

visitor said, with a deep frown. "What do you propose to do about it?"

"I have already taken certain steps," Paul Bell optimistically replied. "The only persons who could possibly know my personal history are the members of the group I left Russia with in 1990."

"But that was over twenty years ago," Lev Leverkov protested. "Surely your former colleagues lost all trace of you after you left for America?"

"I would confidently have expected that to be the case," came the concerned response. "But it is apparently not so."

"Remind me of the names of the members of your chess team who defected from Helsinki, Paul."

His colleague sipped his wine thoughtfully, before saying:

"Maxim Brodsky, Yuri Orlov, Dmitri Smirnov, Mikhail Konev and Pyotr Alenin. The blackmail letters are always post-marked somewhere in London. I have ruled out Alenin, who is now working as a graphic artist in Dublin, as well as Dmitri Smirnov, who has since died."

"So you are concentrating your efforts right here in the British capital?"

Paul Bell nodded, saying:

"Since it could be any one of those persons, I aim to target each person in turn."

"To silence them permanently?" came the wry comment.

"Easier said than done, Lev," the other replied. "I hired a hitman to take out Brodsky at his hardware store in Stepney Green and to place a pipe bomb under Orlov's vehicle outside Cybernetics Institute at Tooting Bec, South London. Neither attack, for different reasons, was an unqualified success. Both victims are, to the best of my knowledge, recovering in hospital."

"The hitman's name?" a curious Lev Leverkov asked.

"Fabien Leroux, a former officer in the Royal Canadian Navy who served on Arctic patrols. A crack marksman, by his own account, also trained in the use of explosives."

Lev Leverkov appraised his associate carefully, while sipping his wine.

"You are taking the right course of action, Paul," he judiciously remarked, "even if your choice of hitman was not all he professed to be. Your cover at the Ministry of Defence must at all costs be preserved. You are the most highly-placed mole we have in Britain, as well as being one of our top agents in Europe as a whole. Only Detlev Brandt, who has penetrated the German foreign ministry, is on a par with yourself."

Paul Bell half filled their glasses with the remainder of the wine, feeling a keen sense of relief at having confided in his senior.

"The steps I have taken," he then said, "may already have produced the desired result."

"Meaning what, exactly?" his visitor asked, with a hint of skepticism in his voice, but a glint of optimism in his eye.

"I have not received a demand for money in over a month," Paul Bell revealed. "That in itself leads me to think that either Brodsky or Orlov is responsible. I intend to take no action against

Mikhail Konev, at least for the time being, in case the lull persists."

"Good thinking," the other agreed. "If the letters resume after the two victims leave hospital – assuming, of course that they fully recover - you will be vindicated. What about our Canadian friend Fabien Leroux, meanwhile?"

"He is currently doing some reconnaissance, in case the letters resume in the near future. He is staking out Mikhail Konev's address and daily schedule."

"Konev lives here in London?"

Paul Bell nodded, saying:

"At Cockfosters, North London."

"Won't the Canadian soon tire of such pedestrian work?" Leverkov put it to him.

"He seems a reliable, discreet and willing-enough character," the spy replied. "I am thinking of using him as a courier to Helsinki, in fact, to keep him on the books."

"I shall arrange for somebody to meet him there," Leverkov said. "One of our most trusted agents."

"That is settled, then," his host remarked. "We can only sit back and await developments."

"Your cover must be maintained, at all costs," his visitor said. "That is the key priority for the foreseeable future."

"Don't I know it, Lev! "came the quick reply. "My whole way of life depends on it."

The two men then relaxed a little, ordering coffee and cognac while absorbing the convivial atmosphere of the pub. A pianist began a medley of popular tunes, among which Lev Leverkov seemed to recognize a few, drumming his fingers on the table in time with the music. When he finally got up to leave for a scheduled visit to the Russian Embassy, Paul Bell asked:

"How is Nadia doing?"

"Your sister is doing very well," the other replied. "Since moving to St. Petersburg two years ago, she has become, I believe, quite active in the local Communist Party."

"Is that still a force in domestic politics?" his host asked, in mock disbelief.

"It is just one party among several nowadays," the other informed him. "Nostalgia for the old days, for the Soviet Union mainly, is what motivates its backers. Many people in the former East Germany, apparently, feel much the same way. Life under capitalism has not done as much for them as they had hoped. They often regard it as crony capitalism, and there is some truth in that."

"Give Nadia my warmest regards, Lev," Paul Bell requested. "I am unable to contact her personally for fear of breaking my cover."

"I shall gladly do so, Paul. Keep your eye on the ball and take good care of yourself."

"Good-bye, Lev Leverkov," the other replied, standing to shake his colleague's hand.

*

The next morning, on his arrival at Scotland Yard, George Mason was summoned to the chief inspector's office.

"You have had quite a busy time of late,

Inspector," Bill Harrington began, "with trips to Dublin and Amsterdam. What have you got to report, for the expense of time and resources?"

"At Dublin, I met with another member of the group who left the Soviet Union in 1990," Mason informed him. "Name of Pyotr Alenin. He confirmed your account of the fate of Igor Nikolayev on Chelsea Bridge."

"Did he come up with an explanation for it?" Harrington asked.

"He told me that Nikolayev had been in charge of the French desk while in the secret service, surmising that he had become too cozy with the French."

"He was a double agent?" his senior pointedly asked.

"Possibly," George Mason replied. "I asked him if he thought there might be a connection between Nikolayev's fate and the recent incidents at Stepney Green and Tooting Bec."

"What was his view on that?"

"He considered it improbable, in view of the time-lapse, Chief Inspector. But he did not rule it out entirely."

"Interesting, Inspector," came the considered reply. "The plot only thickens."

"Doesn't it so!" Mason agreed. "I have, however, made progress in another direction.

"I am all ears," Harrington replied, sitting bolt upright and leaning forward in his chair.

"Walter Stopford managed to retrieve a fragment of the timer used in the bombing incident at Cybernetics Institute. With information from the

F.B.I. about a similar device used in the bombing of an American military outpost, he was able to identify the brand. It was Apex, manufactured by a businessman named Aad Kuipers."

"Which is why you went to Holland, presumably?" his superior asked, serving himself fresh coffee from the tray a young constable had just brought in.

George Mason nodded, saying:

"Aad Kuipers is now being investigated by the Dutch authorities for possible infringement of his export license."

"On the basis of information you were able to give them?"

"While in Amsterdam, I paid a visit to Brigadier Klaas Brouwer," Mason explained, "with whom I had worked on a money laundering case a few years ago. I informed him that Kuipers had admitted providing a timing device to a fellow-Dutchman living at Brighton."

Bill Harrington sipped his coffee thoughtfully for a few moments.

"Good to see you are cooperating with the Dutch police," he eventually remarked, "and doing your bit to counter cross-border crime. Did you follow up this lead?"

"The Dutchman living at Brighton will now be questioned by the authorities on the spot," his colleague explained. "He claimed that he ran a legitimate business, supplying explosives for the civil engineering and construction industries."

"Credible enough, on the surface," his senior commented. "The person's name?"

"Dirk deGroot, Chief Inspector."

"He admitted supplying the bomb used at Cybernetics Institute?"

"That is correct," Mason replied. "He also said he could not supply a name, only a description of the client in question, who he said paid in cash."

At that point, the desk telephone rang. Bill Harrington picked up the receiver and listened for a few moments.

"That was the superintendent, requesting an urgent meeting," he said, quickly draining his coffee. "I see that you have made quite significant progress, Inspector. How do you propose to build on it?"

"The timing device used at Tooting Bec was wrapped in what appears to be a shirt collar," George Mason told him. "Walter Stopford paid a visit to a textile manufacturer at Blackburn, Lancashire, who informed him that it was a special type of material made solely by a Norwegian firm called Norje-Tex."

"So you will be heading off to Oslo any day now?" Harrington queried, as he moved towards the door.

"I need to establish the market for the type of fabric," Mason replied. "It should give us a fair idea of the sort of person or organization who would be likely to buy it, thus narrowing the field of our enquiries."

"Could you not just ring the company and describe it to them, to save expense?"

"Unfortunately not, Chief Inspector," came the reply. "Norje-Tex make various types of specialist fabric, for niche markets. I would need to show them this particular fragment to get a clear idea of its purpose."

Harrington agreed that that made sense.

"You could be there and back in a couple of days," he remarked. "Don't go turning it into a sightseeing trip. You can do the fjords on your vacation time."

"Absolutely not," his colleague said, with a broad smile at his senior's turn of phrase. "Would I ever think of doing such a thing?"

"You might," his senior half-jokingly added, "given the chance."

"May Detective Sergeant Aubrey come with me?" George Mason then asked.

"It would be useful experience for her, no doubt," Harrington said. "I shall have to get clearance from the superintendent first, however. It is a question of cost and priorities, as usual, Inspector."

*

Fabien Leroux slept late that morning, having visited a night club in the West End until the early hours. He took a quick shower, postponed shaving and got dressed. Aware that he had missed breakfast service, he left Leinster Hotel and walked along Queensway for coffee and croissants at a newly-opened branch of MacDonald's. Ensconced at a window table with his simple fare and a copy of the *Daily Mail*, a tabloid newspaper he enjoyed reading for its coverage of the latest scandals, he felt confident that he had met Q's requirements during his hirer's temporary absence. He was also in need of funds. After getting a refill of coffee, he checked his iPhone. There was a text message from Q, requesting a meeting at noon near the Serpentine boat-house in Hyde Park. The Canadian gave a sigh of relief that contact with the mysterious Q had been resumed. Glancing out of the restaurant window, he noted that the sun was breaking through the heavy bank of cloud. It would be fine enough for a stroll through the historic park, which he would access through Kensington Palace Gardens, directly across Bayswater Road from Queensway Underground station.

On the way, he took the opportunity to take photographs of Kensington Palace, elegantly designed by Sir Christopher Wren in the seventeenth century. The home of many former royals, including Queen Anne, the last of the Stuart monarchs, Queen Victoria and Princess Diana, it was now the London address of the Duke and Duchess of Cambridge, heirs to the throne of England, as well of a number of lesser royals. As a French-Canadian, he felt no particular affection for British royals, but he had an eye for good architecture, having recently visited St. Paul's Cathedral, designed by the same famous architect.

Q was already at the boat-house smoking a panatela, when he reached the Serpentine. The older man greeted him in a friendlier fashion than had been his wont, despite the fact that the hits against the two Russians had met with only partial success. They commenced strolling by the shore of the lake, observing the rowing boats and the pedalloes popular at this time of year with visitors to the park. The sky had now almost cleared, with a few banks of cumulus slowly drifting northwards. Q slipped his agent a Manila envelope, which the Canadian took to contain an instalment of his fee.

"This is for services to come," Q said, in genial tones. "Now tell me what you have achieved in my absence."

Fabien Leroux gratefully pocketed the envelope, without counting the contents.

"I have been staking out the address at Cockfosters, as you instructed," he said. "The resident reaches home around five each evening, preceded by his wife who, I gather, works locally. But I have not seen either of them in the past two days."

"They may have gone on vacation," the other said. "Or the husband may have left on a business trip and taken his wife with him. That would not be surprising, since he works as an account executive with an advertising company. In any case, there is no sense of urgency. I have other plans for you meanwhile, Monsieur, if you are agreeable."

That was music to the Canadian's ears.

"You have a new assignment for me?" he asked, as they both noted with some amusement the plight of two young boys whose dinghy had overturned and who were now waist-deep in water.

"I should like you to act as my courier," Q said, observing with some amusement the boys' difficulty in righting the small wooden craft. "I have some important documents I would like you to deliver to a contact at Helsinki. Are you familiar with that city?"

Fabien Leroux shook his head, saying:

"I have long wanted to visit the Nordic countries, but never had the opportunity."

"Finland is in the euro zone. Part of the cash in that envelope I just gave you is in euros. The rest is in Swedish kronor. You are to use cash at all times. No checks or credit cards, is that understood?"

"Because they can be traced?" Leroux asked.

"Exactly, Monsieur," came the reply.

"Shall I be going by Finnair?"

"No, Monsieur, you will travel by surface. Security is less stringent at railway stations and seaports than at airports. Is your passport in order?"

Leroux assured him that it was.

"It needs to be," Q said. "The British authorities catch around ten thousand people each year trying to enter the U.K. with forged or stolen documents. They make routine checks against an international database kept by Interpol."

"A valid Canadian passport should present no problem," Leroux assured him. "We are part of the British Commonwealth."

"In that case," came the reply, "I shall book tickets for you and give you a printed itinerary. Briefly, you will take a train to Newcastle, where you will board a North Sea Ferries service to Gothenburg. From there, you take the train to Stockholm and catch a ship across the Baltic to Turku, on the south-west coast of Finland. From that port, there is a regular bus service to Helsinki. It is all quite straight-forward."

"Sounds good," Leroux remarked. "But I do not

speak Finnish."

Q dismissed his qualms.

"Finns, especially educated ones, generally speak English well," he said. "They learn it at school, as their first foreign language. You should have no difficulty with, for example, hotel staffs. You may, however, have problems with restaurant menus. In which event, I advise you to opt for the pricier dishes. Finns eat a lot of raw, salted fish. Although inexpensive, it may not be to your taste, as it certainly is not to mine. They also tend to serve curdled milk with meals."

Fabien Leroux grimaced on hearing that.

"I take your point," he said, as they turned and retraced their steps.

"I can recommend reindeer steak," Q said, "which most restaurants serve. It is listed as *poro* on menus."

"That is an easy word to remember. Where, in fact, shall I be staying?"

"I shall book a room for you at Hotel Kivi, on Mikonkatu," the other informed him. "It is a short walk from the main railway station."

"It is a notable structure," the Canadian remarked, "designed by the famous architect, Eliel Saarinen."

Q returned a look of pleasant surprise.

"You are quite knowledgeable about architecture, aren't you?" he complimented.

"It is a long-term interest of mine," Leroux replied. "While in London, I have spent my free time photographing famous buildings, such as St. Paul's Cathedral, Westminster Abbey and the Houses of Parliament. On the way here, I stopped by Kensington Palace."

"The home of the Prince of Wales," Q said. "There's lots of great architecture in Finland, too, by such people as Alvar Aalto and Eero Saarinen. But I doubt you will have the opportunity to see much of it."

They had by now regained the boat-house, on completing a circuit of the lake. Two rather wet young boys, who had managed to return the dinghy to its mooring, were being in turn upbraided and consoled by their parents.

"Your contact at Helsinki," Q then said, "will come directly to Hotel Kivi, where you will hand over the documents you are carrying. She may even invite you to dinner."

"The person's name?" Leroux asked, intrigued to learn that his contact was a woman

"That need not concern you, Monsieur," the other said. "She will identify you by your room number, which has been booked in advance."

"After which, I am to return to England?"

"I have booked you at the Kivi for two nights," Q informed him, "to give you a short break from travel. That will allow you some free time in the Finnish capital. I can recommend the Finnish sauna, available at all hotels and swimming pools. The female attendants, called *saunatajat*, will give you a good scrubbing down afterwards."

Fabien Leroux smiled at the idea, not sure if that would be a pleasure or an ordeal.

"When do I leave?" he eagerly enquired.

"In a few days' time," came the reply. Glancing at his watch, he added: "I must be on my way now,

Monsieur. I have a lunch appointment with a colleague in Mayfair. I shall send you a text message about when we should next meet at The Black Prince. You remember where that is, I take it?"

"Of course I do," came the confident reply. "It is a busy pub just opposite Victoria Station."

With that, the mysterious Q bade his agent goodbye and strode briskly off towards the Marble Arch exit.

CHAPTER 9

George Mason and Alison Aubrey, who had been cleared by Superintendent Manwaring to join her senior on this leg of the investigation, took an early-morning flight from Gatwick. As the plane descended towards Fornebu Airport, the young detective sergeant, who occupied the window seat, gazed raptly at the broad fjord unfolding just below them. It was her first trip to Scandinavia. On exiting the terminal, they took a taxi to Hotel Bergstrom on Stranden, a broad promenade skirting the open bay. They checked in, deposited their luggage in adjoining rooms and met up again for a snack lunch in the hotel cafeteria. Afterwards, using a street map, they made their way on foot to Kirkegatan in downtown Oslo, arriving at the head office of Norje-Tex at just turned two o'clock. The general manager, Nils Ahlgren, was expecting them. He greeted them cordially, ushering them into the boardroom, where they took seats at one end of a polished rosewood table decorated with bowls of pine cones and small ferns. Large portraits hung on the wall facing picture windows overlooking the street.

"Those are former presidents of this company," Nils Ahlgren said, noting the detective's interest. "Norje-Tex was founded by my great-grandfather, the gentleman with side whiskers on the far right, in the early eighteen-hundreds."

"What is the exact nature of your business, Mr. Ahlgren?" George Mason enquired.

"We manufacture specialty fabrics for a variety of purposes," the manager replied.

His visitor produced the crumpled shirt collar retrieved from Cybernetics Institute at Tooting Bec.

"This, I believe," he said, "may be one of your products."

A bemused Nils Ahlgren took the piece of cloth and ran it carefully through his fingers, to assess the texture.

"It surely is one of our fabrics," he replied, adding with a frown, "but it seems somehow the worse for wear."

The two detectives could only exchange smiles at that remark.

"It has been in the wars, for sure," Mason informed him. "It was used to baffle the timing device of a type of pipe bomb used recently in South London."

"You don't say so, Inspector!" the other exclaimed, his strong features registering outrage at the misuse of a company product.

"We should be very grateful," Sergeant Aubrey said, "if you could give us some idea of your typical clientele for this kind of fabric."

The general manager sat back in his chair and gathered his thoughts, as a staff member appeared with refreshments. The young woman set the tray on the polished table, poured coffee and set a fresh coffee cake before them.

"Please do help yourselves," Nils Ahlgren said,

placing the shirt collar on the table and adding fresh cream, but no sugar, to his coffee.

The two visitors followed his lead, serving themselves pieces of the appetizing cake topped with sliced almonds. It helped supplement their snatched lunch.

"This fabric," Ahlgren then said, "is one of our newest products. We introduced it to the market early last year. Excuse me for a few moments, while I check with our sales department."

Saying that, he set down his cup and left the boardroom, leaving his two visitors to enjoy their refreshments with a sense of anticipation.

"We should now be able to get some idea of who may have used this type of material, Alison," George Mason said.

"Are you including Dirk deGroot in your calculations?" the young sergeant asked.

"I am working on the assumption that it is not available in England," he replied. "The Blackburn people Walter Stopford met with had not come across it before, so deGroot's client, whoever he is, may have supplied it. We shall see, Alison, in due course."

"This cake is really delicious, George," his colleague remarked, helping herself to a second slice.

"All Scandinavian countries serve something similar with coffee," he replied. "In Finland, it is known as *pulla*."

The general manager reappeared at that point, pleased to note that the refreshment was very acceptable.

"We currently have three main markets for this shirt fabric," he informed them, "which has special thermal qualities. Our main outlet is the Norwegian whaling industry."

"Does Norway still hunt whales?" Sergeant Aubrey asked, in some surprise.

"Whaling has long been a part of our culture," Nils Ahlgren replied. "Certainly since the early nineteenth century. Today, we hunt only Minke, which is not an endangered species. Strict quotas on the annual catch are in force."

"Isn't there pressure from animal rights groups and suchlike to end the practice?" George Mason put it to him.

The general manager returned a rather irritated look at that question.

"It is an issue often raised by conservation groups," he admitted. "But some small communities in the north of Norway rely on whaling for their livelihood, as do inhabitants of the Faroe Islands, for instance. And some Native Americans do too, I might add. Such groups resent what they consider interference from outsiders in their traditional way of life."

The two detectives reacted evenly to that justification of the practice. Whaling was not something they could do much about; the matter was best left to organizations like Greenpeace. To a firm like Norje-Tex, it was just another business opportunity.

Nils Ahlgren refilled their cups, after helping himself to some coffee cake.

"Another market for this material," he added, "is

the Lapland Survey."

"How interesting," Alison Aubrey commented. "What exactly is that, Mr. Ahlgren?"

"Regular surveys of Lapland fauna and flora are conducted," came the reply, "to see which species are keeping a balance and which may be declining in numbers."

"Reindeer?" George Mason asked.

"Reindeer are herded by the Lapps," Ahlgren informed him, "so their numbers are well-documented. The survey focuses mainly on wildlife, such as wolverines, lynxes, foxes, bears, wolves and the several species of birds that frequent the tundra."

"Golden eagles?" an intrigued Alison Aubrey asked.

Their knowledgeable host nodded.

"It is one among several interesting species that nest in, or pass through, our most northerly territory each year," he said. "Others are the willow grouse, the snow goose and the red-necked grebe."

"How fascinating," George Mason remarked, while thinking that people involved in activities such as ocean whaling and Lapland surveys were unlikely suspects in a bomb attack in South London. "I imagine the vast wilderness of Lapland supports a good deal of wildlife."

"Indeed it does," the other replied. "And we aim to conserve it, with an eye to global warming."

"Are those your only outlets for this material?" the detective then asked.

"There is just one other," Nils Ahlgren replied. "We have a contract to supply it to the Royal

Canadian Navy, for use on Arctic patrol vessels."

George Mason's ears pricked up at that news.

"The extra-thermal qualities would come in very handy in the Arctic, I imagine," he remarked.

"The naval authorities seem well-satisfied with it," the general manager replied. "They renewed their order only last month, in fact."

"What type of material is it, exactly?" a curious Alison Aubrey asked, running the shirt fragment through her fingers.

"It is a mixture of heavy-duty cotton and 500 denier nylon," he explained. "Our research department is the most technically-advanced in Europe, certainly as regards thermal wear."

"I can well believe that, Mr. Ahlgren," Mason said. "Thank you very much for your assistance."

"You are most welcome, Inspector Mason," the other replied. "I should like to hear more about this shirt collar's role in the bombing incident you mentioned. Our board members will be much intrigued."

"In due course," the detective assured him, "we shall keep you informed of any developments in the case."

The trio then chatted for a while about more general topics, such as tourism potential and local customs, as the coffee pot emptied and the coffee cake diminished in size.

"Before you leave," Ahlgren said, as his two visitors rose to go, "I should very much like you to enjoy the remainder of your short time in Oslo. I assume you will be staying overnight?"

"We booked in at Hotel Bergstrom," George

Mason replied, "for just the one night."

"A first-rate hotel, overlooking the Oslo Fjord, Inspector," Nils Ahlgren remarked. "They provide an excellent smorgasbord for dinner, with local specialties."

"I shall look forward to that," Alison emphatically rejoined.

"I have two spare tickets for a concert of our national composer, Edvard Grieg," the manager then said, "conducted by the Finnish maestro, Osmo Vanska. I was planning to take my wife this evening, but there is an emergency board meeting scheduled for six o'clock, which is bound to drag on. You are most welcome to have them."

He reached into his jacket pocket and handed a small envelope to his visitors. The detectives were delighted to accept them, as an enjoyable way of spending a free evening.

"That is very generous of you, Mr. Ahlgren," George Mason said, with feeling.

"My pleasure, Inspector Mason," came the reply, as he escorted the two visitors to the main entrance. "The board members will be very interested to learn of a visit from Scotland Yard."

"I can imagine," Mason replied, warmly shaking his hand.

It now being mid-afternoon, the two detectives made their way to the main shopping center. Alison Aubrey was bent on looking for a present for her husband's birthday the following week. Since he was very keen on outdoor pursuits, they entered a large sports' emporium selling hiking, fishing and skiing gear.

"Malcolm needs new ski gloves," Alison said, examining the stock on display. "I might as well buy them here, they seem to be of such good quality."

"They will be," George Mason commented. "Nordic skiing is practically the national pastime in winter. They organize long ski-tours across the fells, staying overnight at strategically-placed cabins, with log fires and saunas."

"That sounds just great," his young colleague replied, examining the price-tags. "Malcolm would really enjoy something like that."

"The gloves seem a bit expensive," Mason remarked, noting her hesitation.

"I think everything is rather pricey in Oslo," she replied, "from what I have noticed in the storefronts on our way down here. But I am going to buy them in any case. Malcolm will be so pleased."

"They should last him a good while," Mason said, encouragingly.

After Alison had completed her purchase with her Visa and had it gift-wrapped, they left the store and walked a few blocks to the National Gallery, where George Mason wanted to view the dramatic paintings of Edvard Munch, along with other examples of Norwegian art. They afterwards made their way back to their hotel, so that Alison could rest up for a while. George Mason headed to the bar, to sample the local brew and read the copy of *The Times* provided by the hotel. He was particularly interested to learn if there had been any further attacks on Russian nationals living in London. The police report on page twelve, covering the last several days, recorded mainly traffic violations. It raised his hopes that that was the end of the matter; the two cases to hand were quite enough to be dealing with, given their complexity. As he quaffed his pale ale and flicked through the newspaper, he fell to wondering how Maxim Brodsky and Yuri Orlov were getting along, especially whether the latter had emerged from his coma.

At just before six o'clock, a much-refreshed Alison Aubrey came down from her room and joined him in the lounge. To sharpen their appetites, they took a half-hour stroll along Stranden, with its panoramic view of Oslo Fjord and its boating activity, before joining the other hotel guests for dinner. On entering the restaurant, the maître d'hotel assigned them a table and a waiter soon arrived to take their order for drinks. The ample smorgasbord stretched the entire width of the room. Piled with food, it offered a variety of fish and meat dishes, plus all manner of desserts and pastries. Choosing a starter of smoked salmon, the two visitors returned to their table.

"They do themselves proud here, don't they, George?" an impressed Alison Aubrey said.

"Norway is a wealthy country," he replied, "mainly from North Sea oil revenues. It used to be the poor relation of Sweden, but their roles are now reversed. Many Swedes have moved here in recent times, often to take the more menial jobs."

"How interesting is that!" his companion said, as they began their appetizing dinner.

Part-way through the first course, George Mason

said:

"What do you think we learned today, Sergeant?"

His colleague glanced up momentarily from her food.

"You mean apart from the high prices at Oslo stores?" she asked, with a disingenuous smile.

"I was actually referring to Norje-Tex," he came back, with raised eyebrows.

"We learned who the customers were for the type of fabric you showed to the general manager."

"And what was your reaction, Alison?" Mason pressed.

"I thought we could likely rule out the Norwegian whaling industry, which I was surprised to learn was still operational," she replied, "as well as the Lapland Survey."

"I have been thinking along the same lines, too, Alison. I recall what Dirk deGroot told me when I went down to Brighton to interview him."

"What was that, George?" she eagerly enquired.

"deGroot admitted assembling the explosive device used at Tooting Bec, but he could not, or would not, provide a name for the client, who paid in cash. He did, however, mention that the buyer spoke with a North American accent and that he had a military bearing."

"The Royal Canadian Navy!" Alison exclaimed.

"Spot on, Alison!" her senior rejoined. "I think my next move, when we get back to home base, is a visit to Canada House on Trafalgar Square."

His companion returned an appreciative glance at her senior's acumen.

"Some pieces of this puzzle are now beginning to

fall into place, George," she remarked.

"You can say that again, Alison," he replied. "I think we may, in fact, have made a significant breakthrough."

With that, they rose from their places to choose the second of what they imagined would be several gourmet courses. George Mason thought he would try the roast elk with red whortleberries, as a typical local dish; Alison opted for reindeer steak with bilberries. Two hours later, they took a brisk walk along the strand, to work off the effects of a full meal. It was already dusk on a clear night, the moonlight reflecting from the vast surface of the fjord.

*

Two days later, George Mason set off early to Canada House, home of the Canadian High Commission on Trafalgar Square. A senior official named Roger Thurgood received him in the library.

"What can we do for you, Inspector Mason?" he genially enquired.

"I have a query regarding your navy," his visitor said. "I have it on good authority from a firm called Norje-Tex at Oslo that a special type of thermal material was supplied for making shirts for mariners serving on some of your naval vessels."

"That would most likely be the Arctic patrol ship, *HMCS Bellhaven*," the official responded, after a moment's thought.

"Can you provide confirmation of that," his visitor asked.

"Certainly, Inspector," came the reply. "If you care to wait here in the library, I shall place a call to Ottawa."

"And if the fabric was so used," Mason added, "I should like to know the names of sailors who left the navy during the past few months."

The official raised his eyebrows at that, while looking questioningly at his visitor.

"Is there some problem with our naval personnel?" he cautiously enquired.

George Mason returned a disarming smile, saying: "It is early days yet, Mr. Thurgood. We are conducting enquiries into some serious incidents that occurred here in London over the past several weeks. It may, or may not be, the case that an individual serving in the Royal Canadian Navy is involved."

"I should sincerely hope not," the official emphatically replied, leaving the library to comply with his visitor's request.

During the man's absence, Mason occupied himself scanning the tourist brochures left on a side-table. He picked one on Quebec City, which he was interested to note was a World Heritage site, probably on account of the well-preserved older section within the city walls. He read with interest that the imposing Chateau Frontenac had been the venue for a top-secret World War 11 conference between Franklin Roosevelt and Winston Churchill. He then crossed the room to examine a large wall-map of Canada, locating Quebec City on the St. Lawrence River, the link between the Great Lakes and the Atlantic Ocean.

After some twenty minutes, Roger Thurgood reappeared, noting Mason's interest in the map.

"Have you ever visited Canada, Inspector?" he asked.

Mason turned and shook his head, with a regretful smile.

"Afraid not," he replied. "But I should certainly like to do so, one day."

"Each province has its own distinctive characteristics," Thurgood said. "I myself hail from St. John, New Brunswick, a major sea-port."

"Next door to Quebec Province?" his visitor asked, indicating the wall-map.

"Precisely, Inspector. Now, to answer your query."

They both sat down again, facing each other across the highly-polished table.

"Our navy has, in fact, been using fabric from Norje-Tex for making shirts for the Arctic patrol vessel, *HMCS Bellhaven*, as I surmised."

"On account of its extra-thermal qualities?"

"Quite so, Inspector Mason. And as to your other query, three servicemen have left the Arctic patrol vessel so far this year."

"You managed to obtain their names?" the detective asked.

"I have them here," the official informed him, consulting a brief list. "Will Tuffnel left in January. He is now apparently employed at a shipyard in New Brunswick, repairing yachts."

"What rank would was he?" Mason asked.

"A midshipman," Roger Thurgood replied. "The second individual left the service a month later, on reaching retirement age. His name is Mark Saville, who is understood to have moved down to Florida with his wife."

"For a more inviting climate, Mr. Thurgood?" George Mason wryly put it.

"Our winters can be a little trying, I admit," the other remarked. "Temperatures can go down to minus thirty Celsius."

"Give me Florida, any day," his visitor quipped.

"The third person to leave the Arctic patrol service was Fabien Leroux, Inspector. He received a dishonorable discharge in March."

George Mason raised his eyebrows at that.

"Do you happen to know on what grounds, Mr. Thurgood?"

The official shook his head, saying:

"That must remain a confidential matter, Inspector Mason, due to protocol."

"Do the naval authorities have any idea of this person's current whereabouts?" Mason then asked, trying a different tack.

"I am afraid not," came the reply. "They have been trying to trace him, as a matter of fact, to recover items of his uniform he did not turn in."

It immediately occurred to the detective that one of those missing items might well have been a shirt.

"How curious," he remarked, noting down the name of the ex-serviceman. "I think we can safely rule out enquiries about both Will Tuffnel and Mark Saville, whose present whereabouts are accounted for. The elusive Fabien Leroux seems a more promising prospect for our purposes, but I doubt your navy will recover his service shirt."

"Why would that be, Inspector?" a mildly-alarmed Roger Thurgood asked, with raised eyebrows.

"That will have to remain a confidential matter too, for the time being," his visitor replied, with a strong hint of irony.

"A most intriguing business, Inspector Mason," the official remarked, "without a doubt. We at Canada House should be very interested to learn the outcome of your enquiries."

"All in due course, my good sir," the detective said, rising to take his leave. "Many thanks for your valuable time."

"Do not mention it," the other replied. "And if you need further assistance, Inspector Mason, do not hesitate to contact us again."

*

Fabien Leroux rose early that morning, in good time for the breakfast service at Leinster Hotel. Afterwards, he made his way along Queensway and took the Tube to Victoria Station, where he caught a train to Brixton to return the rifle he had borrowed from Jeb Sinclair. His fellow-Canadian, who had taken the day off for personal reasons, refrained from asking his former naval colleague the real reason for the loan, accepting with skepticism Leroux's explanation that it was for hunting wild boar. The animal had recently been reintroduced into country areas around London and was valued by chefs at high-end restaurants.

After a friendly chat over coffee with Sinclair and

a promise to meet up again soon for a night on the town, Leroux returned to London. Crossing Victoria Street, he entered The Black Prince soon after it had opened its doors for the lunch-hour trade. Q was already there, seated at a corner table reading a newspaper.

"Good morning, Monsieur," Q said, in affable tones.

"Good day to you," Leroux replied.

Fabien Leroux noticed that the older man was, as usual, smartly dressed in a charcoal-gray business suit and club tie. On the table beside him was a large Manila envelope with a wax seal.

"Sorry I cannot join you for lunch today," Q continued. "I have a prior engagement at the Savoy Hotel."

Saying that, he passed the sealed envelope across the table.

"You are not to let this package out of your sight," he instructed, "not even when you visit the loo."

"I have a leather briefcase with a lock," Leroux replied. "It will be perfectly safe in my custody."

The older man then handed him a smaller envelope.

"Here are your tickets for the North Sea ferry," he said. "You can purchase rail tickets along the way, with the cash I gave you at our last meeting. When you reach Stockholm, book the sea passage to Turku at the Stena Lines kiosk located near the central dock."

"On reaching Turku, I take the service bus to Helsinki?" the Canadian enquired.

"Exactly, Monsieur," came the reply.

"When do I leave?"

"The day after tomorrow," Q informed him. "Take a morning train from King's Cross, to reach Newcastle in good time for the afternoon ferry, which departs at 4.00 p.m."

"You can count on me," Leroux assured him.

"On the day you leave London," Q then said, "check out of your lodgings and leave your effects at the left-luggage facility at King's Cross."

"Why would I need to do that?" Leroux, who had felt quite at home at Leinster Hotel, enquired.

"Routine precaution," the other explained. "The Metropolitan Police have on-going enquiries into the incidents at Stepney Green and Tooting Bec. It is better if you move around. I have reserved a room for you here at The Black Prince, in fact. The proprietor is a good friend of mine. He has a comfortable apartment on the second floor which he uses for short lets, mainly to tourists."

The Canadian's face lit up on hearing that.

"I thought you would approve, Monsieur," Q said, "given your evident fondness for pub life. The entrance to the apartment is a street door to the left of the pub main entrance. You will collect the key from the barman and mount the flight of stairs to a small landing. Your apartment door will be facing you."

"I am to reside here for the foreseeable future?" Leroux enquired.

The older man nodded.

"Assuming you successfully complete this mission," he replied, "I shall consider using your services again in the near future."

Saying that, he drained his glass and got up to go, leaving his agent pondering the contents of the Manila envelope just handed to him. Realizing with a shrug that he would probably never know, he clasped the envelope tightly as he crossed to the service counter and ordered quiche Lorraine for lunch. Afterwards, he would visit his fitness club before returning to the Leinster to make some preparations for his trip to Finland. Despite what Q had said earlier, he would make time to photograph some of that city's notable architecture.

*

The next day, on reaching Scotland Yard, George Mason reported to Chief Inspector Harrington.

"How are your enquiries proceeding, Inspector?" his senior asked, glancing up expectantly from a sheaf of documents.

"Some small progress to report," Mason said. "Our visit to Oslo proved quite useful, in that Detective Sergeant Aubrey and I learned of the outlets for the type of fabric recovered from the parking lot at Tooting Bec."

"Norje-Tex were able to help you?" Bill Harrington enquired.

"Indeed, they were, Chief Inspector," his colleague replied. "The general manager, a Mr. Nils Ahlgren, told me that they supply the material to the Royal Canadian Navy. That seems to be our best bet, all things considered. The Norwegian whaling industry and something called the Lapland Survey also use Norje-Tex fabrics. Alison and I ruled them out as suspects in a bombing incident."

The chief inspector weighed Mason's words carefully, before saying:

"People have been known to catch fish by throwing dynamite into the water. Why rule out the whaling industry?"

George Mason raised his eyebrows at that remark, giving his senior a questioning look. Deciding that Harrington was only half-serious, he said:

"Because they generally use harpoons, Chief Inspector."

"That apparently explode inside the cetaceans," the other remarked, with a grim expression. "But I take your point, Inspector. What else have you got to report?"

"On the strength of the information provided by Nils Ahlgren, I paid a visit to Canada House," Mason replied. "An official there checked with the naval authorities at Ottawa. He came up with the name of the ship used on Arctic patrols, and also the identities of seamen who had recently left the service."

"You have been too modest, Inspector," his senior remarked. "You have turned up quite a lot of useful information."

George Mason smiled to himself on hearing that.

"An individual named Fabien Leroux would seem to be the next focus of our enquiries," he said. "Leroux was given a dishonorable discharge from the navy. The Canadians did not give a reason and they have no idea, apparently, of his current whereabouts."

Bill Harrington leaned back in his chair, lit his briar pipe and pondered the situation. After a while, he said:

"You would need to find out if by chance he came to Britain, Inspector. Assuming he used a valid passport in his own name, check with passport controls at major airports and Channel ports. You should be able to establish exactly when and where he entered this country."

"I shall make enquiries at once, Chief Inspector," his colleague promised.

On reaching his own office, he quickly checked his mail and did some filing before acting on Harrington's suggestion. By the end of the morning, he had discovered that a passport in the name of Fabien Leroux had quite recently been stamped at Southampton, meaning that the subject had arrived in style on Queen Mary 2, the new Cunard liner. The knowledge took the detective's mind momentarily back to his one-and-only trans-Atlantic voyage on the ship's predecessor, Queen Elizabeth 2. On learning that Leroux had indeed arrived in England, the next step was to discover if he had, in fact, come to London. The shirt fragment would then be key evidence against him. He crossed into the general office to speak with Alison Aubrey.

"What news, George?" she amiably enquired, while fixing herself fresh coffee.

"I have been following up on our Oslo trip," he told her. "Yesterday, I visited the Canadian High Commission at Trafalgar Square and got the name Fabien Leroux from the authorities at Ottawa. It seems that he recently served on an Arctic patrol vessel named *Bellhaven*."

"That sounds like a real breakthrough, George," Alison remarked.

"Considering that I have just learned that he arrived in England in April," Mason said, "I think we may well be onto something. The question is, how do we trace an individual in a city of this size, if indeed he is in London?"

The young officer thought about that for a few moments, as she sipped her Java roast.

"Leave that little matter with me, Inspector," she encouragingly remarked. "I shall come up with something."

"I am sure you shall, Alison," he confidently replied, returning to his desk to finish writing a report.

Less than an hour later, Detective-Sergeant Aubrey knocked lightly on his office door.

"Enter," Mason said.

"I think I may be able to get the sort of information you want, George," Alison said. "But it may take a little time."

"I'm listening," he replied.

"I contacted two associations, which together represent most of the hotels in the metropolitan area. They promised to circulate their members to find out if a Fabien Leroux booked in with one of them last month. They do not include small family establishments, however, or bed-and-breakfasts."

"Since Mr. Leroux apparently came over on Queen Mary 2," her senior wryly remarked, "I expect he can afford top-class accommodation. I'd put my money on a hotel. Which organizations did you come up with, Alison?"

"Hospitality Express and Metropolitan Hoteliers," she replied. "It may take several days to hear back from them."

George Mason puckered his brows on hearing that.

"Let us hope," he said, "if Fabien Leroux is indeed our man, that he does not strike again in the meantime."

Saying that, he went down to the staff canteen for a late lunch.

CHAPTER 10

Two days later, Fabien Leroux reached King's Cross Station in good time to catch the 8.35 a.m. service to Newcastle-upon-Tyne, in the far northeast of the country. The train took him through the historic cities of York and Durham, affording him a view of their magnificent Gothic cathedrals, before crossing the bridge over the River Tyne to reach his destination. A shuttle service took ongoing passengers by bus to the North Sea Ferries terminal, where he boarded a vessel named *Birger Karl* for the overnight crossing to Gothenburg, on the west coast of Sweden. Noting as it grew dark that many passengers were settling down on reclining chairs in the main lounge for an indifferent night's sleep, he felt glad that the mysterious Q had had the forethought to book him a private cabin. It was an indication that the man valued his services, auguring well for any future dealings he may have with him.

After lingering over the elaborate smorgasbord with a couple of Swedish beers, followed by a stroll on desk, he slept well enough and felt quite refreshed the following morning, despite being roused during the night by the heavy pitching of the ship. The North Sea, he knew from his time in the navy, was noted for its violent storms. From Gothenburg Central, he took the express train to

Stockholm, where he had time to photograph some of the notable waterfront buildings before boarding the Stena Lines ferry *Allotar* to Turku. From the harbor, he took the regular bus service to Helsinki, checking in at the Kivi, the medium-sized hotel on Mikonkatu where a room had been booked for him in advance. It was late evening by the time he arrived, after almost two full days' travel. It was well past the hour of dinner. He ordered an open sandwich of smoked salmon and cucumber in the hotel bar, helped down with a bottle of export beer, and watched an American comedy with Finnish subtitles for an hour or so, before calling it a day.

Breakfast service the next day began with porridge, followed by hard-boiled eggs garnished with anchovies. It struck him as unusual fare, accepting it as typically Finnish. The conversations at nearby tables intrigued him, since he had never heard spoken Finnish. It was more animated than he had expected in view of the stereotype of the Finn as introverted and rather reserved. The opposite of, say, the Italian or the Greek. His prior impressions of Scandinavia had come mainly from the films of Ingmar Bergman, sometimes screened in the mess-room of the *Bellhaven*. Jeb Sinclair had been a fan of the celebrated Swedish director, placing requests for films such as *The Seventh Seal*, *Wild Strawberries* and *Summer with Monica*. He too had much enjoyed them, as a refreshing change from action movies.

Q had indicated that his contact would approach him on the second evening, leaving him most of the first day to explore this fascinating city. Against advice, he opted to leave his briefcase in his hotel room as he set off on foot to explore his surroundings. Mikonkatu was centrally-situated, just a short walk from the train station, where he paused to take photographs before heading along Mannerheim Way, the main thoroughfare, as far as the Swedish Theatre. From there, he strolled in the spring sunshine along Esplanade, a tree-lined avenue leading down to South Harbor.

There, he came upon a scene of much activity. An outdoor market was in progress. Farmers had sailed down the coast to dock their small craft at the harbor wall. Larger vessels, freighters and passenger ships, berthed farther out in the deeper water. Quantities of fish, flowers and vegetables were unloaded from the boats and set out on long wooden tables manned by the farmers' wives, sturdy, no-nonsense women who brooked no haggling over price. Sales were brisk and the atmosphere lively for what he took to be a weekly event patronized by local residents. The only obvious tourists were a Japanese family group. He took several pictures of the scene and of the onion-domed Russian cathedral on the far side of the bay. He then waited long enough to watch the doughty vendors reload the unsold produce onto their small craft and head out back along the coast, one behind the other, in a curious flotilla formation. Seagulls swooped down, to clean up bits of edibles fallen from the tables.

Concerned that he would not be able to decipher Finnish menus, he chose for lunch a self-service restaurant on Mannerheim Way, where he could select his own dishes from the warm buffet. Helsinki, he soon realized, was a fairly compact city comparable in size to Quebec City. After eating, he was able in the course of the afternoon to take in some of the main tourist sights, including the Lutheran Cathedral, the Parliament building and the National Museum, with its intriguing exhibits of the first inhabitants of this northern country, together with their modes of dress and transport, which seemed to consist mainly of sleds and wooden skis.

Late-afternoon, he returned to Hotel Kivi and spent a relaxing hour in the sauna before retiring to his room, to await developments. At just turned six o'clock, there came a knock on his door, rousing him from a nap. He rose from his bed, threw on a dressing-gown and unlocked the door. A woman of short stature, with shoulder-length auburn hair and clad in a print dress with a loose suede jacket stood in the threshold. He estimated her to be in her mid-thirties.

"Mr. Leroux?" she enquired, with a penetrating gaze.

The Canadian rather self-consciously nodded.

Seeing that he was half-dressed, his visitor tactfully said, in flawless English:

"I shall wait for you downstairs, in the residents' lounge."

"I shall be there in a few minutes," Fabien Leroux assured her, closing the door and hurriedly completing his attire and brushing his hair. He was a little surprised that he had fallen asleep, putting it down to all the footwork he had done that day, plus the rigorous sauna bath. With a final check in the wardrobe mirror, he gripped his briefcase and went downstairs.

"You may call me Alina," the woman said, immediately taking possession of the case holding the Manila envelope.

"And I answer to Fabien," the visitor replied.

She then led the way at a fairly brisk pace towards Station Square, beyond which was a large park with spring flowers in bloom. Speaking little on the way, she in due course led him to a large restaurant on the far side of the park. It was called Kalevala, after a Finnish literary epic, and was already quite full of diners. The interior décor was rustic, with simple pinewood tables and chairs. Glass-fronted display cases at intervals round the walls held examples of typical Finnish fauna, including lynx, fox, wolf, the snowy owl and other species of birds. Fabien Leroux was quite taken with the place, as they occupied a window table overlooking the park.

His hostess glanced at the menu.

"I expect this will mean little to you," she said, with an amused smile.

"If only I could speak your language," the Canadian sighed.

"I shall translate it for you," Alina said. "We can start with today's soup, which is tomato bisque."

"I am all for that," Leroux replied.

"There is a broad choice of entrée," the young woman then said. "For meat, they have beef, elk, reindeer and pigs' trotters."

The visitor's eyes opened wide at the last-named item. He associated trotters with high-end Chinese tables.

"If you prefer fish," Alina continued, "they have cod, salmon, herring or turbot. I can recommend the turbot, which is caught in upcountry lakes."

"Q recommended reindeer," Leroux said. "I think I may like to try that, as I have never seen it before on restaurant menus."

"And I shall have the baked turbot," his companion declared, quickly placing the order with a young waitress clad in national dress to complement the restaurant decor.

"And to drink?" the waitress asked.

Alina glanced towards her guest.

"Any preference?" she asked.

"A good Riesling should go well with both dishes, I imagine," he replied.

"A Mosel Riesling Kabinett," Alina told the waitress, with the air of one well-versed in wine.

Turning to her guest, she said:

"Tell me, Fabien, what you have managed to see of our beautiful city in the short time you have been here."

"I spent an interesting morning at the quayside market at South Harbor," he replied. "I also visited the museum, the cathedral and the parliament building. I am very interested in architecture. I took some great photographs."

"Do you mean the Lutheran or the Ouspensky cathedral?"

Leroux's face registered puzzlement.

"The Ouspensky is the Russian Orthodox building on the far side of the bay," she explained. "You couldn't miss noticing if you were down at South Harbor."

"I figured it was a church of some kind, Alina," he replied, "built in red brick, with bright cupolas."

Alina smilingly nodded.

"So now you know," she said. "Finland was a Russian grand duchy up until the Bolshevik Revolution of 1917. Hence it was also a Russian archdiocese."

"Which would explain things," he agreed.

At that point, the wine was served. The waitress half filled their glasses, placing the bottle in a chiller by the table. Alina raised her glass and proposed a toast.

"To Q," she said, with an artful twinkle in her eye.

"Whoever he may be," her guest said, clinking glasses.

"How well do you know him, Fabien?" she then asked.

"I have met him only a few times," the Canadian replied evasively, sensing that she might be trying to sound him out.

"*I* have never met him," the young woman said, much to his surprise. "Please do tell me what you know about him."

"I would say he is in his mid-to-late fifties," came the reply. "He dresses conventionally, like a businessman. I think he may work in the City of London, possibly in finance or insurance. He always wears a club tie, possibly for golf or tennis...or even cricket."

Alina returned a look of mild amusement at those remarks.

"I doubt he works in the City," she pointedly observed, while adding: "I visit London quite frequently. I love it for the theatre, the bookstores and the fashion boutiques."

"How do you yourself know Q?" Fabien Leroux felt emboldened to ask, since she struck him as guileless enough, despite her involvement in what was evidently a very secretive operation.

"I know of him through his sister, Nadia," she explained. "We met at a conference in Tallinn, the capital of Estonia, early last year. Nadia and I became quite close, in one way. In another way, we remained far apart."

The visitor did not know quite what to make of that enigmatic remark. It reeked of ambivalence and he chose not to probe further. The bisque arrived at that point and they let it cool for a few minutes before tasting it. The waitress topped up their wine glasses, returning twenty minutes later with the entrees. He found the reindeer steak, garnished with red whortleberries, much to his taste. Light in color, it had the texture of prime beef; nor was it gamey, like venison, as he had imagined it might be.

"I imagine, Fabien, that you are very curious as to what is inside the package," his hostess said, as they in due course nudged their plates aside.

"It had crossed my mind, Alina," he admitted, with a rather sheepish grin.

"You are just an errand boy," she teased. "Q is using you."

Fabien Leroux bridled inwardly at that remark, but made no comment.

"What I can tell you," she continued, "in strict confidence of course, is that its final destination is across the border. In a way, I am merely a courier, much as you are. Tomorrow morning, I shall take the train from here to the Finland Station at St. Petersburg, along the same route Lenin took at the onset of the 1917 Revolution, after being whisked out of Switzerland by the Germans."

"What was in it for the Germans?" an intrigued Fabien Leroux enquired.

"In 1917, they were still at war with Imperial Russia. They figured that key dissidents like Lenin would help destabilize the tsarist regime. Since regular routes into Russia were closed during the hostilities, they transported him through Germany by special train and then across the Baltic to Sweden by ferry. From there, he traveled north towards Lapland and crossed the border at Harparanda into Finland."

"How fascinating is that, Alina," he remarked. "I love to hear about European history."

If it had not occurred to him before, however, it now struck the Canadian forcefully that he was engaged in some form of espionage. If the Manila envelope could not be entrusted to the regular mail, it must contain some very sensitive material. He shrugged off the implications of his actions. He was in too deep now to have second thoughts. What was more, he needed the money. Q paid well.

"Would you like some more wine?" he asked.

Alina nodded, nudging her glass forward.

"And to round off a good dinner," she said, "I recommend the cloudberries, a typically Finnish dessert. They are gathered from the forests, mainly in the north of the country."

"Sounds good," an intrigued Fabien Leroux said, sitting back to observe some local children playing soccer in the park, while sipping his Mosel wine.

"Now tell me a bit about yourself," Alina suddenly said. "I am curious about you. American, aren't you?"

"Canadian," he corrected.

"Yet you recently moved to England, I believe?"

"After leaving the navy, in fact. My term of service was completed and I was looking for new opportunities."

"How interesting," she remarked. "What rank did you reach?"

"Chief Petty Officer," came the reply. "I served on the Arctic patrol vessel, the *HMCS Bellhaven*."

Alina's eyes opened wide at that disclosure.

"Did you see lots of wildlife?" she asked. "Polar bears, walruses, beluga whales, things like that?"

Fabien Leroux could only smile at that question.

"Occasionally," he replied.

Cloudberries with vanilla ice-cream arrived, whereupon his hostess promptly offered coffee and a choice of liqueur.

"Amaretto," he said, after a moment's reflection. He liked its almond flavor.

"Armagnac for me," Alina said.

He could see how the fruit he was eating got its name. The berries were the size of large blackberries, but of a cloudy, yellowish-white color and quite succulent. His hostess was pleased to note that he found them to his taste.

"The Arctic is becoming increasingly significant commercially," he remarked. "The ice-cap is melting, opening up new waterways. There will be a scramble for resources."

"Minerals, oil and fisheries?" she enquired. "Do you think there will be conflict?"

"That cannot be ruled out, unfortunately, Alina, given the competing claims by nations bordering the Arctic Ocean. The Royal Canadian Navy is preparing to defend Canada's interests there. New ships with state-of-the-art combat systems have been commissioned. They will enter service over the next few years."

"Russia is already prospecting for oil there," Alina said. "But I think it will be difficult to extract, given the technical problems."

"Which are quite formidable, I believe," the Canadian opined. "Several companies have already given up on Alaskan oil, for example."

With their coffee and liqueurs, they sat back and listened to the house musician playing Finnish folk tunes on the kantele, a traditional stringed instrument resembling a zither. After a while, Alina said:

"You still haven't told me much about Q. What is he like as a person?"

"Agreeable enough, as company," her guest replied. "He likes his food, judging by the lunches we have shared at London pubs. He is also very exacting in his requirements, giving detailed instructions, leaving nothing to chance. I would not wish to get on the wrong side of him."

"I imagine he could be quite ruthless," Alina remarked.

"But you claimed never to have met him," the

other protested. "How would you know something like that?"

"One forms impressions of people, one way or another," she cryptically replied. "I once saw him on Swedish television. He was among a group of people attending a conference at Stockholm. Something to do with international relations, I seem to recall."

"I got the impression he is well up in his chosen field," Leroux said. "But you seem to doubt he is in business of some kind."

Alina returned an artful smile, while chasing her coffee with cognac.

"I know very well what he does," she replied. "But I cannot tell you much, except that he is assuredly no businessman or financier, as you seem to think. As for golf, tennis or cricket, I have no view whatsoever on that. Many people in England belong to sports clubs of one kind or another, unless he wears a club tie just for show."

"You do not seem to have a very high regard for him," the Canadian then said. "Yet you work for him. Is he using you, too?"

Alina gave a nervous little laugh and shook her head, causing an auburn forelock to fall attractively across her brow. Brushing it to one side, she said:

"I volunteered my services after being approached by his sister, Nadia. The work pays well and serves some other useful purposes which I am not at liberty to discuss."

The ex-navy man sat back and sipped his liqueur. Her remarks made him think. This cool-headed, self-possessed young woman was into something, ferrying documents between Helsinki and St. Petersburg for reasons other than purely financial ones. He would have given a lot, even paid for the costly dinner, to learn what those reasons were. He gave her a questioning look, while catching the plaintive strains of the kantele, but she averted her gaze.

As the wall-clock registered eight-thirty, she indicated that it was time to leave. Summoning the waitress, she settled the bill with cash and paid a quick visit to the restroom. On her return, he accompanied her out into the street. If he had been nursing expectations that he would continue to enjoy her company for the remainder of the evening, he was swiftly disabused. A modern sedan pulled up within minutes outside the Kalevala. A tall man with close-cropped gray hair and an athletic build stepped out and greeted them.

"Osmo Lehtinen," he announced, offering his hand.

"Pleased to meet you," Fabien Leroux replied, wincing slightly at the firm grip.

"It was a real pleasure to meet you, Fabien," Alina said, extracting the Manila envelope before handing him back the briefcase. "I enjoyed your company and wish you a safe return to England."

"Thanks for a wonderful meal, Alina," Leroux said, with feeling, "in such attractive surroundings."

"My pleasure," she replied, with a quick wave of her hand.

Leroux watched them get into the car and drive off towards South Harbor. It had been a most interesting encounter, he mused, in very agreeable company. Yet many questions remained unanswered, particularly her relationship to Q, whom she evidently disliked. Heading back to Hotel Kivi through Toolo Park, he remarked how much lighter the sky was at this hour than it would be in England. It must be the northern latitude, he decided. Not yet time for the white nights, when the sun never set, but getting there. Back at his hotel, he filled out the evening in the bar, watching the remainder of an American movie which had begun at eight o'clock. Clint Eastwood and George Kennedy, with Finnish subtitles! American culture apparently spanned the globe.

*

The next day, George Mason made an early start. Leaving his West Ruislip home, he dropped Adele off in the West End to look for a birthday gift for her sister, before heading south towards Dulwich Village. Daphne Orlov was already up and about. On emerging from his parked car, he found her in the front garden, trowel in hand, separating clumps of faded daffodils and hyacinths. She was pleasantly surprised to see him. Removing her gardening gloves and placing her trowel in a small wheelbarrow, she invited him indoors.

"Good news to report, Inspector Mason," she said, inviting him to sit in her spacious kitchen. "Yuri emerged from his coma late last evening."

"I am so pleased to hear that," her visitor said. "What is the prognosis now?"

"He will have to remain at South Wimbledon

Hospital for the time being," she informed him. "There are some internal injuries that need attention. But the outlook is favorable. Yuri should make a complete recovery."

"I can appreciate that is a load off your mind, Daphne," the detective said. "You look much more relaxed than you did when I last saw you."

"It has been an ordeal, Inspector," she replied, "I can tell you that. But we are now coming through the wood. Are you any nearer finding the guilty party?"

George Mason returned an upbeat smile.

"Detective Sergeant Aubrey and I have made some little progress, so far," he told her. "We are hoping to build on it in the next few days."

"Such senseless crimes," Daphne said. "What could someone hope to achieve thereby?"

Her puzzled visitor shook his head.

"Anybody's guess, at this point," he admitted.

Daphne Orlov rose to serve coffee, setting a plate of digestive biscuits on the kitchen diner to accompany it. Her visitor, who had skimped on breakfast, was glad of the refreshment.

"Have you had contact with Linda Brodsky?" he asked.

Daphne paused for a moment and said:

"Maxim is out of danger, too, I believe. Linda intimated as much when I phoned her the other day. He apparently suffered a relapse at East London General Hospital. Some form of internal bleeding, his wife said. He will be going home very soon."

"I expect you and Linda will have cause to celebrate," the detective remarked, "after all you have been through."

Daphne Orlov topped up his coffee.

"You can say that again, Inspector," she emphatically replied. "We have already made plans, in fact. A champagne dinner at the Ritz!"

"Marvelous," her visitor remarked. "That really fits the bill."

"But we are keeping mum about it," Daphne continued. "We want it to be a complete surprise to our husbands."

George Mason could only smile at that. After the welcome refreshment and a friendly chat on more general topics, he left Daphne Orlov to resume her gardening and drove to Westminster. On arrival mid-morning, Alison Aubrey was waiting to greet him.

"Good morning, Inspector," she said.

"Good morning, Sergeant," he responded. "Any news from the hotel industry?"

Alison enthusiastically nodded.

"I think we may have turned up trumps," she said.

"I am listening!" her senior urged.

"Hospitality Express discovered that one of their member hotels in London booked in a Mr. Fabien Leroux on April 10 last."

"Which hotel would that be?"

"The Leinster, on Leinster Square, Bayswater."

"Great work, Alison," an impressed George Mason said. "Now we may really be getting somewhere."

Half an hour later, the two detectives were on their way to Bayswater in a squad car, accompanied by two uniformed members of the Metropolitan

Police. They pulled up, after a short drive through light traffic, outside a Victorian-era establishment. On leaving the vehicle, the quartet entered the premises. The receptionist's face expressed alarm.

"What can I do for you, gentlemen?" the woman anxiously enquired.

"We wish to interview a Canadian national named Fabien Leroux," George Mason explained, producing I.D. "We have reason to believe he booked a room at this hotel early last month."

"That is correct, Inspector," the woman said, after consulting her records. "He also checked out two days ago."

The detective frowned on hearing that.

"Did Mr. Leroux leave a forwarding address?" he asked.

The receptionist shook her head.

"He cleared his belongings and settled the bill in cash," she said.

"Did he give you any indication of where he was heading?" a concerned Sergeant Aubrey asked.

"He remarked that he was going north, to do photography. He seemed very interested in architecture, from the brief conversations I had with him over the past few weeks."

A penchant for architecture struck Mason as an odd pursuit for a hitman.

"Did you notice anything unusual about his behavior?" he asked.

"Not at all, Inspector," came the reply, in a steadier voice. "He came and went as he pleased, just like any other guest."

"Did he use the house telephone?" Sergeant

Aubrey asked, hoping they might be able to trace calls. "Or e-mail?"

The receptionist shook her head.

"I noticed him using a cellphone on occasion," she said, "either in the dining-room or in the residents' lounge. We do not offer Internet access or Wi-Fi."

"Did he receive any visitors during the course of his stay?" George Mason wanted to know.

The woman thought about that for a few moments.

"He did, from time to time, have company for dinner," she said. "That is about it, really."

"Male or female?" Alison was quick to ask.

The receptionist returned a knowing smile.

"In each case, it was an attractive young woman," she replied. "But I never saw him with the same person twice."

A bit of a Lothario, perhaps, George Mason mused, thanking the woman for her help. Turning to the uniformed officers, he said:

"Sorry to drag you both out on a fool's errand."

"Better luck next time, Inspector," Constable Deakins said, with a shrug.

"It's all in the line of duty," his fellow-officer added, as they filed back outside.

On reaching Scotland Yard, Mason said:

"It was a good shot, Alison. And it may well have succeeded if we had gotten the relevant information sooner."

"So what do we do now, George?" his eager young colleague wanted to know.

"We need to come up with a new line of

approach," he replied. "And quickly, too. The superintendent will not like the case dragging on, given the pressures on our department."

"Meanwhile," Alison said, "I shall alert all police forces in the north of England to be on the look-out for Fabien Leroux. He has to eat places and rest his head."

"Very true, Sergeant," he replied. "Go back to Leinster Hotel with a staff artist and get a mock-up of Leroux from the best description the receptionist can provide. You could then circulate the result to police forces in the north."

"I shall attend to it at once, George," Alison assured him.

*

George Mason drove back towards the West End at just turned midday, to join his wife for lunch at Isola Bella, one of their favorite Italian restaurants, named for an island in Lake Maggiore. Some thirteen hundred miles to the north-east a tall, angular woman in her mid-fifties, with chin-length graying hair, strolled along the embankment of the River Neva. She passed the Hermitage, a major art gallery housed in the former Winter Palace of the tsars, and glanced curiously at the *Aurora*, the gun-boat berthed on the opposite bank, which had fired the opening shots of the Revolution. Before turning onto Nevsky Prospekt, she briefly admired the classical lines of the Admiralty buildings dating from the era of Peter the Great. Proceeding along the broad boulevard as far as the canal where

Rasputin drowned, she entered a large park and continued as far as the pavilion. Lev Leverkov, sitting on a bench smoking a half-corona, rose to greet her.

"*Dobri dyen,* Nadia," he warmly greeted.

"Good day to you, too," Nadia replied.

"Let us take a stroll in this fine spring weather," he suggested, falling in step beside her as they headed towards the arboretum.

"What did you make of the package I gave you?" Nadia asked, referring to the Manila envelope Alina had brought from Helsinki.

"Excellent material," the other replied. "Your brother provided us with detailed information on forthcoming NATO military exercises in Eastern Europe. He also wrote that NATO has invited Montenegro to join them."

"That will not go down well in Moscow," Nadia said.

Lev Leverkov gave a grim smile.

"Any expansion of NATO into East Europe presents problems," he remarked. "It is perceived by many of our people as a provocation."

"Because NATO is embracing some of the former Warsaw Pact countries?"

Andreyev nodded.

"Exactly, Nadia," he said. "What with Finland and the Baltic states already members of NATO, that organization will be smack up against our western borders."

They strolled on in silence for a few minutes, admiring the flower beds and the water-lilies on the ornamental pond. The sun broke strongly through the clouds, heralding unusually warm May weather.

"How is my brother doing?" she eventually asked. "I do so miss communicating with him directly, by telephone."

"When I visited London recently," Leverkov replied, "he seemed in fine fettle. He has become almost an establishment figure, interestingly enough, by joining the Conservative Party, Rotary and the local tennis club."

Nadia smiled to herself on hearing that.

"But he has been having a few problems, too" he added. "Over the past few months, he has been receiving blackmail letters, at the rate of one per month, threatening to expose him to the British authorities."

"Then somebody must know of his background?" a shocked Nadia remarked. "How could that possibly be, Lev?"

Her companion merely shrugged.

"That might be very difficult to ascertain, Nadia," he replied.

"So how is he dealing with it?" Nadia asked, much concerned.

"He has been transferring money to a numbered bank account at Geneva, to keep the threat of exposure at bay. He is of the opinion that only one of those members of the chess team who defected with him from Helsinki in 1990 could be aware of his true identity."

His companion thought about that for a few moments, before saying:

"That seems a reasonable assumption, Lev. What other steps is he taking?"

"He has been taking measures to eliminate the threat, Nadia. It is an extreme response, but everything possible must be done to safeguard his position at the Ministry of Defence. He is one of our top agents in the West."

Nadia paused by the pond and threw the scraps of the dry bread she had brought to the ducks.

"You do not need to elaborate, Lev," she remarked. "You can spare me the gory details."

"His initiative may have produced results," the other then said, stubbing out his cigar. "With two of the group at least temporarily out of circulation, he has not had a blackmail letter in over a month."

Nadia gave a sigh of relief.

"Let us hope that is the end of the business," she said, emphatically, glancing at her watch. "Now how about a spot of lunch?"

"I have time for a quick snack," Lev Leverkov replied.

They retraced their steps from the arboretum, exited the park and continued along Nevsky Prospekt. Minutes later, they entered a type of restaurant the Russians call a *stolovaya*. Instead of tables and chairs, there were slender pillars from floor to ceiling at intervals across the room. Each pillar had a narrow, circular shelf about chest-high. The patrons, having collected their meal from the service counter, placed it on one of the shelves and ate while standing. It was an original type of fast-food restaurant, making for quick service and speedy turnover of customers.

Nadia and Lev Leverkov chose pirogi, warm pies filled with meat and vegetables. Endive salad and tea-with-lemon completed their order, which they took to a spare pillar at one side of a spacious room gradually filling up with patrons from nearby offices and shops.

"Are you still involved in local politics, Nadia?" Lev Leverkov asked.

"I act as part-time secretary to the local Communist Party," she informed him, "in addition to teaching violin at the Academy of Music."

"What do you think your prospects are in this new era?"

"I think we shall always be a minority party," she replied. "Our best hope of entering government will be to join some sort of coalition with another left-wing organization, much like the Liberal Party did in England."

Her companion chuckled at that remark.

"The British Liberals waited decades to enter government," he said. "But, after joining the Tories in an uneasy coalition for five years, they were routed in subsequent elections. Voters thought they had compromised their principles."

"British Tories and Liberals were always going to be odd bed-fellows," Nadia wryly commented. "We would expect to avoid that fate by allying with another genuinely left-wing organization."

"You may be right, my dear friend," the other replied. "What is your immediate agenda, may I ask?"

"The next major event is the International Congress at Riga in July. That should be well-attended by representatives from across Europe."

"Which countries will be sending delegates, as a

matter of interest?"

"Firm commitment has come, so far, from the Communist parties in Italy, France, Portugal, Greece and Finland. Others may follow."

"Is the agenda more or less the same as at your last gathering at Tallinn?"

"There will be much attention given to the current social problems," Nadia replied. "Housing will be a key issue, as will state retirement pensions, workers' benefits and immigration."

Lev Leverkov nodded approval, even though it seemed to him that the Communists were not likely to form a government any time soon in any of the countries that were sending delegates. The world had moved on significantly since the fall of the Berlin Wall. Throughout Western Europe, state-owned enterprises, such as railways, airlines and energy-related industries, had been privatized. Even China had become a partly free-enterprise economy, even if centrally controlled.

"Wasn't it at Tallinn that you first met Alina Lehtinen?" he asked, steering the conversation to more neutral ground.

Nadia nodded, wiped her lips on a piece of tissue and said:

"She was the junior delegate of SKP, the Finnish Communist Party, which currently has no representation in either the Finnish or the European parliament."

Leverkov was not surprised to hear that, as they left the *stolovaya* and continued down Nevsky Prospekt, so that Nadia could buy tickets for the Glazunov ballet *Raymonda,* playing that evening at

Mariinsky Teatr.

"You had no problem recruiting her for courier service?" her companion enquired.

"Alina needs the money," came the quick reply. "Her husband Osmo has recently been laid off by Nokia, the giant telecommunications firm faced with cut-backs. They are expecting their first child in October, I believe. Osmo is training to be a school-teacher."

"How dependable is Alina?" Leverkov pointedly enquired.

"She is a dedicated Communist, Lev. That should be sufficient guarantee of her loyalty."

"How well do you know her, Nadia, as a matter of interest?"

"Over the past couple of years," she replied, "we have come to know each other quite well, although there always seems to be a degree of reserve on her part. I mentioned that my brother had taken care of the double agent, Igor Nikolayev, and that he now held an important government post in London."

"You are referring to the incident years ago on Chelsea Bridge?"

"The same, Lev."

"The Metropolitan Police never did solve the crime."

"Which is as well," Nadia rejoined, "in view of my brother's subsequent activities."

"You did not mention the Ministry of Defence by name, I take it?"

"Of course not, my good man," came the reply. "Alina has no real knowledge of the contents of the packages she brings to the Finland Station, but she may have her suspicions. Anybody of reasonable acumen would, in the circumstances, speculate to some extent and draw their own conclusions, whether valid or not."

By now, they had reached the sidewalk kiosk which sold tickets for the ballet, the opera and the symphony, all of which were well-patronized by the denizens of St. Petersburg. Nadia joined the short queue.

"Before I go," Lev Leverkov said, "I should tell you that I recently received some news of Mikhail Konev, a former colleague of mine."

"Wasn't he among the group of defectors?" Nadia asked.

Leverkov nodded.

"Along with Alenin, Smirnov, Orlov and Nikolayev," he confirmed.

"I recall them vaguely," Nadia remarked, "having met them from time to time in my brother's company when we lived in Moscow. So how is Konev doing these days?"

"Very well, by all accounts, Nadia," the other replied. "He has carved out for himself a successful career in advertising, for which he was no doubt well-qualified, since he used to compose propaganda material in the old days. Guess what he is up to now?"

"I could not possibly, Lev," she replied, pocketing her theatre tickets with a quizzical smile.

"He is currently in Moscow with his wife Hillary and another couple from Yorkshire. The husband, named Edward Marsh, manages a prominent brewery. They are over here to promote the company's products, Tadcastle Ales."

Nadia returned a faint smile of amusement.

"They will have their work cut out," she tartly replied, "given the preference of our countrymen for strong liquor. Weaning them off vodka will take some doing."

"I expect you are right," the other humorously agreed. "But do not forget that many Russians nowadays come and go in Britain and may have acquired some British customs and tastes. I suspect there may well be a niche market for premium English beers, if well-promoted."

"Russians would, in my opinion, be more likely develop a taste for Scotch whisky," Nadia remarked, on bidding her friend adieu.

*

Later that same afternoon, Alina Lehtinen began preparations for an early dinner, to coincide with her husband Osmo's return from the teacher training college. The Lehtinens lived on Kulosaari, an island suburb of Helsinki served by an efficient tramway system, which meant that they could often leave their car in the garage for commutes to the city. They rented an apartment in one of the large Victorian houses fronting the ocean that had been divided into smaller units to accommodate the pressing population. Finland, in common with many European countries, had witnessed an exodus from the countryside, as people moved to the cities in search of better-paid work in modern industries, as well as improved living conditions. Good accommodations were therefore at a premium and the young couple considered themselves lucky to have found an affordable place in a natural setting of shoreline, rocky outcrops and pine forest.

Alina was in the act of removing her home-made quiche Lorraine from the oven, to be served with mixed salad, when Osmo breezed in.

"How did it go today?" she genially enquired.

"Champion," Osmo replied. "I got an A- for teaching practice and a B+ for lesson planning."

"You will finish the course next month, Osmo," his wife reminded him. "Hadn't you better start reading the vacancies list in the newspaper? I understand there is a shortage of teachers in your subject."

"There will always be a demand for English teachers," he replied, pouring himself a light beer, while parking himself expectantly at the dining-table. The aroma of freshly-baked quiche wafted into the living-room. It smelled good.

"Is that because businesses rely heavily on the English language to help promote exports?" Alina asked, as she served the meal.

"At one period," her husband said, "German was the main foreign language taught in our schools. It has been largely superseded by English, since World War 11."

"I should like to learn French," Alina announced, slicing and serving the quiche.

"Try the Institut Francais on Topeliuskatu," Osmo suggested. "After I start teaching, our finances will be in much better shape. We could even contemplate taking a vacation in France. I have always wanted to visit the Riviera – Antibes,

Cannes, St. Tropez, places like that."

That was music to Alina's ears. She leant over and kissed him on the cheek.

"And I should like to visit the perfumeries at Grasse," she said, "which would be quite nearby."

"We shall definitely do it," Osmo promised. "Great quiche, by the way."

"It's a recipe I got from Nadia."

"Your odd Russian friend?"

"I would not use that expression," his wife objected. "A bit eccentric, maybe."

"And a very useful one, too, Alina," Osmo remarked. "It was a lucky break for us that you met her at Tallinn. Your earnings as a courier have been a useful stand-by in this past year of teacher-training, supplementing my student loan."

"It certainly pays well," Alina replied. "But I shall discontinue it when you are in regular employment."

Osmo suspended a mouthful of quiche on his fork. With raised eyebrows, he said:

"Do you feel uneasy about those trips, Alina? What I mean is, are you concerned about what those packages may contain?"

"It does cross my mind, from time to time, Osmo," she replied. "But we needed the money. That was the main consideration."

"Do you have any idea at all of the contents?"

His wife returned a wry smile and shook her head.

"No very clear idea," she replied, "to be quite truthful. Except that they originate in Britain. Some sort of classified material, I imagine, too sensitive for the regular mail and not official enough for the diplomatic bag."

"Nobody could pin anything on you, Alina, if questions were asked," Osmo emphasized. "You are just a small link in a chain and you could genuinely claim ignorance of any questionable contents."

"I had other reasons for undertaking the assignments, apart from purely financial ones," she remarked, "but they too will soon cease to be a factor."

"To do your friend Nadia a favor?" he enquired.

His wife smilingly shook her head.

"My motives must remain private, for the time being, Osmo," she said. "At some future date, when all this is behind us, I will tell you more."

Her husband returned a rather puzzled smile at that, while continuing to enjoy his dinner.

"What are your plans for this evening?" Alina then asked, sipping a glass of chilled Soave.

"I need to do some work on my *Macbeth* assignment," he replied. "It should not take more than an hour or so. Afterwards, since it is going to be a fine evening, I suggest we go down to the shore and take out a kayak. We could get to Tapiola and back before dusk."

"A great idea!" Alina responded, as the conversation switched to her upcoming trip to England.

"You had better make the most of it," Osmo said, "since it will be your last trip before our child is born."

"I fully intend to, Osmo," she assured him. "Among other things, I am going to the Garrick Theatre, to see a play by Arnold Wesker. I read some good reviews of it on-line."

"Will you stay with my aunt again, at Epping?" he enquired.

"Absolutely," she replied, "to save on expenses."

"Is Aunt Paivi still in nursing?"

"She will retire in a couple of years' time, I believe," his wife replied. "She was among a group of Finnish nurses hired by the National Health Service in the late eighties, to cover a shortfall in locally-trained staff."

"Does she plan to remain in England?"

"I doubt it, Osmo. You mentioned that she has kept her apartment at Lahti, which she sub-lets to a retired couple from Porvoo. I fully expect she will return to Finland and visit England for vacations. She has made good friends there over the years."

With that, Osmo Lehtinen settled down to his Shakespeare studies, while Alina cleared the table and tended the window boxes, before watching television. Just over an hour later, they were out on the Gulf of Finland, kayaking westwards towards Tapiola, another island-suburb farther along the coast.

CHAPTER 11

The day after George Mason's visit to Leinster Square, Bayswater, he had a morning conference with Bill Harrington, who had been out of the office for a few days.

"How was your trip to Islay, Chief Inspector?" his colleague genially enquired.

"Capital," the other replied, with uncharacteristic bonhomie. "I visited several distilleries on the island, which is noted for the peaty flavor of its single-malts."

"Where exactly is Islay?" Mason enquired, not quite sure where to place it.

"In the Inner Hebrides," his senior informed him. "It was full of tourists admiring the coastal scenery and sampling the local whiskies."

"From which countries do they mainly come, Chief Inspector?"

"Surprisingly, to my mind," came the reply, "many of them were from Germany, with large contingents also from America and Japan."

"Scotch whisky evidently has wide appeal," Mason remarked, thinking that Germans were more into beer, in view of their beer-gardens and Oktoberfests.

"And growing more so, year-by-year," Harrington replied. "In fact, it is Scotland's main export, earning billions of pounds per annum. It is also a mainstay of the tourist industry, drawing some two million visitors annually."

"Good news for the Scots, certainly," his colleague remarked. "Adele and I, however, prefer table wines."

"Each to his own taste," the chief inspector replied. "Now, whisky aside, what have you got to relate about Bayswater?"

"The bird has flown," Mason ruefully admitted. "He apparently checked out of Leinster Hotel just the day before we paid it a visit."

"That was tough luck, Inspector. Did he leave a forwarding address, by any chance?"

George Mason shook his head.

"The suspect, Fabien Leroux, informed the hotel staff that he was heading north," he explained. "We have alerted the authorities in the northern counties to be on the look-out for him. We obtained the best description of him we could from the hotel receptionist. A police artist is working on a mock-up based on that information. We shall circulate it as soon as possible."

"So you are more or less back to square one?" Bill Harrington complained, with knitted brows.

"The only firm lead we have had so far," his colleague said, "has come from Canada House."

"So you are stymied, in fact, until you can trace Leroux?"

"There is one more promising avenue we can pursue," Mason said. "What I would call the missing link."

"Can you enlarge on that, Inspector?" his senior urged.

189

"We have traced all the members of a chess team who defected as a group to Britain in 1990. Except for one."

"And who might that be?" Harrington asked.

"An individual named Pavel Belinsky," Mason replied. "None of the other Russians seems to know much about him. They apparently lost contact with him soon after they entered Britain."

"That is certainly very curious," the senior officer remarked, "especially if the rest of them, as you implied earlier, stayed in fairly close touch with each other."

"It did not amount to much more than exchanging Christmas cards," Mason explained. "At least, that is the impression I got from interviewing the wives."

"How do you propose to track down this Belinsky fellow then?"

"An interesting question, Chief Inspector," George Mason replied. "He may, for instance, have moved on to another country. Or he may even have returned to his native turf."

"A useful first step, Inspector, would be to call at the Home Office, to see if this individual applied for British citizenship."

"I shall make that my first priority this morning," Mason said, rising to leave.

He then helped himself to fresh coffee, exchanged a few words with Detective Sergeant Aubrey and cleared his mail. Half an hour later, he left the Yard and crossed Whitehall to reach the Home Office. After searching computerized records for a few minutes, the clerk on the information desk was able to inform him that a Pavel Belinsky had indeed applied for, and had been granted, British citizenship in 1990. Armed with that knowledge, the detective took the Central Line Tube to Charing Cross and proceeded along the Strand to Somerset House, which kept vital statistics on all residents of Britain. He was interested in any information that would indicate that a Pavel Belinsky had remained in this country. In the event, which he thought unlikely, of the Russian's demise, that fact would also be a matter of record. An administrative assistant, an attractive young woman with chin-length brown hair, eagerly assisted him on noting his I.D.

"A Mr. Pavel Belinsky changed his name by deed poll in November, 1990," she informed him, after a search lasting several minutes. "He took the name Paul Bell."

"How curious!" Mason remarked.

"It is not at all uncommon, Inspector," the assistant said, "for foreign immigrants to anglicize their names, especially their surnames, in order to fit in better in their adopted country."

"They want to blend in, as it were," her visitor surmised.

"Exactly, Inspector."

"That is very useful information," he said. "Do you happen to have anything else on him? A current address, for example, would be most useful."

The young woman re-scanned the on-line records.

"No address is listed, Inspector Mason," she replied, within minutes. "But we do have a marriage license entered for him. The wedding took place in

July, 1994."

"Excellent!" George Mason exclaimed. "Could you please provide me with a copy of the marriage certificate?"

The assistant spent a few more minutes locating the relevant document, before presenting him with a facsimile from the printer.

"Will that serve your purposes, Inspector?" she genially enquired.

The detective glanced at it, a broad smile spreading across his shrewd features.

"Perfectly," he replied, pocketing the document and quitting the building to return to Whitehall. On arrival, he called Alison Aubrey into his office and showed her the document.

"What does this mean, George?" she enquired, with a puzzled expression.

"It means, Alison," he said, expansively, "that we now have a lead to the missing link."

The younger officer returned an ironic look.

"Are you into paleontology these days, George?" she quipped.

"Say that again, Sergeant," her senior said, not quite sure of her meaning.

"The missing link," she came back, with a roguish smile. "The species that is supposed to bridge the gap between the higher primates, like apes and monkeys, and modern humans."

George Mason took a step back and raised his eyebrows on hearing that.

"I think you are pulling my leg, Alison," he said, with a wry smile. "But I can take a joke as well as the next man. That term, I should point out, however, has gone out of fashion among scientists. The popular press is more likely to use it."

"In reference to the yeti, for example?" Alison asked, in the same impish vein.

"Big foot, the yeti, the abominable snowman and whatever else people come up with, mainly for the sensation value. Let us stick to the business in hand, Sergeant."

Saying that, he waited for her to examine the facsimile more closely.

"Paul Bell?" she challenged, now with a more professional demeanor. "I thought we were dealing with Russian nationals."

"This Paul Bell," her senior confidently announced, "is none other than Pavel Belinsky, a member of the original group of defectors, who has so far remained untraced. For some reason, he decided to anglicize his name by deed poll."

"Paul being the English equivalent of Pavel?"

"Precisely, Alison. He also cut off all contact with his former chess team members."

"Perhaps he simply wished to assume a thoroughly English persona," Alison observed, "to make as complete a break as possible with his past."

"He certainly achieved that," George Mason agreed. "But he may have had additional reasons for doing so."

The young officer gave her colleague, noted for his acumen, an appreciative glance. He was evidently several steps ahead of her.

"Such as?" she asked.

George Mason merely shrugged.

"Who knows, at this point?" he replied. "But I

intend, one way or another, to find out if my hunch is correct."

Alison picked up the document again and scanned it thoughtfully.

"His parents are not recorded here," she said. "I find that very odd, George."

"He may have been an orphan," Mason replied. "Many children were, as a matter of fact, following World War 11."

"Or he may have wished to disguise his ethnic origins," Alison suggested.

"That is also a possibility," her senior agreed. "But at least we have the identities of his wife's parents. Cynthia Stead is the daughter of Gerald and Felicity Stead, of Craven Cottage, Musgrave Hill, Dartmouth, Devon."

"Dartmouth being the home of the Royal Naval College," Alison queried.

"Situated on the River Dart, I believe."

"So what is our next step, George?"

"A visit to south Devon, Sergeant," he promptly replied.

*

That same morning, Lev Leverkov arrived at Heathrow Airport on a direct flight from Moscow. His first objective was a visit to Harrod's, the famous department store at Knightsbridge, which he reached on the Underground's Piccadilly Line. His wife Natalia had asked him to look for a Wedgwood China tea service, as a wedding gift for their niece. On finding one, with an attractive floral pattern, he purchased it and made arrangements for shipping to his address in a suburb of Moscow. With a feeling of satisfaction that English china would make a most acceptable gift, he left the busy store and strolled back to the Underground. Studying the complex route-plan on the wall, he devised a simple, if roundabout, way to reach his next objective. He took the Piccadilly Line northwards to Holborn, where he switched to the westbound Central Line, resurfacing thirty minutes later at Marble Arch. From there, it was a short walk to The Wheatsheaf, a pub overlooking Hyde Park.

Paul Bell greeted him with a concerned expression, when the visitor entered the premises and found him at the same alcove table where he had entertained Fabien Leroux some weeks ago.

"Greetings, Paul," Leverkov said, sitting opposite. "From the look on your face, I gather all is not well."

"I have just received another blackmail letter," the other replied. "Post-marked Moscow!"

Lev Leverkov looked aghast.

"How can that be?" he enquired. "I thought you had taken care of that little problem."

"I was hoping so," came the tense reply. "But that is evidently not the case. I think we can safely rule out Brodsky and Orlov, who both recently left hospital. I have it on good authority that they are continuing their convalescence at home."

His visitor said nothing for a few moments, being distracted by a heated argument in the bar area. Suddenly, the light of understanding spread across his shrewd features.

"I have it!" he exclaimed, much to his hearer's astonishment.

"You know something I do not know?" a skeptical Paul Bell quizzed.

"Mikhail Konev!" the older man declared, a gleam of triumph in his eye. "He is currently in Moscow with his wife Hillary and an older couple from Yorkshire."

"What on earth is he doing there?" Paul Bell, alias Pavel Belinsky, enquired, recalling that Fabien Leroux had lost track of the advertising executive.

"Believe it or not, my good friend," the other replied, "they are there to promote English beer."

"You cannot be serious, Lev," Bell remonstrated.

"I assure you that I am, Paul," he emphasized. "I came across the party quite by chance at Beluga Caviar Bar on Red Square. I recognized him immediately, despite the interval of years. We were close colleagues, don't forget, under the old regime."

"That is truly remarkable," Paul Bell said, sitting back to absorb the information. "So we now have a clear suspect for the blackmail letters?"

"It would appear so, Paul," Leverkov said. "When I return to Moscow in two days' time, we shall pull Konev in for questioning. We shall soon get to the bottom of this business and guarantee your cover at the Ministry of Defence."

Paul Bell's features relaxed, as he broke into a half-smile.

"What a turn-up for the book," he remarked. "This casts an entirely new light on everything. Will you fix Konev for good?"

Lev Leverkov returned a conspiratorial smile.

"We shall find enough reason to detain him for a limited period of time," he said. "We can hold him on some technicality. It would be difficult to prosecute him on the strength of one letter, even though it originated in Russia, since most of the blackmailing took place in London. The British authorities would want the lead role in any legal procedures. We must keep them out of the picture at all costs."

"You could dig up something from his past," his colleague said, "and use it to ensure his silence."

Leverkov gave a shrewd nod.

"Good thinking, Paul," he said. "I shall get our research staff working on it on my return. There are gray areas in any agent's record; it's the nature of the game."

He then glanced briefly at the menu, asking:

"What should we have for lunch?"

"They do very good in-house plate pies here at The Wheatsheaf," Paul Bell said. "Steak-and-kidney or cheese-and-onion. Take your pick. It's typical English pub fare, which I can recommend."

"Then slip across to the service counter and order me the steak-and-kidney, with a side salad. And to help it down?"

"A glass of Flower's Bitter," his colleague recommended, it being one of his own favorite beers.

"So be it," the senior man said. "It will be an opportunity to sample the sort of thing Mikhail Konev and his client are trying to foist on us Russians."

As Paul Bell crossed to the service area, the visitor's eye rested on an attractive brunette amid a group of admiring males. How beautiful English women were, he mused, thinking how his wife Natalia had been putting on weight in recent years. He would suggest a slimming regime. He was not a ladies' man, in the accepted sense of that term, but he always had an eye for attractive females, as enhancing the scenery.

On his colleague's return, they sipped their ale and waited patiently for the food to arrive.

"Next item on the agenda," Leverkov said, "is your next report. The last one you sent, via your Canadian friend, was very well received in Moscow. They commend you for it."

"I am very gratified to hear that, Lev."

"We now have a very sensitive matter to consider," the other continued. "We need to get some idea of how NATO would respond if we deployed land-based, medium-range cruise missiles along our western borders."

Paul Bell returned an ironic look.

"They will regard such action," he answered, "as a breach of the so-called INF accord, which has been in force since the end of the Cold War."

"You are referring to the agreement negotiated by Mikhail Gorbachev and Ronald Reagan, to eliminate all intermediate-range nuclear missiles?"

"The very same, Lev."

"Try to sound out at the Ministry of Defence what their reaction might be."

The bogus civil servant thought about that for a few moments.

"In my current role of liaison officer with NATO, I shall certainly be able to give you a firmer opinion in due course," he assured his visitor. "Off the cuff, just for now, I should imagine that the West would not take kindly to any significant shift in the balance of power in Europe."

"So they would very likely increase military spending," Leverkov asked, "and bolster troop deployment in East Europe?"

"The British, pressured by the Americans, have already increased military spending under the new Conservative government. I doubt they would raise it further, owing to parliamentary opposition by the Labour Party, and to on-going budgetary constraints."

"But other members of NATO might be inclined to spend more on defense?" Lev Leverkov asked.

"That remains debatable, Lev," the other replied. "They have been slow, up to now, to spend two per cent of G.D.P. on the military budget, the amount constantly urged by the Americans. Leave the matter in my hands, for the time being. I should be able to send a report on the matter through the usual channels, before the end of the month."

"We should also like to learn of any planned naval maneuvers in the North Atlantic," his visitor said.

"In view of our vested interests in the Arctic region?"

"Precisely, Paul."

The steak-and-kidney pies with endive salad arrived at that point. The two friends tackled them with good appetite, finished their ale and ordered coffee. Lev Leverkov recounted his visit earlier that morning to Harrod's department store.

"Natalia has excellent taste," Paul Bell complimented. "Wedgwood China is exactly what Cynthia's parents gave us as a wedding present ten years ago."

"Do they also live in London?" a curious Lev Leverkov asked.

"They used to, until her father retired from the Civil Service. It was he, in fact, who helped me obtain a position at the Ministry. Little did he suspect that he was aiding a spy."

Leverkov chuckled at that remark.

"My wife and I requested Sevres porcelain for our dinner service," he added. "She is sold on all things French."

"As, apparently, was our late-lamented former colleague, Igor Nikolayev."

"He was too Francophile for his own good," the other remarked, "which raised a question about where his true loyalties lay. Excellent beer, by the way. What did you say it was called?"

"Flower's Bitter."

"No chance of it appearing in Russian restaurants, I suppose?"

Paul Bell smilingly shook his head.

"You will have to make do with Tadcastle Ales," he replied, "which I believe are quite good."

*

The following day, George Mason and Alison Aubrey took an early-morning inter-city express from Paddington Station through the attractive rural counties of Berkshire, Wiltshire and Somerset to arrive at Exeter St. David's. From there, they caught a local connection southwards to the city of Dartmouth, on the Devon coast. Making their way on foot along the embankment of the River Dart, mingling with early-season tourists, they paused to observe a training ship from the Royal Naval College glide down to the ocean. Onlookers waved at the smartly-dressed young cadets on board, who did not wave back. After a hundred yards or so, the detectives quit the riverside and headed up Musgrave Hill towards Craven Cottage. Gerald Stead, wearing a wide-brimmed hat, was pottering about his front garden, trowel in hand. He turned in some surprise to greet his visitors. When George Mason showed ID, his sunny expression clouded.

"Scotland Yard!" he exclaimed. "What brings you to our neck of the woods?"

"Routine enquiries," George Mason matter-of-factly replied.

"Then you had better come inside," the other said, stepping through the ivy-covered porch to open the oaken front door.

The visitors followed him in, to be greeted by an equally-surprised Felicity Stead, who showed them into a living-room featuring reproduction antiques. Bookshelves lined one wall and chintz curtains, matching the chair covers, hung at the leaded windows. With its thatched roof, it was a typical English country cottage, the sort often favored by well-heeled retirees.

"Could you not have made an appointment beforehand?" Cynthia's father said, with a questioning look.

George Mason knew full well that he was out on a limb, to some extent. But, as he had explained to his colleague on the way down, a prior telephone call could have been reported to Paul Bell, whom the detective wanted to remain unaware of a visit to his in-laws.

"I preferred to take a chance on finding you at home," he replied, omitting to say that he had found the Steads' telephone number from Directory Enquiries. He had dialed it last evening and replaced the receiver immediately the line became live, assuring himself that the occupants of Craven Cottage were in residence.

"You could easily have had a wasted journey," Felicity said, inviting the visitors to sit.

"Let me explain myself, Mrs. Stead," George Mason said. "My colleague, Detective Sergeant Aubrey, and I are trying to locate a Mr. Paul Bell, whom we understand is married to your daughter Cynthia. They are not listed in London-area telephone directories, nor could we find their names on the electoral rolls."

Gerald Stead returned an uneasy smile.

"That would be because their number is ex-directory," he explained. "They also moved recently to an address in a different London borough. I expect the electoral system has not yet caught up with them. Bureaucracy, you know."

"Can we offer you some refreshment," Felicity politely enquired.

"Tea or coffee would be very acceptable," he replied.

"We generally take tea at this hour," the woman remarked. "I shall make a pot."

With that, she withdrew to the small kitchen at the rear of the premises, returning minutes later with a tray bearing cups and saucers, milk and sugar, plus a plate of assorted biscuits. Her second trip to the kitchen produced a large pot of tea, which she let stand for a few moments before pouring.

"So what is all this really about?" a puzzled Gerald Stead queried. "I can give you Paul and Cynthia's address, but I should like to know the reason for it."

The two detectives sipped their tea, while helping themselves to a couple of biscuits.

"We are investigating two serious assaults in the London area," Sergeant Aubrey explained. "Both victims were members of a chess team who defected to Britain in 1990."

"What could this possibly have to do with Paul and Cynthia?" Felicity Stead asked, in some bewilderment.

"We are trying to trace all the members of that same group of chess players," Mason said. "Your son-in-law appears to be one of them."

"That is preposterous, Inspector Mason!" Cynthia's father remonstrated, as his wife's face turned a few shades paler.

"You were not aware that your son-in-law was of Russian origin?" Alison Aubrey pointedly asked.

"I deny it absolutely," came the reply. "Paul is an American citizen. Granted, his parents were naturalized Russian immigrants. From the Caucasus region, I believe he said."

That assertion immediately explained to George Mason something Pyotr Alenin had suggested, namely that Pavel Belinsky had probably moved on soon after arriving in England, losing contact with the other members of the group. Could his motive, he mused, have been to obscure his true origins? And, if so, for what purpose?

"Your son-in-law may well have spent time in America," Mason then said. "But he definitely moved from Moscow to England beforehand. Our sources are quite firm on that score."

Cynthia Bell's parents exchanged uneasy glances. Felicity sipped her tea nervously; Gerald left his untouched.

"What does all this mean, Inspector?" Gerald Stead then asked.

"It may mean something, or it may not," Mason replied. "As I explained earlier, this is just a routine investigation. We have been able to trace all members of that original group of chess players, except for Paul Bell. We should like to know his present whereabouts, so that we can interview him and possibly rule him out of our enquiries."

"I can certainly do that for you," Felicity said, crossing to a small desk beneath the leaded window and jotting down her daughter's current address on a slip of notepaper, which she then handed to the detective.

Gerald Stead, meanwhile, had been mulling over this revelation about his son-in-law's true origins.

"I suspect you are keeping something from us, Inspector Mason," he testily remarked. "A group of people leaving the Soviet Union at that time would presumably be defectors?"

George Mason drained his cup and set it down on the tray, noting Alison's wary glance. He felt, nonetheless, that he had no option but to come clean.

"They were all former agents of the secret service," he said.

Gerald Stead got up and paced the room agitatedly.

"Are you telling us that Cynthia's husband was once a Communist spy?" he asked.

"That seems to be the inescapable conclusion, Mr. Stead."

"This is extremely worrying, Inspector. Had we known that, we would have done our level best to dissuade our daughter from marrying him."

"How did the couple meet?" Alison asked.

"They met on a Danube cruise, from Vienna to the Black Sea," Felicity informed them. "That was ten years ago. Paul was already living in England at the time."

"Do they have children?" the detective sergeant enquired.

Felicity shook her head.

"Cynthia wanted to adopt," she explained, "but Paul did not favor the idea. He preferred to concentrate on his career."

"Which is?" George Mason prompted.

"The Civil Service," Gerald replied. "Ministry of Defence, to be precise. I was instrumental in getting him the job, as a matter of fact, based on his knowledge of Slavonic languages."

"You were in the service yourself?" Alison

immediately asked.

A more composed Gerald Stead, who had regained his seat, nodded curtly.

"I worked at the Ministry of Trade," he said, with evident pride. "But this is an odd kettle of fish, to be sure. A former Communist working at the Ministry of Defence!"

"He very likely changed his views," Mason offered, as a palliative. "People defected from Communist countries because they rejected the system. I imagine, too, that your son-in-law obtained security clearance from MI5. The vetting of civil service applicants is a very thorough process."

"Let us hope that is the case," Felicity soulfully remarked, starting to clear away the tea service, as her husband seemed visibly more relieved by the detective's remarks.

"All the same," Mason then said, "it would be helpful if you could regard our meeting today as strictly confidential. Until, that is, we are able to take our enquiries a stage further."

"I spent a long career in government service," Gerald Stead replied. "I fully understand the need to preserve integrity in the public sphere. You can count on our absolute discretion in this matter, Inspector Mason."

"We shall not inform either Paul or Cynthia of your visit today," Felicity assured him.

"We are very grateful for your cooperation, Mr. and Mrs. Stead," the detective replied, as the two visitors rose to take their leave.

"But you will let us know, Inspector, for our

daughter's sake, if anything adverse should turn up?" Gerald said, with a concerned look, as he accompanied them as far as the garden gate.

"Absolutely," came the reply.

Since it was now turned noon, the Scotland Yard pair had a spot of lunch in mind. They retraced their steps to the riverside and found an outdoor café serving light refreshments. Opting for warm Cornish pasties and coffee, they spent a pleasant hour in fitful sunshine observing the tourists and the river traffic.

"What did you make of all that, Alison?" George Mason asked his young colleague.

"The Steads were certainly surprised to learn of their son-in-law's true origin," Alison remarked. "Paul Bell must have spun them quite a yarn, in fact, to become acceptable as a member of the family."

"And to think that his father-in-law helped secure him a job at the Ministry of Defence!" Mason exclaimed.

"Are you thinking what I am thinking, George?" she asked.

"That Paul Bell may be a security risk? Hard to say at this stage. Nothing points to that, Alison, and our brief is not about national security. It is about discovering who attacked Maxim Brodsky and Yuri Orlov."

Alison Aubrey could only agree with that statement.

"Supposing we could establish a link between Paul Bell and Fabien Leroux?" she said, with sudden inspiration.

"You do not seriously think they could be connected, do you, Alison?"

The young officer finished her appetizing pastry and delicately wiped her lips on a tissue.

"I was wondering about it while we were at Craven Cottage," she replied. "What a whole new hornets' nest it would open, if they did turn out to be in league with each other."

George Mason returned an ironic smile.

"You can say that again, Sergeant!" he replied. "But we should stick to the facts as we know them, Alison. If your intuition, which has served us well in the past, should prove to be correct, I would not be very surprised."

"We have no leads so far, however, on the current whereabouts of Fabien Leroux," Alison remarked. "Maybe he has left the country altogether."

"In which case, we would be well and truly stymied," George Mason wryly concluded.

Rising from their table, they strolled along the embankment to the train station in good time for the 3.10 p.m. service back to Exeter St. David's. From there, they would catch the inter-city express to Paddington, occupying window seats in the dining car, to catch the first dinner service.

CHAPTER 12

That same evening, Mikhail Konev joined Edward Marsh, the Yorkshire brewer, for a drink before dinner in the bar of Hotel Minsk, just off Red Square, the cobblestone area that formed the center of Moscow, as of much of its history. Noting that Boddington's Bitter was on tap, they opted to support the British brewing industry, rather than the German and Czech lagers also available. They perched on bar stools and ordered half-pints from Sergei, a barman with whom they had become quite friendly during the course of their stay.

"There is evidently some potential here for English beer," the brewer remarked, appreciatively sampling his ale.

"Boddington's is a global brand," his companion said. "You will even find it on cruise liners."

"They had a head-start on Tadcastle Ales," Edward Marsh said. "We aim to play catch-up."

"That will take some doing, Ted," the advertising executive considered. "But so far the signs are promising that we could enter the Russian market in a meaningful way."

"I liked your approach to the media, Mikhail," the other said. "They seemed to go for your highlighting London tourist sights and country pubs."

"English soccer, too, is a useful plug," his friend

rejoined. "Clubs in the Premier League, such as Manchester United, have many fans in Russia and throughout the world. Remember that game on television a few days ago?"

"United versus Real Madrid?" his client replied. "It was a great European Champions League win for the home team."

At that point their wives, tastefully dressed for dinner in the gilded dining-room, joined them. The men quickly drained their glasses and accompanied them to their usual table. With a good appetite after a day's sight-seeing, they eagerly scanned the menu.

"For starters," Hillary Konev said, "I think I shall try the noodle soup called *lapsha*. It says here that it originated with the Tatars."

"Having invaded large areas of Europe in bygone times," her husband quipped, "they must have left their mark in some way."

"Many Tatars live in the Crimea," his wife Marjorie said, "the region recently annexed by Russia."

"Are you having soup, too?" Mikhail Konev asked.

"I would prefer the vegetable soup they call *botvinya*," she replied. "Cucumber, scallions, beets – sounds good."

"I shall go along with Marjorie's choice," Edward Marsh said, after lengthy deliberation.

"And I shall opt for the hors d-oeuvre," Mikhail Konev added.

The waiter came to take their order, as the dining-room gradually filled with patrons. Many of them were visitors, the English party noticed with interest, from China and Japan.

"What have you ladies been up to today?" the Yorkshireman asked, "while Mikhail and I have been trying to earn a rouble."

"We did some shopping," Hillary replied, laughing at his comment, "at the Ismaylovsky Market."

"It is well-known for traditional handicrafts and antiques," Marjorie added. "I particularly liked the wooden carvings of native fauna, such as arctic fox, lynx and chamois."

"But you refrained from buying?" her husband asked, in some surprise.

"I hesitated," she replied, "because they seemed a bit too bulky for our luggage. I have already bought clothes and we have limited space."

"A pity," Edward Marsh said. "I like wood sculpture."

"You could always find something similar in Scotland," his account manager suggested.

"True enough," came the reply, "in view of all the deer and other wildlife in the Highlands."

"Native fauna, such as wild boar and elk, are staging a come-back in many parts of Europe," the brewer said. "A good thing, too."

"But will global warming affect them?" Hillary Konev asked.

"It is predicted to have adverse consequences for certain species," Marjorie replied, "that may not adapt very well to a warming climate. Some will move northwards, or to higher elevations, to avoid the heat; others will simply die out."

"Global warming will also affect agriculture and water supplies," Edward Marsh added.

On that rather dour note, they tackled the newly-served first course.

"What have you enjoyed most of your stay in Moscow?" Mikhail asked, to turn the conversation to a more cheerful topic.

"The scenic river cruise," their wives said, in unison. "It took in Red Square, St. Basil's Cathedral and several medieval convents. Marvelous architecture, all told."

"Did you actually enter the Kremlin?" the Yorkshire brewer asked.

"We certainly did," Hillary replied. "I was surprised to learn that the Kremlin was originally the headquarters of the Orthodox Church. "It houses several museums covering different aspects of Russian history."

"We also climbed the tower," Marjorie said, "to get a panoramic view of the city."

"I should like to have visited Gorky Park," her husband said. "I enjoyed the movie of that name, with William Hurt and Lee Marvin. But we are practically out of time now."

"I believe *Gorky Park* was actually filmed in Helsinki," Mikhail Konev remarked.

"Because they probably wouldn't let film crews in here during the Cold War, I expect," his client replied. "It was a great movie, nonetheless."

"What time is our flight home tomorrow?" Hillary asked, changing the subject.

"11.45 a.m.," her husband informed her. "We must be at Sheremetyevo Airport by around nine-thirty."

"It will mean an early breakfast then," Marjorie complained, since she preferred a leisurely start to the day. "We shall have to get most of our packing done tonight."

"There will be time," Mikhail Konev assured her. "The Bolshoi Ballet program ends around ten o'clock."

"Remind me what the program is," Hillary said.

"*Petrushka*," came the prompt reply.

"Isn't that the ballet by Stravinsky, about the love lives of puppets?" Marjorie asked.

"Something on those lines," Konev replied. "It is supposed to be one of the all-time great ballets."

"I am keenly looking forward to it," Hillary remarked.

"Here, here," the others rejoined, in chorus.

Ordering a main course of *shish kebab*, with a bottle of Crimean red wine to help it down, they quickly finished their dinner, passing up dessert. They then paid visits to the restroom, before requesting taxi service in the hotel foyer.

*

Next morning, the English visitors were down early for a traditional breakfast of porridge and cold cuts. Afterwards, they quickly finished packing and met up again in the foyer, where they booked a taxi to the airport. As they waited for its arrival, a short, dapper figure, with dark hair sleeked back, accompanied by two uniformed police officers, entered the hotel. The advertising executive

213

recognized him immediately, his features registering surprise mixed with alarm.

"Mikhail Konev," Lev Leverkov said, "I must ask you to surrender your passport and accompany us to police headquarters."

Konev stared back at him, in disbelief, as his companions looked on with alarm.

"But we have a plane to catch," Konev remonstrated, "in two hours' time."

"The remainder of your party may proceed to the airport," Leverkov said. "You are to come with us."

Mikhail Konev turned helplessly towards his companions, at a loss for words.

"I cannot possibly leave Moscow without my husband," Hillary said.

Lev Leverkov was completely unmoved, as her husband quickly recovered his poise, saying:

"Ted and Marjorie, you had both better leave. This matter, whatever it is, cannot possibly be of any concern to you. Hillary and I shall stay behind."

"Your wife can remain here at the Minsk, in the meantime," Leverkov tersely remarked. "You are not under arrest, Mikhail, I hasten to add. After our interview, you will be free to return to your hotel until further notice, but you will not be able to leave the country."

"Ted and I would be loath to take leave of you in these circumstances," Marjorie Marsh said, as the taxi driver entered the foyer.

"I think we should cancel our flight and stick by you, old chap," the brewer said, with conviction.

Mikhail Konev sadly shook his head.

"There would be no point," he replied. "This

matter, in my experience, could drag on indefinitely and you have your job to do at Tadcastle Brewery."

The taxi driver, not understanding a word of the tense conversation, hovered impatiently by the main exit.

"I suppose you are right, my friend," his client reluctantly conceded. "The best of luck, my good friends! Do keep in touch."

With that, the Yorkshire couple regretfully let the driver grip their luggage, following him out into the street with a sad wave back at the Konevs. Mikhail handed over his passport, hugged his tearful wife and accompanied the police agents to a black sedan parked outside. They drove through the back streets of Moscow to a large, functional building set well-back from the sidewalk. On alighting, Lev Leverkov led his erstwhile colleague to a small room at the rear.

"I imagine you are surprised to find yourself back at your old stomping-ground," Lev Leverkov said, with a look of amusement.

"It certainly brings back memories," the other ruefully commented. "What the Dickens is all this about, Lev?"

Leverkov cleared his throat and said:

"We have reason to believe that you have been in communication with your former colleague, Pavel Belinsky."

The advertising executive returned an incredulous smile.

"I haven't seen him, or heard anything of him, in well over two decades," he replied.

"That remains to be seen," the other remarked.

"You were caught on CCTV at the central post office about a week ago. I do not imagine you were mailing to an address here in Russia."

"I was sending postcards to my wife's family and to my colleagues at Philpot Advertising Agency," Konev adamantly replied. "Do you have a problem with that?"

Lev Leverkov gave him a hard, scrutinizing look.

"You have been mailing letters to Pavel Belinsky," he said, with a challenging look.

"I can only repeat, Lev," Konev replied, "what I have already told you. I have had no contact whatsoever with Pavel Belinksy. Our paths parted very soon after we arrived in Britain. None of the other members of the chess team have kept in touch with him, either, to my almost certain knowledge."

"Are you in contact with those other defectors?" his interviewer asked.

"Only to the extent of exchanging greetings cards at Russian Christmas," came the reply. "Except for Pyotr Alenin, who moved to Ireland."

"What is your relationship with him?"

"A purely professional one," came the reply. "He is a graphic artist. I give him commissions from time to time for some of our advertising projects. He does posters and magazine work, but no television."

Lev Leverkov thoughtfully weighed the other's remarks, as he poured spring water from a flask, filling two glasses.

"Does Alenin still play chess?" he asked. "I recall that he was a keen exponent of end-game theory."

Mikhail Konev smiled on hearing that, recalling

that each member of the team had his own particular strengths.

"We did not discuss chess when I last met him," he said.

His interviewer took a drink of water, before saying:

"Let me level with you, Mikhail, since we were quite close in the old days and I thought of you as much as a friend as a colleague."

"It pleases me that you remember me in that way, Lev," the advertising executive said, feeling a little more at ease.

"Pavel Belinsky is being blackmailed," the other informed him. "It has been going on for the past six months. Until recently, demands for substantial amounts of money have been made by letters postmarked in various parts of London."

"Belinsky is still in London?" a much-surprised Mikhail Konev asked.

Lev Leverkov slowly nodded.

"The last letter he received, quite recently in fact, was sent from Moscow," he said. "You, my friend, are normally based in London and you are now here in Moscow. That makes you a prime suspect. Only a former agent could know anything of Pavel Belinsky's past. You fit the bill perfectly."

Mikhail Konev shifted uneasily in his chair, fixing his interlocutor with a look of utter disbelief.

"That is purely circumstantial evidence," he said. "I am here mainly on a business venture."

"To promote English beer, I understand," Leverkov said.

Konev nodded.

"I hope it catches on," the other continued. "I have tried one or two brands myself, while in London, and quite liked them. They had a good, malty tang."

Konev returned a look of amusement at that unexpected remark.

"It is certainly news to me that Pavel Belinsky is living in London," he said. "If that is the case, why would he have remained incognito all these years?"

"He has his own reasons," came the reply, making his hearer instantly suspect that he was back in the world of international espionage. Belinsky could well be in the pay of the secret service, not that Lev Pavlovich Leverkov would ever admit as much.

Lev Leverkov then changed tack.

"Do you have a bank account in Switzerland?" he asked, aware that the blackmailer used one.

Mikhail Konev shook his head.

"I use the Cockfosters branch of Barclay's Bank," he said. "That is the only account I own, jointly with my wife."

"We shall see about that," the other pointedly remarked. "We shall make enquiries with the Swiss Banking Authority. They will be able to tell us if a Mikhail Konev is a registered account holder in their country."

"What about the much-vaunted Swiss banking secrecy?" Konev objected.

"That is much less rigorous nowadays," Leverkov informed him, "following pressure from America and the European Union to pursue tax dodgers who have been salting money away for decades in Switzerland and many other tax refuges."

Mikhail Konev, for the first time that morning, essayed a thin smile.

"I imagine the Swiss only reluctantly acquiesced," he remarked.

"They dug their heels in all right," Leverkov replied, "and tried their best to stall official enquiries, but they gave significant ground in the end."

"Go ahead, Lev, if that is your intention," his former colleague taunted. "Waste your time pursuing a bum lead. What am I to do, meanwhile? Kick my heels here in Moscow?"

"You are free to return to your hotel for the time being," his interrogator said, feeling a little deflated by the advertising executive's response. "This matter will take a few days. If your denial proves to be correct, I shall return your passport and you shall be free to return to England. There are many wonderful things to see and do here in Moscow. I expect, having spent your time thus far on business matters, you have not availed yourself much of these opportunities."

"That is certainly true," Mikhail Konev replied. "Hillary and Marjorie, on the other hand, managed a full program of sight-seeing...and shopping."

"A car is waiting for you outside," Leverkov then curtly said, lighting a filter cigarette.

The detainee thereupon quit the premises and returned to Hotel Minsk. A surprised and much-relieved Hillary Konev greeted him.

"Mikhail!" she exclaimed, as he entered the hotel lounge, where she had been writing postcards. "How relieved I am to see you back. I have been beside myself with worry all morning. I was afraid they might put you in prison."

Her husband gave her a huge hug and an ironic smile.

"They are withholding my passport for the time being," he said, "pending further investigations."

"Investigations into what, for heaven's sake?" Hillary anxiously enquired.

"Someone has been blackmailing one of our former chess team members now living in London," he explained, "and salting the proceeds away in a Swiss bank account. I shall tell you more about it later. For now, we must stay put here in Moscow until this matter is cleared up."

"Which it will be, won't it, Mikhail?" she was quick to ask.

"I fully expect so, Hillary," he replied, "since I have never owned an account in Switzerland. But it may take several days before Lev Leverkov realizes he is on the wrong track. They are desperate to nail somebody, to safeguard their agent's cover. "

The penny suddenly dropped for Hillary Konev. They were talking, she realized, about a secret service agent active in London. That was an area she wished to avoid thinking about. The subject gave her the creeps and she decided not to probe further, saying instead:

"What are we to do meanwhile, Mikhail?"

"I should like to become just a regular tourist," he rejoined, "to see some of sights you and Marjorie visited. When I was stationed here in the 1980s, after a transfer from Novgorod, I never seemed to find the time."

"A great idea, Mikhail," Hillary enthusiastically agreed. "It will take your mind off things. How are we for funds?"

"We have enough roubles for everyday needs," he replied. "And we can use our Visa for entrance fees and the like. Ted is generously writing the hotel bill down as marketing expenses. He is a good old sport and won't mind if we are obliged to extend our stay, especially in the current circumstances."

"Thank goodness for that!" his wife remarked, gathering up her picture postcards to take to the nearest post office.

*

Around the same hour that the Marshes reached Sheremetyevo Airport, Alina Lehtinen arrived at Helsinki-Vantaa Airport in good time for the 11.25 a.m. flight to London Heathrow. On arrival, she cleared customs and took the Piccadilly Line Tube northwards to South Harrow. On the long Underground trip, with nothing more than tunnel walls and fellow-passengers to look at, she fell to musing about past events in her life. She recalled how her father, Igor Nikolayev, had left Moscow in 1990, to seek a new life for them in the West. With her mother, she had accompanied him to Leningrad and waved him good-bye from the platform of the Finland Station, as he took the express train to Helsinki. That was the last she had seen of him. How she had waited for his return, month after month, to assure them that everything was fine and that he was making arrangements for them to join him in Great Britain.

Suddenly without sufficient income, she and her mother had been unable to keep up the rent on the upmarket apartment they had long occupied in a prime residential area close to Artists' Village, where her father often played chess. They moved in with her mother's sister, Sofia, who had spare rooms. This arrangement enabled her to continue her education through high school and university on her mother's meagre earnings as a piano teacher. Less and less mention was made of her father as the years went by, even though a wedding picture graced the mantelpiece.

By the time she reached adulthood and began working as a librarian at the university, she was more fully versed in the ways of the world. Several of her friends' parents had divorced. She came to the conclusion, very reluctantly, that her father had deserted them. He had probably made a new life for himself in England with a new partner. Western newspapers were not available in Russia at the time, so there was no way she could have been aware of an event in 1990 that had caused such a stir in the British press, namely that a Russian immigrant had met his death in suspicious circumstances while crossing Chelsea Bridge.

Her well-paid job at the university enabled her to take vacations abroad. In the post-Soviet era, few restrictions were placed on foreign travel or on the purchase of foreign currencies. She took advantage of the new freedom to visit London several times, with the objective of trying to trace her father. Igor had often spoken of his love for France, the focus of his operations in the secret service. Like him, she discovered an affinity for the French way of life, visiting Paris and Grenoble in the Savoy Alps.

It was on a visit to Antibes, where she stayed at a Club Mediterranee hotel, that she first met her husband, Osmo Lehtinen. He asked her for a dance at an outdoor venue on the miles-long sandy beach, where she was intrigued to note that female bathers often went topless. Their friendship developed in the course of time into a firm relationship. Osmo would take the train from Helsinki some weekends, to meet her at St. Petersburg, where they liked to stroll the broad boulevards, visit the city parks and the variety of restaurants, before rounding off the evening at the ballet or the symphony. The relationship prospered and they eventually married there. Aunt Sofia's partner Alexsei gave her away at a small church in the suburbs.

As her mother Anna had died the previous year, she had decided to make a clean break with her past and start a new life with Osmo in Helsinki, where he seemed at the time to have good prospects at Nokia. They occupied a medium-sized apartment on the island suburb of Kulosaari, often visiting Osmo's ageing mother, who lived in a cottage deep in the countryside, about an hour's drive from the capital. At the bottom of her rambling garden, she had a sauna hut. Osmo would go down ahead to light the wood stove, while she chatted with his mother in her rustic kitchen. When the sauna was heated up, they would take thick sausages named *saunalenkki* with them, to cook while they enjoyed the bathe. She recalled the pungent aroma of prime pork sizzling on the metal stove-top and tasty suppers back in the cottage, often by an open fire. What good times she and Osmo have had, she mused, as her train pulled into Ealing Common Underground station, marking the half-way stage of her journey. The automatic doors clattered open. Some travelers got out; others stepped in, with all the urgency of city-dwellers and their frenetic way of life. The doors closed and they were soon speeding to the next stop at Park Royal, she noted from the route-map above the carriage window. She had made this trip several times before in recent months, becoming familiar with the route and the timing. She would reach Aunt Paivi's around four o'clock, just in time for afternoon tea, a ritual that the Anglophile nurse adhered to religiously on her days off. Someone had left a copy of the *Daily Mail* on the seat opposite. She picked it up glanced at it cursorily, finding little of particular interest.

Resuming her reverie, she reflected on when the key breakthrough had come regarding her long-absent father. It had been the occasion of her meeting with Nadia Belinsky at the Communist International in Tallinn two years ago. They had been members of the same steering committee, taking their meals together between sessions. She and Nadia had quite taken to each other and she had accepted, with some reservations, the older woman's invitation to act as a courier between Helsinki and St. Petersburg. The financial aspect had persuaded her, especially since Osmo was facing redundancy at Nokia, the giant telecommunications firm that had been losing market share and laying off employees. It was at one of their subsequent meetings at St. Petersburg that Nadia had confided to her that her twin brother Pavel had taken care, as she pointedly put it, of the double agent, Igor Nikolayev. Hearing those words had struck her like a thunderbolt. She had gasped aloud, but betrayed none of her innermost feelings.

The older woman had gone on to explain that her brother had anglicized his name and was living in England. Nadia Belinsky had not, of course, revealed the new name, nor had she mentioned the city where he was now living. The inference to Alina was obvious. Pavel Belinsky was still an active spy and his supposed defection a front. It was at that juncture that she had decided to track down the man responsible for her father's death, for the long years of wondering what had happened to him, and for the agonizing doubts she had nursed about his attitude towards his only child and to his devoted wife, Anna. The question then had been how to act on Nadia's information. How could she possibly locate the brother?

About twelve months after that fateful meeting with Nadia Belinsky, she and Osmo had taken a weekend trip to Stockholm, to visit one of his university friends whose law firm had transferred him to the Swedish capital. After a full day's sightseeing in a fascinating city open to the Baltic Sea, where ocean liners docked alongside the busy streets, they had settled down in the friend's apartment to watch the television news before a seasonal dinner of grilled crayfish.

Her attention had become riveted on a report of a

conference of NATO ministers of defense. Their spokesman was the British delegate, named Paul Bell. He faced the cameras to discuss NATO policy on a number of key issues. Looking at him, Alina noted that her bore a striking resemblance to Nadia Belinsky, his twin sister! Paul Bell, she immediately realized, was an anglicized version of his real name. She had jumped up from her comfortable seat on the sofa, almost spilling her beer, waved her arms and shouted Eureka! at the top of her voice.

She could smile to herself now at the effect that had produced on her conventional husband and his even more buttoned-up lawyer friend. Expecting some explanation of her eccentric behavior, they were disappointed. At no point in their relationship had she mentioned to Osmo her interest in Paul Bell, alias Pavel Belinksy. Nor would she ever do so.

On previous visits to London over the course of the past few months, she had addressed a letter marked 'personal' to Paul Bell at the Ministry of Defence. She was determined to make him pay for what he had done, and had visited Geneva to open an account at Union Bank, to receive wire transfers from London, confident that he would pay up rather than risk exposure. Her hunch proved correct. She was now over fifty thousand pounds to the good, a sum she would reserve for her child's future, since higher education was costly in Finland. If Osmo became curious and began to ask questions about the source of the money, she could always invent a story about a long-lost relative who had migrated after World War 11. She had mailed the final blackmail letter from Moscow, after continuing by rail to that city to visit her ageing Aunt Sofia, following her recent trip as a courier to St. Petersburg.

The Tube duly arrived at South Harrow. She alighted, resurfaced on High Street in uncertain weather and walked as far as the post office, where she took a left turn into Windsor Street, to reach the semi-detached house Aunt Paivi rented. The nurse, on opening the front door, greeted her warmly.

"You made it, Alina!" she said, "Just in time for afternoon tea. I shall put the kettle on."

The visitor stepped inside, left her suitcase in the hallway, removed her loose jacket and followed her aunt into the kitchen. The rear window overlooked an enclosed garden with small flower beds and a rockery with alpine plants.

"Your garden is coming on nicely," Alina remarked.

"Isn't it so?" Paivi replied. "But it is getting a bit too much for me to cope with, so I hired a gardener this year to clear the borders and plant new stock. He is a young immigrant from Poland, very helpful and obliging."

Placing four measured spoonfuls of tea in the pot, she added boiling water and let it brew for a short while before placing it on a tray with the cups and saucers. She added a few slices of fruit cake and entered the living-room, where her guest was admiring some prints of Lakeland scenes.

"I just found a great new blend," Aunt Paivi remarked. "Lipton's orange pekoe. We shall let it stand for a few minutes, to give a good brew. So how is my nephew doing?"

"Very well, Paivi," her visitor replied. "He has nearly finished his teacher training course and shall soon be looking for a position in Helsinki."

"Unfortunate, that business at Nokia," Paivi replied. "He seemed to be doing so well there."

She poured the tea and nudged the fruit cake towards her guest. After a long trip, with only a light lunch on the plane, Alina Lehtinen was glad of the refreshment.

"You have adapted so well to life in England, Paivi," she remarked. "Shall you stay on here after your retirement?"

Her aunt contentedly sipped her tea, as she weighed the question.

"There is a lot about this country that I like," she said, eventually. "Even the wet weather, which makes everything so green. And I like the people. Their sense of humor is very similar to the Finns'. But I have always agreed with the Russian proverb."

"Which is?" an intrigued Alina asked.

"*East is good, and West is good. But home is best.*"

The younger woman returned a broad smile.

"There is a lot to be said for that," she remarked. "I take it then that you shall be returning to Lahti?"

"I fully expect so, my dear, but I shall visit England as often as resources allow," Paivi assured her. "I have made good friends here, mainly in the nursing community. Several of them, in fact, moved here from Finland around the same time as I did."

"I may well like to come here with you," Alina

said, "soon as our child is in kindergarten."

"That is some years down the road," Paivi opined. "I should always be glad of your company, however. I am in line for a good retirement pension from the National Health Service."

"They have done very well by you, Paivi."

"The health service has its problems," the other said, "but on the whole free universal health care has worked very well in Britain for the past eighty or so years."

"Isn't that something!" her visitor remarked.

"And in Scotland, even prescriptions are free."

"The welfare state," Alina commented. "I am all in favor of it."

Paivi drained her cup, poured herself a re-fill and slipped back into the kitchen to replenish the tray with McVitie's chocolate digestive biscuits, seeing that Alina had already eaten most of the fruit cake.

"Do you think Osmo will take to school teaching?" she asked, on her return.

"I think he will manage very well," Alina thoughtfully replied. "He loves his subject, English literature, and should have the necessary patience and tact."

"Is Finland still top of the educational attainment league?" the other asked.

"I think South Korea may have pipped us into first place, Paivi," Alina replied. "There is a great deal of pressure to succeed in that country, as in Asia generally, I believe."

The two women continued chatting for a while, bringing each other up-to-date on various matters of mutual interest. When the tea ritual was over, Alina took a good walk in the neighborhood, to offset the hours spent traveling, and to work up an appetite for dinner. Paivi switched on the television and watched the early-evening news for a while, before returning to her tidy kitchen to begin preparations for an evening meal of spaghetti carbonara. She selected a bottle of Muscadet, her favorite Loire wine, from the wine-rack and placed it in the refrigerator to cool for an hour or so, thinking that tomorrow she would take Alina on a shopping trip to the West End, to look for a suitable gift for the expected addition to the family. They would have dinner in the West End and go to the theatre.

*

Fabien Leroux had spent most of the afternoon at Hyde Park. In fitful sunshine, he had played mini-golf and taken a rowing-boat out on the choppy Serpentine. Since his trip to Finland, which he recalled with pleasure, time had hung rather heavily. He had settled in at his new quarters near Victoria Station. It suited him just fine to be living above The Black Prince, which did a busy trade at most hours of the day, especially in the evenings, when regulars came to play darts or dominoes in the tap room. It often amused him to observe these games over a pint of beer, but he declined their frequent invitations to take part. Q had advised him to keep his own company, saying that a few drinks at a pub could easily loosen the tongue and he might let slip some critical piece of information that could be used against him. He had therefore spent a deal of time at the fitness center, making good use of the amenities there, including the sauna. He had also paid several visits to Brixton, to spend time with his old navy colleague, Jeb Sinclair.

At just turned five o'clock, he directed his steps towards Speakers' Corner, a venue which became alive on Sundays with soap-box orators of all stripes, plus a few cranks, addressing the motley crowd. He did not stop to listen, exiting the park by Marble Arch, a triumphal arch in Carrara marble designed by John Nash in 1827, and covering the short distance to The Wheatsheaf. Q, who was sitting at his usual alcove table solving a crossword puzzle, had already ordered a round of drinks.

"Greetings, Monsieur," he said, inviting his agent to join him, while laying his newspaper aside. "How was your trip to Helsinki?"

The Canadian, thirsty from his afternoon exercise, took a swig of Watney's Bitter before replying.

"It went very well," he said. "I met with Alina Lehtinen, as arranged, and handed over the Manila envelope."

"So you learned her surname, after all?" Q asked, with raised eyebrows. "I work on the principle that the less one knows the better, especially in this line of work."

"Alina's husband collected her from the restaurant afterwards," Fabien Leroux explained. "He introduced himself as Osmo Lehtinen."

"She entertained you to dinner, in fact, as I suggested she might?"

Leroux nodded.

"A typically Finnish menu," he replied, "at a

place called Kalevala."

"What did you make of our young associate?"

"She was much friendlier and more outgoing than I had expected, to tell the truth," the other told him. "We had a good long chat, while enjoying several courses and the music of the kantele."

"Did she at any point refer to the contents of the package?" Q pointedly asked.

Leroux shook his head, saying:

"She intimated that it was destined for St. Petersburg. I got the impression that she would be taking it there herself, by train."

"Nadia," the other continued, "who is my contact at St. Petersburg, told me that Alina is an attractive, well-educated young woman and a dedicated party worker, like Nadia herself."

The Canadian returned a questioning look.

"She works for the Communist Party," Q clarified.

"Are the Communists still a political force in Russia?" Leroux asked, in some surprise.

"Not so much as in former times," came the reply. "But they do retain a significant presence, along with several other political parties. Communists are also active in some European countries, such as France, Italy, Portugal and Greece."

"Will they ever regain power?" came the next question.

Q took a swig of beer and returned a doubtful look.

"Their time is past, in my view," he said. "Nostalgia for the old days gets them a degree of support."

""Interesting," the Canadian remarked.

"Now listen carefully, Monsieur," the older man said. "I have limited time. It is my wife's birthday today. We are organizing a small reception at our home this evening and I have yet to buy in the champagne."

"Give her my best wishes," Leroux said, keen to keep in the other's good graces.

"Thank you. Monsieur. I shall make a point of it," Q replied. "Are you prepared for a second trip to Finland?"

As he posed the question, he wondered if the Canadian had divined the nature of these assignments, and whether he had sensed that they were treasonable. Alina Lehtinen was unaware of the contents of the Manila envelopes, so she could not have told him anything. All the same, the man facing him, savoring his English beer while enjoying the pub atmosphere, was of above-average intelligence. He may have drawn his own conclusions and entertained misgivings.

"The compensation would be the same?" Leroux enquired.

Q emphatically shook his head.

"It increases with each trip," he replied, with an artful smile. "All expenses paid, plus three thousand pounds in your pocket."

"In that case," Fabien Leroux promptly declared, "I gladly accept the next assignment."

"Excellent!" the other said, now more convinced than ever that the ex-navy man was in his control.

"When do I leave?" Leroux asked.

"Within the next few days," Q said. "Nadia has

been having some difficulty contacting Alina Lehtinen. When that little matter is resolved, I shall send you a text message about where we can next meet and hand you the package."

"Do I follow the same route?"

"I should think so," the older man replied. "There are alternative surface routes, such as by rail via Hamburg and Copenhagen. But I think that would be rather tedious in comparison to two sea voyages."

"I especially liked the crossing from Stockholm to Helsinki," Fabien Leroux remarked, "through the skerries off the coast of Sweden, and on through the islands of the Finnish Archipelago."

"I imagine that is a wonderfully scenic trip," Q said. "One I have never had the opportunity to make myself, but I have heard positive accounts of it from several quarters. I was in Stockholm for a conference last year, as a matter of fact. Some of the delegates went yachting on the Baltic during their free time."

Leroux wondered what kind of conference the mysterious Q would take part in, but refrained from asking. He gladly accepted the wad of banknotes, as Q drained his glass and rose to leave. He himself decided to stay put for the next hour or so, to watch the Arsenal vs. Chelsea soccer match on television. He crossed to the bar and refilled his glass with a keen sense of satisfaction. Things were going well, he considered, as he counted the money and placed it in his wallet. And a return trip to Finland was just the ticket.

CHAPTER 13

The next day dawned clear and sunny after overnight rain. Paivi and Alina enjoyed a simple breakfast of cereals and fruit at the kitchen table, after which the older woman pottered about the garden for a while, leaving her niece to do a few personal chores. Towards noon, Paivi took a shower and changed her clothes for a trip to the West End. Alina Lehtinen laid down the newspaper she had been reading, went to the bathroom to apply a little make-up and fix her hair, before donning a loose jacket and accompanying her aunt outdoors. They strolled down to the High Street, greeting a couple of the nurse's acquaintances near the shops before entering a café for a quick snack.

"Who were those people we just met?" Alina asked.

"The woman about my age is also a nurse," Paivi replied. "She moved here from Poland last year. She barely speaks English, but seems to manage her job nonetheless, without too much difficulty."

"I thought I detected a foreign accent," her niece said.

"The gentleman I spoke to is the manager of my local bank. As British as they come. Harrow and Cambridge University."

"Isn't Harrow another of those famous public schools, like Eton?" Alina asked.

Aunt Paivi nodded.

"It is quite near here," she said. "I am not sure why they call them public schools, since they are private, fee-paying institutions for the upper strata of English society."

"Plus quite a few wealthy foreigners, I imagine," Alina added.

"Schools for the general public are called state schools," the nurse added.

"That makes sense," Alina rejoined.

After a light lunch of tuna salad and Perrier water, the two women left the café and made their way to South Harrow Underground station, taking the Tube to Bond Street. Alina Lehtinen always made a point of visiting the West End on her trips to England. She especially liked the large department stores, such as Harrod's and Selfridge's, not necessarily to purchase their rather expensive wares, but mainly to keep abreast of current tastes and trends. She was conscious that such establishments conflicted to some extent with her egalitarian principles, but saw no great harm in browsing.

"I should like to buy something for your upcoming event," Paivi announced, as they regained street-level after a fairly long Underground trip. "Do you have a preference, or shall you leave it up to me?"

"That is very kind of you, Paivi," Alina replied. "Forget about baby clothes. Osmo's parents will be giving us some, as their main gift. His mother especially likes to shop at Stockmann's in downtown Helsinki."

"I was thinking along the lines of a cuddly toy,"

Paivi then said. "It would be suitable for a boy or a girl."

"A great idea," Alina replied.

They filled out the afternoon doing the rounds of the various stores, weighing up the latest fashions and also dropping by Foyle's bookshop, so that the visitor could choose a paperback to read on the journey home. Paivi then led the way to a toy store, where she purchased a small panda. Alina was delighted with the choice.

"It looks so life-like," she said. "It will make a wonderful gift."

"I think so, too," the other said. "Given the remarkable array of cuddly animals on view, I was quite spoiled for choice."

"Hadn't we better be thinking about an early dinner?" Alina said, as the toy was being gift-wrapped. "The play begins at seven."

"What have you booked for us?" Paivi asked.

"An Arnold Wesker play at the Garrick."

"Then we had better get a move on," Paivi said, glancing at her watch. "It is nearly five o'clock. I suggest we try Isola Bella, an Italian restaurant just off Piccadilly Circus, handy for the theatre district."

"I am in your hands, Paivi," Alina enthusiastically rejoined.

Placing the wrapped panda in a carrier-bag, they made their way to the restaurant. At that early evening hour, it was less than half-full and service was relatively quick. From the menu they chose a Sicilian pasta dish with a glass of Barolo to help it down, followed by tiramisu for dessert. They reached the Garrick in good time for the performance of *Chicken Soup with Barley*, an anti-fascist play that greatly appealed to Alina. Two hours later, they were on their way back to South Harrow.

"What an interesting full day we have had," Paivi remarked, as they reached her home on Windsor Street.

"Did you enjoy the play?" Alina asked.

"Very much so," came the reply. "I generally like modern theatre, but Shakespeare has always been my favorite."

"I should like to visit Stratford-on-Avon," Alina said, "and the Royal Shakespeare Theatre."

"One day, in the future, we shall do that," Paivi replied, putting the kettle on for a night-cap.

After she had served tea and biscuits, she said:

"Oh, and I almost forgot to tell you, Alina, that I helped nurse a Russian gentleman a short while ago. His name was Maxim Brodsky. He was transferred to our local hospital from East London, to complete his recovery."

"How unfortunate," her niece replied. "How did that come about?"

"He was struck with a rifle bullet, while closing his hardware store one evening at Stepney Green."

"How did you come to be involved in his treatment, Paivi?"

"The wound caused water to collect in his lungs," the experienced nurse explained. "One of the leading pulmonary specialists in England, a Professor Aspi Rajput – Indian, I believe – is based at South Harrow Hospital. Brodsky was placed under his care."

"A gunshot victim in London?" Alina asked, with a skeptical look. "I thought knife attacks were much more common here."

Aunt Paivi nodded agreement, sipped her tea and said, almost conspiratorially:

"I happened to overhear Mr. Brodsky discuss the incident with a representative from Scotland Yard. Brodsky told the detective, whose name escapes me for the moment, that there had been an attack on one of his former colleagues on Chelsea Bridge in 1990, which had proved fatal. He was wondering if there might be a connection between the two incidents, even though they are decades apart."

"Did Brodsky mention the name of his former colleague?" Alina asked, sitting bolt-upright.

"He may have," the nurse replied. "But I do not recall it. I was only on the ward for a few days, preparing and administering medications."

With that, Paivi quickly cleared away the tea service and retired for the night, leaving her visitor to wonder if there was, in fact, a connection between the two incidents. What a remarkable scenario that would be. She too retired shortly afterwards, lying awake in bed for a long while, pondering her aunt's remarks. Before she closed her eyes, she had decided on a course of action for the next day.

She rose early, sitting at a table in the living-room with a cup of strong coffee to write a letter, which she addressed to The Prime Minister, 10 Downing Street, London SW1A 2AA. She then made herself poached eggs for breakfast and read *The Guardian* newspaper until her aunt came down.

"Aren't you the early bird!" Paivi said, surprised to see her niece had already breakfasted.

"I woke early," Alina replied, "and made a pot of coffee. It should still be warm."

"That was thoughtful of you," Paivi said, pouring herself a cup and joining her niece at the table. "What plans do you have for today?"

"Since it is my last day," came the reply, "I want to take things fairly easy. At some point this morning, I will stroll down to the post office to mail a letter. This afternoon, I could help you out a bit in the garden, if you wish."

"That would be great, Alina," her aunt said. "For dinner, I shall make your favorite Swedish meatballs with baked potatoes. I expect you have a busy day ahead tomorrow."

"I shall be leaving first thing, Paivi," Alina informed her. "I shall take the Tube down to Heathrow Airport and catch a mid-morning flight to Geneva, where I have some business to attend to."

"That sounds interesting," Paivi said, her curiosity piqued about what kind of business her niece might have in that country. "Shall you be staying in Geneva?"

Alina Lehtinen did not rise to the bait. There was no way she could reveal that she would be withdrawing the substantial deposit built up there over the past few months. She could not even tell her husband, who would be curious about the source. A private account in her name at Karelian Pankki, Helsinki would do the trick.

"There is an early-evening direct flight to Helsinki with Finnair," she replied. "I should be in time to catch it, to avoid the expense of an overnight stay. Osmo will meet me on arrival."

Aunt Paivi tactfully did not pursue the matter. On finishing her coffee and the two slices of toast-and-marmalade she had quickly made for breakfast, she went back upstairs to shower and dress.

*

Two days later, Chief Inspector Bill Harrington urgently summoned George Mason into his office, as soon as the detective arrived mid-morning, following a routine call he had made in the North London borough of Islington.

"Please take a seat," the senior officer said.

From his chief's demeanor, Mason sensed that something big was afoot.

"I have just received a telephone call from M.I.5.," Harrington continued. "The Security Service informed me that the prime minister has received a letter mailed at South Harrow claiming that there is a Russian mole at the Ministry of Defence!"

"Indeed, Chief Inspector?" an astonished George Mason said. "Do they know the author of the letter?"

Bill Harrington shook his head.

"It was sent anonymously," he said. "M.I.5 have asked us to be on the look-out for anything that might lead either to the suspected mole or to the author of the letter."

"It could be a hoax," his colleague suggested. "Or even a prank. There are all sorts of weirdos around these days, conspiracy theorists, fake news freaks. You name it."

His senior returned a wry smile.

"That is always a possibility, I agree, Inspector," he rejoined. "But the government is treating it as genuine, ahead of critical discussions about the role of NATO in East Europe."

George Mason sat back in his chair to weigh that information.

"So what precisely is expected of us, here at the Yard, Chief Inspector?" he enquired.

Bill Harrington leaned forward, looking his colleague directly in the eye.

"I mentioned to M.I.5," he said, "that you have been investigating attacks against two former members of the Russian intelligence services who defected to Britain over two decades ago. They were wondering if those incidents might have some relevance to the matter in hand, to the presence of a mole, in fact."

A smile played about George Mason's shrewd features.

"I can think of one individual who might possibly be of interest," he said. "His name is Paul Bell, alias Pavel Belinsky."

At that point, the chief inspector's morning coffee was brought in by a junior officer. As she laid the tray on the walnut desk and withdrew, Bill Harrington reached down to his bottom drawer for his flask of Islay single malt. He poured himself a tot, to chase his coffee.

"I believe you have mentioned that name to me previously, Inspector," he said. "What did you manage to get on him?"

"We discovered," Mason replied, "that he changed his name by deed poll soon after arriving in Britain. I also turned up his marriage certificate at Somerset House to a woman named Cynthia Stead. We quickly traced her parents to Dartmouth, Devon. Detective Sergeant Aubrey and I recently paid them a visit."

"Excellent work, Mason," Harrington enthused. "What did that yield?"

"Gerald and Felicity Stead were under the impression that their son-in-law was of American extraction. They were amazed to learn that he was, in fact, born in Russia."

"What else did they tell you?" an alert Bill Harrington wanted to know.

"Among other things," George Mason replied, "they told us that he worked at the Ministry of Defence, a position Gerald Stead helped him obtain, based on his fluent knowledge of Slavonic languages!"

The chief inspector slammed his palm down on the table, causing his coffee to spill into the saucer.

"By Jove, Inspector!" he exclaimed. "You're probably on to something there. I shall ring my contact at M.I. 5 straight away."

"We should need firm evidence," Mason cautioned. "That might not be very easy to obtain."

"We shall work on it," Harrington said, lifting the receiver of his desk-phone and quickly dialing.

George Mason waited patiently for the outcome of the telephone conversation. Minutes later, his senior informed him that M.I.5 were very interested in what he had found out. They would be sending an experienced agent over to Scotland Yard this very afternoon, to coordinate enquiries.

"M.I.5 need the assistance of the Metropolitan Police?" Mason enquired, with an ironic smile.

"It is a big compliment to you, Inspector," Bill Harrington said. "Your reputation must be spreading."

"Pull the other leg, Chief Inspector," his colleague replied, sensing that his superior was ribbing him a little bit. On his way back to his own office, he caught up with Detective Sergeant Aubrey, who was busy with routine paperwork.

"Our investigation may have taken a decisive step forward, Alison," he told her. "More on that this afternoon. Make yourself available after you have had lunch."

"You bet, George!" she responded, with a genial smile.

*

Around two o'clock, Susan Newcombe arrived. She was a tall, slender woman with chin-length brown hair and finely-cast features, dressed in a gray two-piece suit. George Mason received her in his office, inviting Alison Aubrey to join them. He explained to the M.I.5 agent the nature of his enquiries so far, regarding the incidents at Stepney Green and Tooting Bec. He also mentioned his visits to Amsterdam, Brighton and Oslo, as well as his interest in Fabien Leroux.

"You think, Inspector Mason, there may be a link

between these incidents and the individual you have claimed is now working at Whitehall?" she asked.

"I have only coincidental information so far," the detective replied. "Mainly from the fact that this Paul Bell, together with Maxim Brodsky and Yuri Orlov, is a former secret agent who supposedly defected from the Soviet Union in 1990."

"How does this Fabien Leroux fit into the picture?" Susan Newcombe asked.

"We are fairly sure he obtained the explosive device used at Tooting Bec from a person named Dirk deGroot at Brighton," Mason replied. "But all attempts to trace him have so far proved unsuccessful."

"We managed to track him to an hotel in Bayswater," Alison Aubrey added, "but he had checked out the day before we arrived."

Agent Newcombe pondered their remarks for a few moments.

"Let us concentrate our resources on the mole," she said, after a while. "This is a very sensitive matter in view of the upcoming NATO conference."

"If Paul Bell, alias Pavel Belinsky, is in fact the mole, he has evidently been in place many years," George Mason said. "Who knows what damage he has done to our country's interests and to those of the western alliance?"

"All the more reason to root him out now," Newcombe said, with conviction.

"What course of action do you propose, Susan?" Mason asked.

"We shall put him under close surveillance, Inspector," came the reply, "with the active cooperation of your department, I trust."

"Alison and I are both at your service," the detective assured her, intrigued at the idea of being involved in secret service work.

"Then we shall make a start straight away," the M.I.5 agent said, in business-like fashion. "This very evening, in fact. Do you happen to have the suspect's address?"

George Mason consulted his files, having rung the Steads at Dartmouth soon after his visit there, in order to obtain that information.

"35 Briarwood Lane, West Acton," he informed her. "His home is just a few blocks from the Underground station."

"We need to know where he goes after working hours and whom he meets," his visitor said.

"I can volunteer for that duty," Alison said. "I know the area quite well."

"Can you start as early as this evening?"

"Absolutely," the young sergeant replied.

"Will the Ministry of Defence be informed of our suspicions?" Mason asked.

"I think that would be premature, at this stage," Newcombe replied. "Paul Bell might very well get wind of it, especially since he is working there. Meanwhile, I shall have his recent ministerial duties carefully vetted."

That course of action being agreed upon, the trio broke up. Susan Newcombe paid Bill Harrington a quick courtesy visit before leaving, mainly to enquire about his wife, who had been a friend of hers at Queen Mary College. George Mason told Alison not to take undue risks and to contact him immediately if there were any problems or developments.

*

Three days later, Fabien Leroux received a text message from Q, asking him to join him in the bar lounge at The Black Prince at seven o'clock that evening. The Canadian was reclining on a bed drinking tea in the dressing-room, after taking a sauna-bath at the fitness center he frequented in Bayswater. At 120 degrees Celsius, it had been hotter than usual and he had stayed a bit too long. A half-hour's rest and the complimentary tea service revived him. He checked his Rolex. It was almost five o'clock. Rising from the firm mattress, he quickly dressed, left the fitness center and took the Tube to Victoria Station, dodging the busy commuter traffic on Victoria Street to reach the pub. He decided to take an early dinner ahead of Q's visit and look up on his laptop some of the tourist sights he had missed on his first visit to Finland.

Paul Bell left home that evening at 6.15 p.m. and walked briskly to West Acton Underground, unaware that a young woman was following him at a discreet distance. He took the Central Line to Notting Hill Gate, where he switched to the Circle Line to reach Victoria. Alison Aubrey found a seat in the compartment behind the one her target occupied, so that she herself could exit immediately after he did, in the small window of time when the train doors were open. Confident that Paul Bell had not noticed her presence, she observed him cross Victoria Street and enter The Black Prince. Before following him in, she contacted George Mason by cellphone.

"I am still here at the Yard," he informed her. "I can reach you within minutes, if you should need me. Take good care, Alison, to remain unobserved."

The young sergeant did not wish to enter the pub alone, thinking that a lone female would immediately attract attention. She phoned Susan Newcombe, who drove down swiftly from her home at nearby South Kensington, parking her car illegally on the forecourt of Victoria Station. The two women casually entered The Black Prince, bought drinks at the bar and took them to a table near the alcove Q invariably chose for his meetings with the Canadian. They chatted about neutral topics, while keeping an eye on the alcove. Its two occupants, with pints of beer, seemed engrossed in conversation. Alison knew that the older man was Paul Bell. His younger companion, she surmised with growing confidence, fit the description of Fabien Leroux, the Canadian who had eluded them for so long. She watched Paul Bell remove a large Manila envelope from his briefcase and pass it across the table. Alison rose from her place and crossed to the restroom, where she phoned George Mason.

Within minutes, the detective appeared on the scene, accompanied by two uniformed officers of the Metropolitan Police. They met up with Aubrey and Newcombe, before approaching the alcove to confront the two drinkers.

"Paul Bell," Mason tersely announced, "I have a warrant for your arrest under the Official Secrets Act, 1989."

The older man rose to his feet, in an attempt to face down the detective.

"This is preposterous," he indignantly protested. "I am a senior civil servant fully accredited at Whitehall."

"We know all about your activities at the Ministry of Defence, Mr. Belinsky," Susan Newcombe remarked with heavy irony, while taking possession of the Manila envelope.

At mention of his real name, the Russian's faced turned pale. Fabien Leroux looked on helplessly. While much alarmed at the sudden appearance of the police, he was at the same time intrigued to learn the name of the person he had hitherto known only as Q. Mention of the Official Secrets Act confirmed his previous misgivings that he had been involved in some form of espionage. He took a large swig of his beer, to help calm his nerves.

As the uniformed officers, accompanied by Susan Newcombe, led Pavel Belinsky, alias Paul Bell, outside to the waiting squad car, George Mason and Alison Aubrey turned their attention to the Canadian.

"Your passport, please," Mason peremptorily requested.

Leroux rose to his feet, withdrew the document from his breast pocket and handed it over.

"Fabien Leroux," Mason then said, "formerly of the Royal Canadian Navy, from which you received a dishonorable discharge?"

Leroux knit his brows, puzzled about how that piece of information had come to light, since he had been so careful to cover his tracks. He nodded, saying:

"I was merely an errand boy, Inspector. I had no knowledge of the contents of the Manila envelope."

"But you did have knowledge of a firearm attack on a person named Maxim Brodsky at Stepney Green," Sergeant Aubrey said. "And also of an incident involving explosives in the parking lot of Cybernetics Institute, Tooting Bec, which seriously injured Yuri Orlov."

The Canadian felt an inner panic.

"I deny it absolutely," he said.

"Did you ever meet a person named Dirk deGroot?" George Mason put it to him.

The suspect merely shook his head, with a cynical look.

"Dirk deGroot will identify you," the detective said, "as a person for whom he helped prepare a pipe bomb at an address in Brighton. He will turn Queen's Evidence against you, in the expectation of reducing his own prison sentence, when his case comes to court next week. I am therefore arresting you, Fabien Leroux, on suspicion of attempted murder, illegal possession of a firearm and explosives.

The Canadian, realizing that the game was up if the Dutchman was prepared to identify him, gave the detective a look of hostility mixed with grudging respect, before he in turn was led outside and taken to a holding cell at Scotland Yard.

*

Three days later, George Mason and Susan Newcombe were summoned to the Ministry of Defence at Whitehall. The minister, William Kendall, wearing a grim expression, invited them to sit facing his desk for a brief meeting before he was due in the House of Commons.

"I have read your report on this disturbing case," he began. "It is an extremely serious matter. The contents of the package you seized at Victoria contain sensitive information about NATO's policies in East Europe. The prime minister is beside himself. Our allies will feel betrayed."

"A clear-cut case of espionage, Minister," Susan Newcombe remarked.

"Where is the person I know as Paul Bell at this moment?" Kendall asked.

"At Pentonville prison," George Mason informed him. "Bail was not granted, because of the obvious flight risk. He will stay put until the Crown Prosecution Service builds its case against him."

"To think that he has gone undetected all these years!" Kendall ruefully remarked.

"How do you assess the damage, Minister?" Susan Newcombe asked.

"Not so bad as it might have been had you not exposed him," the minister replied. "Paul Bell has been our representative at NATO for the last three years. My right-hand man, in fact, in many ways. Before that, he was party to fairly low-level information. All the same, the damage is considerable and may explain certain setbacks I am not at liberty to discuss at the present time."

"He would not reveal anything about espionage activity during my sessions with him," the M.I.5 agent said. "He did reveal, however, that he was being blackmailed."

William Kendall raised his eyebrows in surprise at that remark.

"We seized his iPhone," George Mason added. "Text messages between him and Fabien Leroux, the person we apprehended along with him, reveal that together they planned the attacks on Maxim Brodsky and Yuri Orlov."

"How do those individuals fit into the picture?" the minister wanted to know.

"It was in connection with the blackmail," the detective replied. "Brodsky and Orlov, together with three other men, were part of a group of former secret agents who defected from the Soviet Union in 1990."

"Paul Bell was also part of that group," Susan Newcombe added.

"My reading of this," George Mason continued, "is that Paul Bell would consider that only a member of that group could possibly suspect that he was actively involved in espionage. He would therefore assume that the blackmail letters were sent by one of them. So he set about eliminating the threat."

"An interesting theory, Inspector Mason," William Kendall remarked. "Did he succeed?"

"The two individuals named had narrow escapes," the detective replied. "Both were badly wounded,

Orlov more so than Brodsky. They have, however, recovered well enough to leave hospital and continue convalescence at home."

"There is enough evidence here in your report," Kendall said, "together with the content of the text messages, to obtain a conviction for espionage. Can we also get Bell for attempted murder?"

George Mason reserved judgement on that score.

"First thing tomorrow morning," he said, "I am organizing an identity parade at Scotland Yard. Fabien Leroux will line up with nine other men of similar age and build. The person who assembled the pipe bomb used at Cybernetics Institute at Tooting Bec is Dirk deGroot, a Dutchman living at Brighton. He has agreed to come up to London to identify the person he sold it to. It is a slam-dunk case, Minister. Dirk deGroot is himself due in court later this month for his dealings in explosives, which he claims are used mainly by the construction industry. "

"So he will cooperate," the Minister of Defence said. "Tell me, Inspector, was Leroux Bell's hitman in the incidents you referred to?"

"It would appear so, Minister," came the reply. "The text messages do not mention the intended victims by name, but they do give the venues for the incidents, which took place at Stepney Green and Tooting Bec, respectively."

"Is this Fabien Leroux also implicated in espionage?"

George Mason nodded.

"He was caught red-handed at The Black Prince," he said, "accepting a compromising package from

Paul Bell. Text messages exchanged by iPhone confirm his role as a courier as far as Helsinki."

"The material to be conveyed on to Moscow?"

"Apparently so, Minister. But we have no idea of the route he took. Enquiries at travel agencies, railway termini and airports turned up a blank."

"He probably used cash," Susan Newcombe said, "to avoid leaving a trail."

"I should imagine he went by surface," William Kendall observed. "Security is much laxer than at airports, where he would have been more closely vetted."

"There are several ways one can reach Finland by surface travel," George Mason pointed out. "It is anybody's guess which one he took."

"That seems to conclude matters for now," the minister then said. "We shall see in due course what the trial reveals. Meanwhile, my sincere thanks to you both for the excellent work you have done. It will be up to me now to smooth relationships with our allies, not least with the Americans, and to answer some awkward questions in Parliament."

At the conclusion of the meeting, George Mason invited Susan Newcombe for coffee in the ministry cafeteria.

"William Kendall will have his work cut out," the M.I.5 agent remarked, adding cream to her Italian roast, "explaining all this to his counterparts in Europe and America."

"A fine kettle of fish, to be sure," the detective replied. "What we need now is to get to the bottom of the blackmail business. If the culprit is not one of those original defectors, that raises a most interesting question. Who else it could be."

"I think I can help you there," Newcombe said. "Paul Bell gave me the number of the bank account he has been wiring money to, in the hope that some or all of it could be recovered."

"The Swiss authorities should be willing to identify the owner of the account," George Mason said, "in view of the criminal activity involved."

The M.I.5 agent wrote the account number down on a slip of paper and handed it to him.

"The account is held at Union Bank, Geneva," she said.

"Many thanks, Susan," Mason said. "I shall contact my friend Leutnant Kubler at Zurich Polizei Dienst. He has assisted me before on some cross-border cases."

"Useful to have friends in high places," the other remarked.

"Isn't it so!" the detective agreed.

The cafeteria began to fill with civil servants arriving for lunch. George Mason surmised, on weighing them up, that most of them would be Oxbridge graduates working their way up the promotion ladder.

"Before we go our separate ways, Susan," he said, as they rose from the table and moved towards the exit, "there is one other matter that may, or may not, relate to our current enquiries."

"What would that be, Inspector?" Newcombe enquired.

"One member of that original group of chess-playing defectors, a Pyotr Alenin living in Dublin, mentioned a seventh individual, named Igor

Nikolayev. Does that name mean anything to you?" The woman firmly shook her head.

"Can't say I have ever heard of him," she replied.

"Pyotr Alenin told me that Nikolayev died in rather curious circumstances," the detective continued. "I mentioned that to Chief Inspector Harrington. He seemed to recall the case, vaguely, from an earlier phase in his career. Nikolayev collapsed while walking across Chelsea Bridge. Poisoning was suspected."

"Like a passer-by pricked him with a loaded needle, Inspector?" the other asked, with an ironic smile.

"Something on those lines," Mason replied. "Enquiries were shelved years ago, for lack of firm evidence. I have been wondering if that incident is not in some way connected to the case in hand."

"If it was decades ago, Inspector Mason," Newcombe considered, "I doubt you will be able to get to the bottom of it. If Paul Bell was involved, he would never admit to it. He is in deep enough trouble as it is. Murder is a much more serious charge than attempted murder."

"You are surely right, Susan," the detective said. "I may have to be content with the success we have had so far."

"Plus solving the blackmail incidents," she reminded him.

With that, they quit the building, promising to keep in touch. George Mason, on reaching his office, placed an international call to Zurich. Rudi Kubler was as pleased to hear from him as he was surprised.

"How is the world treating you, Inspector?" he genially enquired.

"Not too badly, Leutnant, on the whole," came the reply.

"What can I do for you on this occasion?"

"I am investigating a case of blackmail," the detective explained. "I need to discover the owner of a numbered account at Union Bank, Geneva."

"I can approach the Swiss banking authorities on your behalf," Kubler replied, "if criminal activity is involved. It may take several days, going through official channels."

George Mason read him the account number Susan Newcombe had given him earlier.

"Leave it with me, Inspector," Rudi Kubler said. "I shall do what I can."

"I have every confidence in you, Leutnant," Mason said, ringing off.

CHAPTER 14

Alina Lehtinen, shortly after arriving back in Finland, took the tram from her home on the island suburb of Kulosaari to downtown Helsinki. On clearing her account at Union Bank, Geneva, she had changed half her haul of Swiss francs into euros, the currency Finland had adopted on joining the European Union. On now reaching Helsinki's financial district, she called at two currency exchanges to convert her remaining Swiss francs into euros, so that the Swiss banknotes she had withdrawn from Union Bank could not be traced back to her. She had taken the double precaution of using false I.D. at Geneva, so that her blackmailing activities would not be discovered, should her victim ever reveal the scheme to the British authorities, a development she considered very unlikely.

Armed with her haul of euros, she went to Karelian Pankki on the Esplanade, where she opened a new account. The large sum of money could sit there and earn interest, until the day arrived when she and Osmo would be faced with higher education costs for their child. She could then explain to her husband that she had been saving regular amounts over the years out of housekeeping and her own earnings. She could even invent a distant relative in Australia, claiming that he had left her a legacy. Osmo knew very little of her Russian family and would accept anything she said about them, true or false, at face value. Feeling well-satisfied with herself, she left Karelian Pankki and continued on foot along Esplanade to the outdoor market in full swing at South Harbor.

Strolling among the wooden stalls for a while, much taken with the variety of wares on offer from the farmers and fishermen arriving in small craft from higher up the coast, she paused for *nakit ya semp*, roughly translated as 'hot dogs with mustard', and a coffee at one of the refreshment stands, while observing the towering crane being pulled along the quay by a steam locomotive, in order to load timber onto a freighter. The vessel, the *Menai Strait,* was flying a British flag, she noted; it reminded her of her recent visit to London. On finishing her lunch snack, she purchased a dozen large sea scallops from the fish stall and a pound of oranges and a bulb of fennel from a greengrocer. She then walked back to the tram-stop on Esplanade, waiting in warm sunshine for the next tram to Kulosaari.

On reaching her home, she relaxed for a while before her close friend Virpi Killinen arrived. They spent part of the afternoon going through various catalogs on nursery items and maternity clothes. Virpi, who had two young children now in kindergarten, proved a big help in making appropriate choices. When her friend finally left, just before five o'clock, Alina began preparations for dinner. She was going to surprise Osmo with a new culinary creation, pan-seared scallops in orange Pernod sauce. The aniseed flavor of the liquor would offset the rather bland taste of the seafood. Dicing the fennel, she sautéed it in olive oil, before treating the scallops in similar fashion. Combining the ingredients in a baking pan, she added reduced orange sauce and a dash of Pernod, before placing the dish in the moderately-heated oven, to bake for ten minutes.

At that point, Osmo breezed in, hungry after a taxing day in teacher training. Leaving his textbooks on the sideboard, he quickly freshened up in the bathroom, before sitting down expectantly at the dining-room table. While waiting for the food, he poured himself a glass of Muscadet.

"Smells good, Alina," he remarked, as the aroma wafted through from the kitchen. "What's cooking?"

"A surprise!" his wife said, briefly joining him for a glass of Loire Valley wine. "Had a good day at college?"

"It went well enough," he replied, less perky than usual. "But the sooner it is all over, the better. I am keen to be earning again."

"Only a few weeks left, Osmo," Alina said. "You'll soon be on the job market."

"I noticed several vacancies for English teachers at local schools," Osmo said. "I am going to file some applications over the weekend."

Alina set down her wine glass and went back to the kitchen, returning moments later with her new creation, accompanied by brown rice and French beans. Serving two generous portions, she waited for her husband's reaction.

"It tastes wonderful," he said. "Compliments to

the chef!"

"It is a new recipe I found on-line," his gratified wife said, as she commenced eating. "I thought it might appeal to you."

"Any time," he replied. "It has a great tangy flavor. So how was your trip to England?"

"It went very well, Osmo. Aunt Paivi and I went shopping in Bond Street, where she bought that panda I have put aside for the baby shower. It is a really cuddly toy."

"Our new-born will surely love it," Osmo remarked. "What else did you get up to?"

"After shopping, we had dinner at an Italian restaurant called Isola Bella, just off Piccadilly Circus, before going to the theatre."

"What was on the bill?"

"Arnold Wesker's *Chicken Soup with Barley*," his wife replied. "You would have enjoyed it."

"I bet," Osmo replied.

After their tasty meal, Alina cleared the table to do the dishes, leaving her husband to finish his second glass of wine while watching the television news. A few minutes later, he called to her.

"Come and watch this, Alina," he said, his eyes glued to the screen.

His wife came back into the living-room and stood by the table.

"The British have exposed a Russian spy at the Ministry of Defence!" he said. "Isn't that something?"

"Does it give his name?" an inwardly elated Alina Lehtinen asked.

"He goes by the name Paul Bell," Osmo replied.

"But his original name, apparently, was Pavel Belinsky."

"That is truly amazing," Alina said, adding disingenuously: "I wonder if he is related to Nadia Belinsky, my contact at St. Petersburg."

"Possibly, I imagine," her husband considered. "This Paul Bell, they just said, has been in place as a mole for over two decades. The authorities are only now beginning to assess the extent of the damage he has caused. It turns out that he was their chief representative at NATO."

"A good job they latched on to him," his wife remarked, with genuine satisfaction.

"Not before time, either," Osmo said. "There have been questions in the House of Commons. Some members of Parliament are even calling for the resignation of the Minister of Defence, William Kendall."

"I never intended that," she said, with feeling.

"What did you just say, Alina?" Osmo asked, giving her a curious look.

Alina Lehtinen quickly realized her mistake.

"I mean I would never have expected something like that," she corrected.

"But you said *intended*."

"A slip of the tongue, Osmo."

The trainee teacher gave his wife a long, questioning look.

"What they call a Freudian slip, perhaps," he remarked, with a puzzled expression.

"Stop playing the amateur psychologist, Osmo and finish your drink," his wife remonstrated. "I should like to go kayaking again, if the weather holds."

"Give me an hour," Osmo replied, "to work on my thesis. It looks fine enough to me. We could try making it as far as Tapiola again."

"The exercise will do you good," she replied, biting her tongue at the stupid slip she had just made, "after being cooped up in college all day."

*

In the late-afternoon of that same day, Chief Inspector Bill Harrington called George Mason into his office, a few minutes before he was due to leave for a conference on community policing at Maidstone, Kent, an hour's drive away.

"My congratulations, Inspector," he began, inviting his colleague to sit. "You and Sergeant Aubrey have done a great job on a remarkable case."

"Who would have thought it would have such ramifications," Mason said. "A long-term mole at the Ministry of Defence, would you believe it!"

"There is pressure on William Kendall to resign," his senior then said. "That is a genuine pity. He has served his country well over the past several years, including updating our nuclear deterrent."

"The *Trident*, based on submarines at the Firth of Clyde, Chief Inspector?"

Bill Harrington nodded.

"He has also negotiated the continued use of Scottish lochs to accommodate them, in the face of strong opposition from some sections of the Scottish public."

"The Scottish Nationalists and the not-in-my-backyard types?"

"Precisely, Inspector," Harrington replied, with a grunt of disgust. "I take it that your case is now closed?"

"There remains the blackmail aspect," George Mason explained. "Alison and I are still trying to get to the bottom of it."

"You have ruled out the other members of the chess team who moved to England with this Bell, or Belinsky, whatever his real name is?"

"We have, Sir," his colleague replied. "Susan Newcombe obtained from the detainee the number of the Swiss bank account used for wire transfers he made from National Bank, London."

"You were able to get the Swiss authorities to cooperate and reveal the name of the account holder?" Harrington asked, in some surprise.

"I contacted Leutnant Rudi Kubler, of the Zurich Polizei Dienst," his colleague said. "He has always been most helpful, especially in dealings with Swiss bureaucracy."

"You have collaborated with him before, I seem to recall."

George Mason nodded.

"We worked together on two major cross-border cases in recent years," Mason replied. "Leutnant Kubler came up with the name Tuuli Siivonen."

"Sounds Finnish, Inspector," his senior remarked.

"Quite so, Chief Inspector," Mason confirmed. "I then contacted Major Viljo Forsenius, of the Helsinki police, with whom I have also previously had successful cooperation."

"And he has managed to trace this Tuuli Siivonen?"

George Mason regretfully shook his head.

"The only person he could come with bearing that name is an elderly, partly-disabled woman living in a care home in a town north of Helsinki called Porvoo. The blackmail letters, with one exception, were postmarked in London, which effectively rules her out."

"The blackmailer has evidently used an alias, then?" Harrington put it to him.

"That would seem to be the case, Chief Inspector," his colleague agreed. "We have another lead, in fact, which also may prove fruitless."

"I am listening, Inspector."

"Paul Bell told Susan Newcombe that the last letter he received was postmarked Moscow."

Bill Harrington thought about that for a few moments, before saying:

"That is rather curious. It adds a whole new dimension to the enquiry."

"That is what I think, too, Chief Inspector."

Bill Harrington, deep in thought, said nothing for a few moments.

"If the blackmailer was indeed a Finnish national, that poses a very interesting question," he eventually suggested. "Do we call it a Finnish crime that we can safely leave to Major Forsenius to investigate? Or do we consider it a British crime, since most of the letters were mailed on British soil?"

"That is an interesting conundrum, Sir," George Mason agreed, wondering why he hadn't thought of that angle himself.

"I think," the senior man said, with an air of finality, "it will save us a deal of time and trouble if we classify it as a Finnish matter. We shall consider the case closed, Mason. I shall inform the superintendent of the fact."

"And I shall get in touch with Viljo Forsenius again and place the ball in his hands," his colleague rejoined.

*

George Mason's and Alison Aubrey's final duty in this complex and intriguing case was to accept an invitation to dinner at the Ritz Hotel. On the evening of the Saturday following the arrest of the mole, the two detectives arrived by taxi at seven o'clock. With Mikhail and Hillary Konev, they joined Yuri Orlov, Maxim Brodsky and their wives, to celebrate recovery from their injuries.

"It was quite fascinating to see the television news item about the arrest of Pavel Belinsky," Mikhail Konev said, as they took their places round a large table covered with a crisp linen cloth and decorated with red carnations.

"Did either of you two suspect that he remained operative after his arrival in England?" George Mason asked.

Belinsky's former colleagues shook their heads.

"We lost contact with him completely," Maxim Brodsky said. "Almost from the word go."

"I was surprised he left Russia at all," Mikhail Konev added. "He always struck me as a dedicated

Communist, the least likely person to defect."

"So you were not aware," Alison Aubrey said, "that he went to America and obtained a post-graduate degree in Slavonic Studies?"

That disclosure caused considerable surprise, tinged with irony.

"That would have been a cake-walk for him," Yuri Orlov remarked, "since he already spoke fluent Russian and Czech."

"He returned to England some years later," the detective told them, "presenting himself as the son of Russian immigrants into America. He married an upper-class English girl named Cynthia Stead, whose father got him his start in the Civil Service."

"His knowledge of languages would have been very useful in either the Foreign Office or the Ministry of Defence," Hillary Konev commented.

"Cynthia Bell must be quite devastated," Linda Brodsky said, "to have been taken in like that."

"Her parents, too," Alison Aubrey put in. "Initially very skeptical of our enquiries, they in fact helped us locate the couple."

"More credit to them," Yuri Orlov said, "for putting national above family interest."

Studying the menu, they opted for French onion soup, to be followed by Angus roast beef. A Burgundy red wine was chosen to help it down.

"I imagine you two gentlemen," George Mason said, addressing Brodsky and Orlov, "have no idea why you were attacked."

"I can perhaps explain that," Mikhail Konev interposed. "On our recent business trip to Moscow, just as we were about to leave our hotel for the airport, in fact, I was apprehended by a former colleague of mine named Lev Leverkov!"

That disclosure produced a surprised reaction from the other diners, apart from Hillary.

"Leverkov took me in for questioning," the advertising executive continued. "I felt like a gamekeeper turned poacher."

That remark produced much merriment, as the first course arrived. They let their soup cool for a few moments before tackling it.

"Leverkov was quite open with me," Konev went on. "He said that Pavel Belinksy had been receiving blackmail letters mainly mailed in London. The most recent missive, however, was sent from Moscow. To Leverkov's mind, I was an obvious suspect."

"How did you get out of that fix?" Daphne Orlov asked him.

"They realized, after making certain enquiries, that I was not the owner of the account at Union Bank, Geneva that received regular wire transfers from London. The upshot was that Hillary and I had a few extra days sightseeing in Moscow. Ted Coverdale generously helped with expenses."

The light of understanding dawned across Yuri Orlov's intelligent features.

"Belinsky would figure that only one of our group could possibly have known of, or suspected, his ongoing role in international espionage," he said.

"Quite so, Yuri," George Mason added. "He needed to preserve his cover at all costs, so he employed a Canadian hitman to remove any possible threat. You two gentlemen were the obvious targets, I am afraid."

That disclosure took some time to sink in. The main course was served, accompanied by new potatoes and asparagus tips. The wine waiter filled their glasses, as the group concentrated on their appetizing food. The resident pianist began playing a selection of popular classics.

"The interesting question now," Yuri Orlov said, half-way through his roast beef, "must be who, in fact, was responsible for the blackmail. Do you have any leads on that, Inspector Mason?"

The detective thoughtfully sipped his glass of Chambertin 2005.

"That is indeed the $64,000 question," he replied.

"*Someone* must be behind it," Maxim Brodsky emphatically remarked.

"All I can tell you on that score," the detective said, "is that the owner of the numbered account at Union Bank, Geneva was a person of Finnish nationality. Chief Inspector Bill Harrington is content to let the Finnish authorities handle that. He considers that we have done our bit in exposing the mole at the Ministry of Defence and apprehending his accomplice, who apparently also acted as some form of courier."

"I imagine it will all come out in the media, eventually," Daphne Orlov remarked.

"I expect so, too," Mason said. "But I would not count on it. The blackmailer, whoever it is, strikes me as a very elusive and resourceful person."

Their entrée finished, the group of diners nursed their vintage wines for a few minutes before scanning the dessert menu. Eventually, to round off the meal, they opted for blueberry cheesecake with large espressos.

"One thing I discovered in the course of my enquiries," Mason said, during the brief hiatus, "was that a member of your group who defected in 1990 was assassinated on Chelsea Bridge not long after arriving in this country."

"Igor Nikolayev!" the others said, in unison.

"That case was never solved," Alison Aubrey added. "Do any of you think Pavel Belinsky may have been involved?"

"That is certainly a possibility," Yuri Orlov opined, on considering the matter. "Especially if Belinsky was not a defector after all, but only made the pretense of being such."

"We shall never get to the bottom of that particular incident now," Mason commented, "after so much time has lapsed. But why do you think Nikolayev was targeted?"

Konev and Brodsky exchanged puzzled glances.

"What is your view on that, Mikhail?" Maxim Brodsky asked his immediate neighbor.

"Nikolayev was in charge of the French desk," Konev replied. "Some people considered that he had become too cozy with the French."

"I recall," Orlov added, "that two Frenchmen operating as double agents were detained by the French authorities on Nikolayev's watch. They were subsequently given long prison sentences."

"Did your superiors figure that Igor Nikolayev betrayed them?" Alison asked.

"One problem," Mikhail Konev remarked, "was that Igor owned a villa on the French Riviera, at St.

Tropez, I believe. That would have raised flags in Moscow, in view of the strict controls on foreign exchange in force at the time."

"Foreign currencies were tightly rationed," Maxim Brodsky added. "Very few people traveled outside the Soviet Union. Government officials, mainly, as well as orchestras, the Bolshoi Ballet, athletes and chess teams."

"So your superiors might have figured that Nikolayev betrayed the two undercover agents to the French authorities?" George Mason asked.

"They may very well have thought that," Yuri Orlov concurred. "Paranoia was the name of the game, in those days."

"It still is, in my opinion," Maxim Brodsky ruefully remarked.

The group of diners exchanged smiles of amusement at that disenchanted observation.

"I vote we put all this behind us," Daphne declared, before tasting her dessert. "Let sleeping dogs lie and let us look to the future."

"Amen to that," the others said, in chorus.

On finishing the dessert, the group chatted about more neutral topics for a while. The advertising executive regaled them with an account of his activities in Moscow and the progress of his campaign, alongside Edward Marsh, to promote Tadcastle Ales. He also conveyed Pyotr Alenin's regrets at not being able to join them from Dublin, owing to a prior commitment. As the hand of the wall clock moved towards nine o'clock, Yuri Orlov rose to his feet.

"I now propose a toast," he said, raising his glass:

"To Inspector Mason and Sergeant Aubrey, for your sterling work in solving this very complex puzzle."

"Here! Here!" echoed the two wives, with a rousing handclap, as other patrons of the Ritz dining-room glanced round in curiosity.

George Mason, visibly moved, also rose to his feet.

"And I propose a toast to you survivors in particular," he declared, with a nod to Maxim Brodsky and Yuri Orlov. "And to all the present company, for a safe and prosperous future in this green and pleasant land!"

*

One month after she returned from London, Alina Lehtinen gave birth to a baby boy, whom they named Alvar. The christening was delayed until Aunt Paivi retired from nursing and took up residence in her home at Lahti, some distance north of Helsinki. Following the baptismal ceremony at Ouspensky Cathedral, across the bay from South Harbor, Paivi treated them to a lunch at Fisherman's Cabin, a popular restaurant on the sea-front, facing the Yacht Club. Shortly afterwards, Osmo took up a teaching position at a high school in the suburb of Roihuvuori.

Alina was gratified to read in *Helsingin Sanomat*, the city's main broadsheet, that Pavel Belinsky had been sentenced at the Old Bailey, under the Official Secrets Act, to twenty years' imprisonment for espionage while employed at the Ministry of Defence. The time was to be served at Pentonville

Prison. What would her friend Nadia, who had always set her twin brother on a pedestal, make of that, she wondered? She would have given a lot to see the look on her face.

She was also intrigued to read that a Canadian ex-serviceman named Fabien Leroux had been convicted at Westminster Crown Court of attempted homicide and illegal possession of explosives. The additional charge of conveying classified material out of the country was dropped. He was sentenced to fifteen years' jail-time, to be served at Wormwood Scrubs. She recalled a pleasant dinner with him, accompanied by kantele music, at the Kalevala, some weeks ago. The man she had deemed a mere errand boy evidently had, to her surprise and disappointment, some more questionable attributes, namely those of a hired assassin.

She mentioned the fact to her husband, who only vaguely recalled him. Osmo expressed relief that the courier business was behind them. His wife could concentrate on raising Alvar, he considered, now that he was in line for a regular income. School-teaching in Finland was a well-paid profession, which would afford them a good standard of living and the possibility of a larger apartment on the island of Kulosaari. That would be desirable, if their family should increase in size. Aunt Paivi could then move in with them, to help raise the children and permit his wife to return to part-time employment.

On visiting South Harbor one day, to buy fresh supplies at the open-air market for a repeat of

Alina's culinary masterpiece of orange Pernod scallops, he was surprised to notice a poster in the window of police headquarters. It was a rather grainy image of a youngish woman, with the caption: *Tiedeteko tama rouva? - Do you know this woman?* He peered at it for a while, thinking it bore a vague resemblance to Alina. How curious was that, he thought, shrugging his shoulders and moving on. It could not possibly, he concluded, be his dear wife and helpmeet.

*

Three days before Osmo noticed the Wanted poster, George Mason received a telephone call from Major Viljo Forsenius, of the Helsinki Police.

"Good day, Inspector Mason," the Finnish officer said.

"Good to hear from you, Major," Mason rejoined.

"I thought I would bring you up-to-date on the blackmail incidents we discussed earlier," the Finnish officer said.

"You have found the culprit!" the detective exclaimed.

A distinct chuckle was heard at the other end of the line.

"Nothing so dramatic as that, Inspector," Forsenius remarked. "But we have had a poster printed of a possible suspect, to be displayed at police stations throughout Finland."

"How did you come by that, Major?" an intrigued George Mason enquired.

"We contacted Union Bank, Geneva," came the

reply, "mentioning the exact sum of money you told us had been demanded of the spy known in London as Paul Bell, over a period of months. The bank informed us that on the day before the blackmailer's letter reached Downing Street, a sum equal to that amount in Swiss francs was withdrawn from their branch at 2.32 p.m. precisely. They also confirmed the account number."

"I get it," Mason said, quickly latching on. "The customer was caught on a security camera as he or she was withdrawing the money?"

"Precisely, Inspector," Viljo Forsenius said. "Except that, as you well know, such images tend to be rather grainy. Moreover, it was only three-quarter face. The bank gave us an off-print, which our experts enlarged to produce a passable image. It is the best we can do, but I personally think we shall be lucky to get positive results from it."

"Let us hope for the best, Major," the detective said. "Chief Inspector Harrington and I are very grateful for your assistance."

"At the very least, Inspector Mason, our compatriot has performed a useful service by exposing a serious lapse in British security."

"With significant ramifications at NATO," Mason was quick to add.

"If the culprit is apprehended in due course," the Finn continued, "you might, in the circumstances, consider dropping charges. Any court case must of course be conducted in England, where the offences were committed, despite Chief Inspector Bill Harrington's curious notion that it was a Finnish matter."

"You are right about that, Major," George Mason replied, smiling to himself. "The ball is well and truly in our court, in the event of an arrest. The pardon you suggest might be worth trying out with the Home Secretary. It would be unprecedented, as a matter of fact, but it might just work. Good day, Major, and good hunting!"

CPSIA information can be obtained
at www.ICGtesting.com
Printed in the USA
BVHW030214251120
594176BV00022B/86

9 781657 637542